James J. Waring

The Epidemic at Savannah

1876 - its causes, the measures of prevention adopted by the municipality during

the administration of J. F. Wheaton, mayor

James J. Waring

The Epidemic at Savannah
1876 - its causes, the measures of prevention adopted by the municipality during the administration of J. F. Wheaton, mayor

ISBN/EAN: 9783337314859

Printed in Europe, USA, Canada, Australia, Japan

Cover: Foto ©Andreas Hilbeck / pixelio.de

More available books at **www.hansebooks.com**

THE EPIDEMIC AT SAVANNAH,

1876.

ITS CAUSES, THE MEASURES OF PREVENTION,

ADOPTED BY THE MUNICIPALITY DURING THE ADMINISTRATION OF HON.
J. F. WHEATON, MAYOR.

BY JAMES J. WARING,

CHAIRMAN DRY CULTURE COMMITTEE.

" Let every one physician or not freely declare his own sentiments about it ; let him assign any credible account of its rise, or the causes strong enough, in his opinion, to introduce so terrible a scene."—THUCYDIDES, " *Plague at Athens.*"

The history of yellow fever teaches that the mortality is great, even under the most favorable circumstances. When recording the eighteenth case I also recorded the thirteenth death. This would seem to indicate a necessity of turning our attention from the vain endeavor to combat the disease, or to try any improved treatment of the sick, to the other alternative, PREVENTION.—*Page* 4, *Analysis of Record of Yellow Fever in* 1876, *by Joseph Holt, M. D., Sanitary Inspector for the Fourth District, New Orleans.*

SAVANNAH, GA. :
MORNING NEWS STEAM PRINTING HOUSE.
1879.

DEDICATION.

IN THE BELIEF THAT A MORE EXTENDED AND CORRECT
KNOWLEDGE OF THE NATURE AND CAUSES OF
EPIDEMICS IS THE SUREST MEANS OF
THEIR PREVENTION, THIS
COLLECTION OF SCIENTIFIC DATA IS HUMBLY DEDICATED

TO THE PEOPLE OF SAVANNAH.

A VIEW OF SAVANNAH as it stood the 29" of March 1734.

To the Honorable Trustees for establishing the Colony of Georgia in America.
This view of the town of Savannah is humbly dedicated by their Honour's
Obliged and most obedient servant,   PETER GORDON.

"It was known that whilst these lands remained in a state of nature they were unproductive of disease, and that some seventy-five years ago, as I have been informed by Dr. Jones, Savannah was resorted to in Summer by some of the inhabitants of Charleston on account of its salubrity."—*Autumnal Fevers of Savannah, page* 20, *W. C. Daniel, M. D.*, 1826.

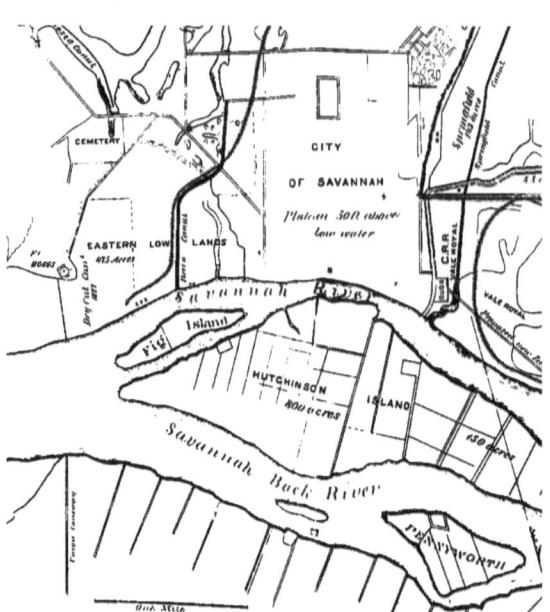

DESCRIPTION OF MAP OF SAVANNAH.

Green—Elevated sand plateau upon which the city is built.

Red—Zone of dryness upon surrounding lowlands, created by dry culture contract in 1817–20, and perfected in 1877.

Blue—Rice lands subject to irrigation.

Yellow—Back swamps, now drained.

***—Atlantic and Gulf Railroad wharves, upon which was deposited the Cuban ballast.

00—Deposit of dredge mud in 1854.

*, *, *—On green, first cases of yellow fever within seven days, in 1876.

oo, oo—On Springfield, points of deposit of scavenger's garbage from 1865 to 1877.

The map also shows the relations of the elevated plateau of the city to the surrounding low lands, which have been in every epidemic (1820, 1854, 1876) and (in lesser epidemics of 1817, 1819, 1821, 1858, 1864), in exceptionally bad condition and intensely malarial, a condition which existed when yellow fever between 1780 and 1820 occurred annually. The red shows the effective labors of the municipality in creating the zone of dryness originally projected by the dry culture contracts of 1817-20, and the blue shows the present rice lands subject to irrigation.

TOPOGRAPHY AND DESCRIPTION OF SAVANNAH.

Savannah is a city of 28,000 inhabitants, one-half of whom are white and one-half colored, covering an area of two miles square, standing on a plateau fifty feet above tide water, flanked on each side by low lands *three feet below* high water mark of tides, and fronted by a long island of the same low alluvium. It stands on the 32d parallel of latitude, having a mean temperature of sixty-eight degrees, Fahrenheit, being the same as the Bermudas. The winter is a short one of six weeks duration, extending from the middle of December to the first of February, with occasional light frosts and rarely a film of ice—never snow. The immediate proximity of the Gulf Stream affects the temperature, and hence the cold and cold dry winds come from the north and west. In summer the prevailing winds are south and southeast, and are the cooling sea breezes. It is within the circle of West India hurricanes, which have struck this city with great violence several times since the close of the war, notably in 1871-73-75-78. The tropical rains which fall in June, July and August are marvelous for the quantity of water which falls. The rainfall of June, 1876, reached the enormous amount of sixteen and one-half inches, and was the indirect cause of the epidemic, converting Springfield low lands on the west into an unbroken sheet of water.

The accompanying map will show at a glance the influences surrounding the town in 1876. The green represents the elevated plateau upon which the town is built; the red the low lands placed under dry culture in 1817-20, but which during the epidemic were intensely malarial, in June, and July and August soaking wet, and a large part of that period partially submerged and offensive. (See official report of John B. Hogg, City Surveyor, p. —.)

The yellow represents the back swamps recently drained. The yellow and red represent those lands which this administration has thoroughly drained and dried, amounting to 1,200 acres.

The blue represents the rice lands still subject to irrigation and harvest water. The three crosses on the green show the points at which the *first* cases of yellow fever occurred, August 21st, 22d, 26th. The three stars (***) on the left mark the Atlantic and Gulf railroad wharves, upon which were deposited the Regla ballast from Cuba, supposed to have been the possible cause of introducing yellow fever. Immediately back of this point are the 130 acres of dangerous harvest water lands in close proximity to the city, successfully drained by this administration. A little to the right of the three stars are two ciphers, marking the point of deposit of dredged mud, supposed cause of yellow fever in 1854. The yellow border on the east side of Springfield low lands is the point of extensive deposit of all the garbage and scavenger debris of the city during the epidemic and for several years before it. This slope was unusually wet and reeking with water, and covered by hundreds of turkey buzzards seeking their food in the offal during the whole period of the epidemic. (See letter addressed to Health Officer during epidemic.)

PREFACE.

The existence of an epidemic at Savannah was not known to its absent citizens until September 1st. Upon learning of its existence the writer returned to Savannah and had the honor to submit to the Mayor and Council, in an interview with them, the following :

SEPTEMBER 20th, 1876.

GENTLEMEN : I have the honor to lay before you a practical method of arresting the epidemic which is now visiting Savannah with fatal effects. It is an accepted fact that such diseases as yellow fever, bilious fever and their congeners are produced by the seeds of living organisms. These living organisms are classed as cryptogamic plants, and their seeds are called spores. * * *

It will be observed that this work necessarily divides itself into two parts—first, to clear and clean, and put in perfect working order the drains around Savannah, which are now keeping back large masses of water ; second, to attack every particle of green mould wherever found in the interior of the town. The trunk of every tree should be whitewashed, so also every wooden fence and old wooden house, scrape old shingle roofs and whitewash them ; this will last till frost. Pour the gas washings (diluted carbolic acid) upon all damp, mouldy yards, and rake them well with iron rakes. * * * (Carbolic acid to privies and its free use was not mentioned.) * *` * I predict with absolute confidence that if this work is finished by October 1st the disease will have so far ceased that with the first light frost on October 10th or 15th, everybody will be returning home. * * *

JAMES J. WARING.

The proposition was accepted, money by private subscription was raised, the drainage was fairly done, but whilst Alderman Douglas was organizing a large force for disinfection, divided counsels discouraged the municipal authorities. The work was arrested at this point, and disinfection by the New Orleans method abandoned. Whilst malarial fevers markedly subsided in October, no perceptible impression was produced upon the progress of yellow fever until *frost* and *cold* closed the painful scenes of the epidemic.

WHAT SHALL THE PEOPLE OF SAVANNAH NOW DO TO PREVENT IN ALL FUTURE TIME THE REPETITION OF THE DISASTERS OF 1820, 1854 AND 1876?

And, incidentally, what has this administration done towards the accomplishment of so desirable a result.

To this end, in this report have been gathered together material and facts which, if fairly considered, become a guide to an intelligent and vigilant protection of the public health.

To this end, have been gathered in readable form, material to make up, for the reasonable mind, answers to these questions :

1. Can these epidemics originate in Savannah ?

2. Is importation essential to the existence of yellow fever in Savannah ?

3. What is the poison of yellow fever ?

To this end is submitted herewith :

1. An analysis of the epidemic of 1876, and other papers bearing upon the epidemic of 1854 and 1820.

2. Considering the exceptional causes and the general predisposing causes of the epidemic of 1876.

3. The malarial element of that epidemic, and

4. The question of its importation,

Embodying in a brief report the labors of the present administration, both as to possible importation and possible local origin ; a condensed report of the most approved opinion upon the subject of water closets and privies ; a condensed history of the development of knowledge of the germ theory of disease ; and, finally, a translation from the German of F. Cohn upon bacteria, a subject attracting much attention at the present time.

First, these papers will show :

1. That there is no proof of importation in 1820, 1854 and 1876.

2. That yellow fever occurred annually up to 1820.

3. That yellow fever can occur in Savannah at the most dangerous period of the year, as in 1877, without the spread or propagation of the vital organisms, (bacteria), and without spread of the infection and consequent sickness or death of the people.

4. That the recent discoveries of science leave little doubt as to the nature of the poison of yellow fever—indeed, of all pestilential diseases ; that they assimilate in form to the lowest algæ, (see Cohn page), and in function to the lowest fungi (see Cohn page) ; that they are for convenience called bacteria, and are classified by F. Cohn according to their forms, and by Pasteur according to their functions ; that they cannot abstract carbonic acid and other elements from the air, but abstract elements of their structure from organic matter, both dead and living, producing putrefaction in dead organic matter, and *disease* in lying matter, both vegetable and animal ; that they live without air, and must live on organic matter because they have no chlorophyl like the algæ ; that hence the removal of dead organic matters, resulting in *cleanliness*, is the certain prevention of their existence and propagation.

5. That there is the amplest evidence that bacteria, like all other plants, can be transplanted from place to place, and have persistent forms and persistent functions ; hence the necessity of quarantine, if towns have within their limits any quantity of putrefaction materials, and as certainly quarantine is needless if *cleanliness* is assured.

6. That there is nothing more certain than that innocent forms of bacteria can rapidly expand into varieties or *culture races* (Cohn), like all other plants in proportion to the rapidity of their propagation and the intensity of their vitality and the consequent shortness of their life, according to a well recognized law that the greater the intensity of vitality the shorter the life. This is the polymorphism which renders reasonable the theory of domestic origin, and which necessarily admits the possibility of the transplanting or importation of these bacteria, especially when intensely active and virulent.

To paragraph second, page 11, add—

A Sanitary Commission was also created which has carefully watched the appearance of any contagious diseases or of any conditions threatening epidemic sickness, and vigorously applied all well recognised methods of relief and prevention. The Council has also had the advantage of the active coöperation of a Commission of Drainage, created by State law, which has faithfully and effectively expended an appropriation by the State for the proper drainage of this county. This commission has left a monument of its wisdom in the admirable work it has done upon Springfield low lands, and the southeastern swamps.

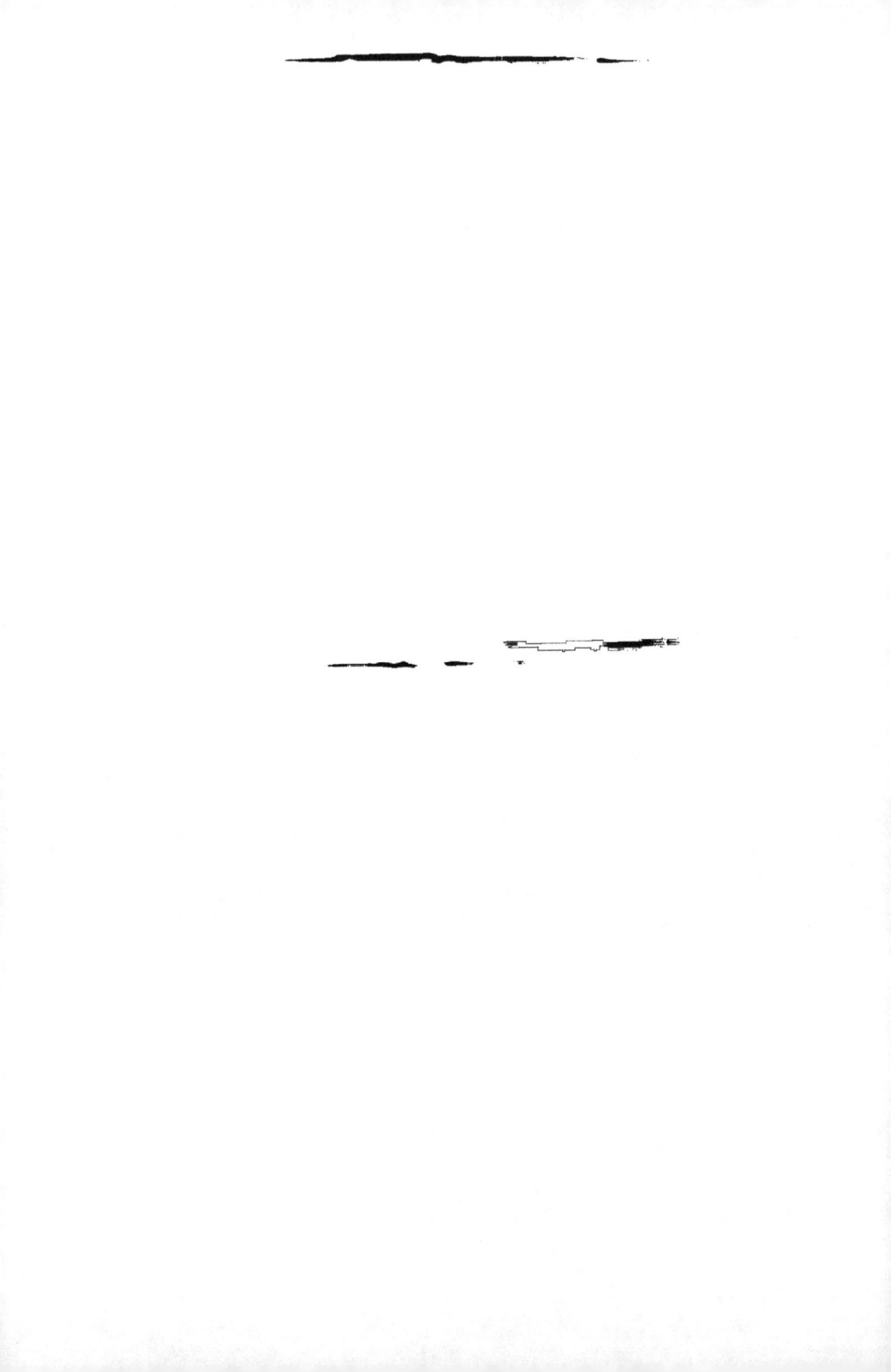

REPORT

LABORS OF THE ADMINISTRATION IN 1877 AND 1878.

When the present Board of Common Council took charge of the
municipal government on January 22, 1877, it was their duty to
admit the possibility of importation and guard the city from this
possible danger, but at the same time to respect the traditions
and experiences of this town, and pursue the invariable policy
of the wisest and best legislators the people of Savannah have
ever had, and treating the possible cause of epidemic yellow fever
as of local origin. For these reasons :

It entrusted the danger of importation to the committee known
as Health and Cemetery, and entrusted the danger of a possible
local origin to the committee known as Dry Culture, created in
1821. The following was the condition of the city and its surroundings at this date, and which it has been the aim of the proper
departments to remove or ameliorate :

1st. All the low tide lands around the city were intensely malarial and imperfectly drained, or not drained at all.

2d. The western and eastern slopes nearer still to the city were
sobbed and dripping.

3d. The western slopes and Springfield lowland were the places
of deposit of almost the entire garbage and refuse of the city
for the past twelve years.

4th. *Two hundred acres of the western lowlands*, including these
garbage slopes, *within the corporate limits*, had been, just before
the epidemic, the scene of one vast overflow, resulting in the conversion of this large area into an extensive rotting surface of the
most offensive character. (See report of John B. Hogg, page —).
Though relieved of this, an important work was necessary to
prevent a similar disaster by the raising of dams, opening drains
and establishing a new system of brow drainage for the western
slopes.

5th. The dry culture contract lands on Hutchinson's Island had
been neglected for fifty years, and these were to be restored.

6th. The power to enforce upon property-holders the drainage and drying of their lands around the city being a doubtful one, it was necessary to obtain from the Legislature a public act empowering Council to enforce it. This was obtained.

7th. The Bilbo canal was fouled and silted up, its dams protecting the adjoining lowlands were entirely too low, and the provision by trunks to drain these low lands into this canal was a constant mischief. Moreover, the Atlantic and Gulf Railroad had planted itself upon one of these drains—the eastern one—and it was necessary to bind, by agreement and contract, this road to take care of, and keep up to grade, this dam. All this has been thoroughly remedied and the needed contract with this road executed.

8th. Within the area of dry culture, established in 1817, were certain lands of John Waters, upon which the Mayor (Daniels), in 1826, had failed to enforce the measure in a law suit. These dangerous lowlands, amounting to 130 acres, yearly covered with harvest water, have been placed under dry culture contract, by purchase, for the sum of $5,200.

9th. The southeastern swamps, in close proximity to the city and in the direction of the prevailing winds of summer, had never been drained, were intensely malarial and indescribably desolate and dismal. These have been thoroughly drained and fitted for agriculture.

10th. Certain ponds, formed by excavations of brickyards, were offensive masses of stagnant water, covered always with a green film. These have been dried by partial filling.

11th. The privies of Savannah are a sore evil, always offensive and foul, simply because left to the private citizens to keep clean. After the failure of very many schemes, this administration has placed the cleansing of them on a footing with the scavenger department, and the public authorities will do the work, charging an annual tax upon every privy.

12th. The scavenger has been compelled, by a change of contract, to remove the garbage to a distance of one mile.

13th. The ventilation of waste pipes and sewers, so much needed, has been enforced by ordinance.

14th. The Bilbo canal had never been properly flushed by the high tides. Since the dams have been raised to a proper high grade and strengthened, the tides are now fearlessly turned in on this receptacle of filth.

In few words, by reference to the map accompanying, the eye at once appreciates the work done by this administration. The area of sweet and healthful dry lands has been expanded into a *broad zone one mile in width*, extending around the whole circuit of the city, and to accomplish this, 1,200 acres of land have been redeemed within this zone of dryness, which had never been properly redeemed, and, indeed, it may be safely said no citizen believed, two years ago, *could* have been redeemed. We allude more particularly to the John Waters' rice land on the east and Hutchinson Island on the north.

By reference to the map also, the blue coloring will show the source of malaria now existing and its distance from the town, whilst the red shows the work of this administration and the state of things existing here preceding and during the epidemic.

THE HISTORY OF DRY CULTURE.

The late Dr. W. C. Daniell published in 1826 a little volume on fever. On page 21 is the following extract :

" In 1817, at a town meeting, it was resolved that about seventy thousand dollars should be appropriated by the city to the purchase of the right of cultivation, 'in wet culture, of such of the tide swamps as were adjacent to the city. These lands were accordingly subjected to a dry culture, by contract, at the price of forty dollars per acre ; and the system went into operation the following year. Its success at first surpassed the expectations of its warmest friends. The want of attention to the cleanliness of the city, the introduction of a laboring class of whites unaccustomed to our climate, the great mortality of 1820, the reputed unproductiveness of the dry culture lands, with other circumstances, gradually brought the system into considerable disrepute, and in 1821 it was determined that the propriety of continuing it should be decided by a vote of the citizens. Upon counting the ballots the majority in favor of its continuance was only sixty-nine votes. Those opposed to the dry culture system now became more clamorous than ever. About this time new efforts were made to sustain the system ; a new train of measures was adopted ; a Board of Health, which had been previously established, took under its special care the condition of our streets, lanes, etc., and great attention was paid to cleanliness.

" The proprietors of the dry culture lands were gradually induced to pay more regard to their contracts. One of the largest tracts, and immediately opposite to the city, came into the possession of T. Spalding, Esq., of Darien, who placed it, at great labor and expense, in very fine order. His example was followed by several of the other contractors, and most of these lands are now in good condition. Its benefits being most obvious, public opinion is now almost unanimous in favor of the dry culture system.

" Elevated above the adjacent country, situated upon a dry sandy soil, and the cultivation of rice in its immediate vicinity restrained, Savannah will be considered as enjoying advantages for health superior to any Southern city, and it must become a place of summer retreat for those residing in its vicinity, whether upon the sea shore or in the interior, as it was some seventy years ago.

" Subjoined is an extract from a report made by the Dry Culture Committee to the City Council early in 1824 :

" Six years have now passed away under the operation of the dry culture system. Imperfectly as that system has been enforced, it has given proofs the most conclusive of a favorable influence upon the health of Savannah. It is the object of your committee, in their report, to refer to these facts, and to show by them how important it is that the City Council should persevere in rigidly enforcing the dry culture contracts ; and, to pursue, by all lawful means, those who, alike regardless of their engagements with the city and the dictates of humanity, set at naught the deep and permanent interest of the community in which they live, and to which they are indebted for the protection of their property. It cannot have escaped the attention of the most careless observer, that since the introduction of the dry culture system our summer and autumnal atmosphere have undergone a great and favorable change in its sensible qualities. The fogs which heretofore rising from the lands, now subjected to the dry culture system, and penetrating to the heart of our city, gave a high degree of humidity to our atmosphere, have since disappeared, and with them that humidity. Heavy fogs may now occasionally, in an autumn morning, be seen rising from lands cultivated in rice. Sometimes they approach the eastern and western ends of the city, but do not advance further. During the long flow which was made the last season upon the rice fields recently opened upon

the southwest extremity of the city, the atmosphere became more
heavy and damp, and in a short time a very disagreeable stench
was remarked by the inhabitants of that portion of the city ; the
trunks conveying the water to the rice suddenly gave way, and
the putrid water escaped its confinement before the trunks could
be repaired. The offensive stench was not perceived after this.
Previous to the introduction of the dry culture system, such was
the humidity of the atmosphere of this city during the long flow
upon the rice, that a person being exposed for a short time at
night, could wring water from the locks of hair hanging below his
hat. Now, throughout the whole season there is a dryness and
an elasticity of atmosphere, the very reverse of what existed previously. It will be obvious that this great improvement in the
sensible qualities of our atmosphere must be salutary to those
who breathe it."

In the same report is a comparative table of the proportion of
deaths to population. Here is the published testimony of 1824 :

1815, 1 in 15 ⎫
1816, 1 in 18 ⎬ Wet culture.
1817, 1 in 9 1·2 ⎭
1818, 1 in 62 3-4.
1819, 1 in 13—(Dry culture contracts violated.)
1820, 1 in 5 1-10—(Epidemic.)
1821, 1 in 37 ⎫
1822, 1 in 33 4-5 ⎬ Dry culture.
1823, 1 in 32 1-6 ⎭

In 1817 the dry culture contracts were made and carried into
effect, and in their ordinance the city authorities said : " It does
appear to Council that these measures recommended will have
the effect of so ameliorating the health of this city as to check, if
not to prevent, the ravages heretofore produced by autumnal
fevers, and to render it a safe and healthy residence, which, from
its high, dry and advantageous situation, nature intended it to be."

In 1818, when the rice-field system of drainage with trunks, and
gates, and ditches were in perfect order, the mortality fell to one
in sixty-two. Every rice planter knows the rapidity of decay and
ruin to the drainage of rice lands by one season of neglect ; and
the second condition of Springfield, two years after the neglect by
the owners, became worse than the first. The epidemic of 1820
succeeded as a consequence, and in 1822 our fathers created the
now well-known Committee on Dry Culture, in order to enforce
the observance of these contracts.

When the dry culture contracts were made in 1817-1820, Vale Royal plantation, 250 acres low land (see map), was subjected to dry culture, but Springfield plantation, 142 acres low land, was not so contracted for, and not subjected to dry culture. These were rice plantations, and the latter continued to be a rice plantation until 1850, when the city authorities purchased it from the heirs of Joseph Stiles.

These two bodies of land were the property of this Joseph Stiles, an emigrant from the Bermuda. The Springfield tract consisted of 963 acres, 142 acres of which were low tide lands, below the level of high water in the Savannah river. The Vale Royal tract consisted of one thousand acres, 250 acres of which were low tide lands below the level of high water in Savannah river. In February, 1762, second year of George III, the plantation of Royal Vale, in the province of Georgia, 1,000 acres in extent, was granted to Pickering Robinson, Esq., upon condition that he clear and cultivate three acres for every fifty acres granted, and by him sold to Laclan McGilliveay for five shillings, and by him sold to a Bermuda family, by name Stiles. In 1850, Springfield had become such a public nuisance, in consequence of the obstruction to its drainage, caused by (in 1826) the digging and embanking across the line of its drainage of the Ogeechee canal, and in 1830 the building of the Central Railroad embankments, that in that year the city was induced by Dr. James P. Screven to purchase the whole tract, and the generation of men who have just passed away enacted an ordinance, dated 29th of August, 1850, with this solemn and authoritative declaration :

"WHEREAS, The city of Savannah has recently become the purchaser in fee simple of that tract of land called Springfield, lying on the southwestern border of the city, which purchase was made for the sole purpose of reducing to and keeping in a state of dry culture the said tract of land, which is low and swampy and has been, in its wet state, the cause of disease to the people of Savannah ; and, whereas, it is the *duty* of the City Council to remove the said cause of disease, and to place the said tract of land in a *dry* and *healthful* state ; and, whereas, the Legislature of the State have conferred upon the city government *ample power* for the discharge of that duty ; and, whereas, it is essential to the dryness of the said lands and to the protection of the health of the citizens that the said tract of land should be *perfectly drained* in the natural course of the water, to the extent of its drainage capacity, and that the flow of the water through the said drains should not be *impeded*."

In 1864 it is well known that Springfield was overflowed for defensive purposes, and the Andersonville prisoners were placed on the parade ground, General Lafayette McLaws being in command of Savannah. It is well known that there was a marked outbreak of yellow fever in that year.

In 1871 Springfield was overflowed and made one vast sheet of water by the breaking of the banks of the Ogeechee canal during the cyclone of August 18 ; and, though the city authorities made vigorous efforts to drain and restore to a dry condition these lands, a marked outbreak of yellow fever occurred in the middle of October, the first victims being the three members of the Garroway family, who had been *three weeks* in Savannah, and had come from Augusta.

In 1876 Springfield was again overflowed by that wonderful rainfall of sixteen and a half inches, which fell between the 9th and 18th of June, and these waters were allowed to leak off and be evaporated slowly as best they might, during this past unprecedentedly hot summer. The drains had not been touched for one year, and the wild growth of Springfield during and after the epidemic, covered by the water grass, asmart, instead of, as in eight years previously, by the kesina weeds, which only grow on very dry ground, is the best evidence of what existed during this summer of epidemic.

The officials and passengers of the Central Railroad bear testimony to the offensive odor of Springfield during June and July. John McGrath is the lessee of the tract bordering on Gwinnett street ; he testifies that his land was useless to him until I drained it on September 25th, and that a party of pleasure, which he conveyed on July 23d to the residence of Captain Dooner, who lives on the western high ground of Springfield, refused to return that night until compelled by him to do so, because of the sickening and offensive atmosphere of this spot.

Now couple together two more facts with this one : The late epidemic reached its height and prevailed in marked virulence only in the month of September, and the Signal Bureau report, which is herewith published, shows that the southwest wind, blowing from off this pestilential swamp, prevailed in this month, whereas, for the three years previously, the northeast wind had prevailed in each of those years. Can we shut our eyes to these facts ? The dispassionate observer will not fail to note them, and give them a proper consideration.

2

TABLE.

MORTUARY FEVER RECORD OF SAVANNAH.

Years.	Population.	Total Death for Year.	Fever.	Yellow Fever.	Inter., Remit. and Bil. Fevers.	Rates of Fever Deaths to Total Mortality.	Meningitis.	Remarks.
1804	5,046	223	56	...	* 27	1:2.6	..	
1805	......	255	34	...	* 72	1:2.4	..	*Bilious.
1806	......	158	14	...	* 38	1.3	..	*Bilious and remittent.
1807	......	230	73	...	* 16	1:2.6		*Bilious and remittent.
1808	......	218	65	...	* 21	1:2 4	..	*Bilious and remittent.
1809	......	185	50	...	* 11	1:3	..	*Remittent.
1810	5,195	163	38	...	* 7	1:3.6	..	*Remittent.
1811	......	211	65	...	* 19	1:2.5	..	*Malignant bilious.
1812	......	226	85	...	* 5	1:2.5	..	*Bilious.
1813	......	213	48	...	* 10	1:3.7	..	*Worm fever.
1814	......	299	171	...	* 7	1:1.7	..	*Worm fever.
1815	......	232	122	...	* 5	1:1.7	..	*Worm fever.
1816	......	275	128	...	* 11	1:1.9	..	
1817	......	466	308	..	* 6	1:1.5	..	
1818	......	212	50	...	* 26	1:2.8	..	*Bilious remittent.
1819	......	516	312	...	* 7	1:1.6	..	
1820	7,523	820	*640	...	* 8	1:1.2	..	*Marked black vomit.
1821	......	382	108	...	* 12	1:3.2	..	*Bilious and remittent.
1822	......	302	60	...	* 67	1:3	..	*Bilious and remittent.
1823	......	207	65	...	* 26	1:2.3	..	*Bilious and remittent.
1824	......	136	37	...	* 9	1:3	..	*Worm fever.
1825	......	126	14	...	* 12	1:5	..	*Remittent and bilious.
1826	......	238	37	...	* 17	1:4.4	..	*Remittent and bilious.
1827	......	324	13	...	* 62	1:3.5	..	*Remittent and bilious.
1828	......	146	5	...	* 11	1:9	..	*Remittent and bilious.
1829	......	210	17	...	* 14	1:7	..	*Remittent and bilious.
1830	7,773	158	13	...	* 15	1:5.6	..	*Remittent and bilious.
1831	......	147	11	...	* 5	1:9	..	*Remittent and bilious.
1832	......	219	28	...	* 35	1:3.4	..	*Bilious.
1833	......	207	31	...	* 6	1:5.5	..	
1834	......	197	26	...	* 7	1:6	..	
1835	......	230	37	...	* 13	1:4.6	..	*Bilious.
1836	......	249	21	...	* 32	1:4.7	..	*Scarlet.
1837	......	358	89	...	* 31	1:2.9	..	*Scarlet.
1838	......	335	91	...	* 15	1:3	..	*Remittent and bilious.
1839	......	376	97	...	* 55	1:2.5	..	*Malignant bilious.
1840	11,214	381	114	...	* 9	1:3	..	*Malignant and bilious.
1841	......	262	72	..	* 13	1:3	..	

TABLE.

MORTUARY FEVER RECORD—CONTINUED.

Years.	Population.	Total Deaths for Year.	Fever.	Yellow Fever.	Inter., Remit. and Bil. Fevers.	Rates of Fever Deaths to Total Mortality.	Meningitis.	Remarks.
1842		243	33	...	* 34	1:3.6	..	*Scarlet.
1843		259	84	...	* 8	1:2.8	..	
1844		248	35	...	* 22	1:4.3	..	
1845		229	31	...	* 25	1:4	..	
1846		240	47	...	* 9	1:4.3	..	
1847		195	23	...	* 5	1:7	..	
1848		295	16	...	* 38	1:6.7	..	*Bilious.
1849		380	41	...	* 30	1:5.3	..	
1850	14,000	329	27	...	* 25	1:6.3	..	*Bilious and remittent.
1851		330	28	...	* 17	1:7.3	..	*Bilious and remittent.
1852		298	16	...	* 32	1.6.2	..	*Malignant and bilious.
1853		302	24	...	* 19	1:7	..	*Malignant and bilious.
1854		1,111	....	639	*138	1:1.4	..	*Malignant and bilious.
1855		410	...	...	* 69	1:6	..	*Malignant and bilious.
1856		434	...	...	* 96	1:4.5	..	*Malignant and bilious.
1857		646	5	...	* 38	1:15	..	*Malarial.
1858		514	...	114	* 83	1:2.6	..	
1859		746	1	...	* 65	1:11.3	..	*Bil., malig. and cong.
1860	18,000	775	...	...	* 97	1:8	..	*Bilious and scarlet.
1861		856	6	3	*131	1:6	..	*Intermit'nt and remit.
1862		966	4	...	*156	1:6	..	*Intermit'nt and remit.
1863		867	...	...	*124	1:7	..	*Intermit'nt and remit.
1864		1,236	18	11	* 87	1:10.6	4	*Bilious and malarial.
1865		1,985	4	1	*146	1:13	4	*Bilious and malarial.
1866		1,439	8	4	*106	1:10	9	*Bilious and malarial.
1867		1,039	8	...	* 94	1:10	4	*Bilious and malarial.
1868		1,114	10	1	* 95	1:10	17	*Bilious and malarial.
1869		845	4	1	* 66	1:11.9	..	*Bilious and malarial.
1870	28,000	1,026	10	...	* 91	1:10	..	*Remit. and intermit.
1871		1,132	11	3	*100	1:10	..	*Remit. and intermit.
1872		1,155	10	...	* 93	1:11	..	*Remit. and intermit.
1873		1,347	4	...	* 72	1:18	..	
1874		1,036	4	1	* 83	1:11.8	..	*Bilious and malarial.
1875		996	....	8	* 43	1:23	..	*Remittent and bilious.
1876		2,249	...	896	* 47	1:2.4	..	*Remittent and bilious.
1877		998	...	1	* 56	1:17.5	..	*Remittent and bilious.
1878		980	2	...	* 51	1:18	..	*Remittent and bilious.

TABLE.

SEPARATING DEATHS OF WHITE AND COLORED.

Years.	Whites.	Colored.	Total.
1866.......	534	903	1,439
1867...........	476	563	1,039
1868..........	518	596	1,114
1869......................	414	431	845
1870.................	450	576	1,026
1871..............	526	606	1,132
1872......	519	636	1,155
1873...........	558	789	1,347
1874.......	394	642	1,036
1875............	394	602	996
1876...............	1,265	984	2,249
1877...........	375	623	998
1878, to December 1st............	335	585	920

On page 21—

The rate of deaths to population steadily fell in each decade as 1 in 14, 1 in 17, 1 in 24, 1 in 33, 1 in 46; but since the late war and the emancipation of the colored people, the death rate has risen to 1 in 25, and 1 in 26. The death rate for all the decades, except the two last, were taken from Joseph Bancroft's Statistics of Savannah, 1848. He says: "It would be proper to remark, however, that the mortality among that class (blacks) of the population, who through the years set forth in the table have numbered but little less than one-half of the entire population, is but as 2 to 3 of whites; and the months of the greatest and least mortality, the reverse of the whites." On page 20, it is seen that the deaths of the colored people have risen to nearly double that of the whites, thus in 1877 there are 375 white deaths to 623 colored, and in 1878, 335 whites to 585 colored.

THE FOLLOWING TABLE WILL SHOW THE EFFECTS
OF DRY CULTURE SINCE 1804.

DECADE.	Rates of Fever Deaths to Total Motality.	DECREASE OF FEVER DEATHS.	Rate of Deaths to Population.
1st.—1800 to 1810.	1 in 2.6		
2d.—1810 to 1820.	1 in 2.3		1 in 14
3d.—1820 to 1830.	1 in 4.1	This decrease of fever deaths is under influence of the dry culture contracts 1817-20.	1 in 17
4th.—1830 to 1840.	1 in 4.7	No further labors, no further results.	1 in 24
5th.—1840 to 1850.	1 in 4.4	No further labors, no further results.	1 in 33
6th.—1850 to 1860.	1 in 6.7	This decrease of fever deaths is under influence of dry culture labors of Aldermen Dr. Scriven, Dr. Saussy and Dr. Posey.	1 in 46
7th.—1860 to 1870.	1 in 9.2	This decrease of fever deaths is under the influence of the dry culture labors of Alderman Dr. James J. Waring.	1 in 25
8th.—1870 to 1879.	1 in 15	Is under the influence of labors of Mayor Screven and Alderman Haywood, 1871-4; and for 1871 to '79 under influence of dry culture committee, J. J. Waring chairman, and State Commissioners of Drainage.	1 in 26

TABLE.

SHOWING THE EFFECTS OF DRY CULTURE ON THE NUMBER OF PRESCRIPTIONS MADE UP AT CITY DISPENSARY FOR THE POOR.

1875..........................	September Prescriptions, 1,947
1876..........................	September Prescriptions, 3,670
1877..........................	September Prescriptions, 2,600
1878..........................	September Prescriptions, 1,697

THE EPIDEMIC OF 1876.

A MALARIAL AND YELLOW FEVER—A FEVER OF INTERMITTENT, REMITTENT AND CONTINUED (MONOPAROXYSMAL) MALIGNANT TYPE.

In the month of August, 1876, a fever of intermittent, remittent and continued malignant (yellow fever) type gradually developed itself into an epidemic of the utmost fatality at Savannah. The language of the report to the City Council upon the epidemic of 1820, of Dr. Wm. R. Waring, is the exact language applicable to this epidemic of 1876 :

"The epidemic began then as mild and manageable intermittent and remittent bilious fever. In the course of its march it became a remittent, more severe and fatal ; at another step, a *continued fever*, most ungovernable and destructive, at first of short, but afterwards, in some instances, of considerable duration, and, finally, concluded with a relapse into the primary intermittent and remittent types."

The epidemics of 1820 and 1854 can alone be compared to it. In 1820 there were 729 deaths in an average population of 3,000 for the period of seven months of its duration, or a death rate of one to four of the population. In 1854 there were 1,040 deaths in an average population of 6,000 for the period of four months, or a death rate of one to six. (See Mayor's report, John E. Ward, 1854.)

In 1876 there were 1,594 deaths in an average population of 20,561 for the period of five months of its duration, or a death rate of one to thirteen. The first case, the sailor Schull, July 26th ; last case, Mrs. M——, December 5th ; height of the epidemic September 20 ; mortality 48 ; temperature at mid-day 92 degrees ; wind southwest.

In that brief period, the population was diminished from 28,000 to 20,561. In 1854, the diminution of population was from 14,000 to 6,000, and in 1820 from 7,500 to 3,000, and, for a short period, to 1,500.

The monthly mortality and comparative table of the three epidemics is as follows :

COMPARATIVE TABLE OF MORTALITY IN THREE EPIDEMICS.

Year.	1820.		1854.		1876.	
Population	3,000		6,000		20,000	
Mortality	729		1,040		1,591	
Death rate.....	1 in 4		1 in 6		1 in 13	
MONTHS.	Yellow fever.	Other Diseases	Yellow fever.	Other Diseases	Yellow fever.	Other Diseases
May...........	3	13	.....	......	.....	......
June..........	14	15	.....	......	.....	......
July..........	39	14	.....	......	.....	......
August........	111	8	133	124	37	139
September.....	214	18	390	256	533	227
October........	196	32	71	66	287	187
November	10	19	12	50	64	81
December	3	24	.....	......	1	35

The epidemic of 1876 did not spread from foci, and became general and all-pervading within seven days from August 21st, date of the first pronounced case of the continuous disease. Though conveyed to distant points by currants of air, e. g.: along the clean cut swathes of the forests around the city, made by the Savannah, Skidaway and Seaboard Railroad and Central Railroad ; though conveyed by box and passenger cars, or by boxes of merchandise to Isle of Hope, Macon and points intermediate, as Whitesville, etc., yet in no instance did this epidemic exist, propagate itself, and thrive, except within the corporate limits of the town. The Atlantic and Gulf Railroad passes out upon open fields and marshes, and the Charleston Railroad crosses the Savannah river and a short open country, hence the occurrence of cases along their routes was rare, whilst on the Central Railroad cases occurred in persons who had not been exposed in Savannah. On the other hand, the orphan school at Bethesda is located two miles from Isle of Hope and seven from Savannah, isolated in the midst of a forest, and though I cannot ascertain that a special quarantine was kept up during the epidemic, not a case occurred in this large school of 100 persons.

At least 500 citizens lived at Isle of Hope, going in and out morning and evening, enjoying excellent health during the epidemic, showing that the place in itself was healthy, though the poison, carried out, plainly and strikingly attacked several persons who had not been to Savannah for a long period. The only explanation here is that the poison was conveyed from Savannah, but did *not propagate itself.*

The summer opened with an extraordinary rainfall of 16½ inches, and afterward the rainfall exceeded the rainfall of previous years ; the summer was hotter than for several years, and the winds prevailed from the southwest in September, across the low rotting fields of Springfield, (see report of J. R. Hogg), whilst for the three years previous the northeast winds had prevailed.

The atmosphere was so loaded with spores of fungi and algæ that all surfaces were attacked. Brick walls, wooden structures, both new and old, paths untrodden were attacked by mould and algæ, not weeds and grass. Paint oxidized and blackened ; milk soured so rapidly that it was with difficulty carried around unchanged to customers ; meat spoiled so rapidly and kept upon ice with such difficulty as to be matter of common comment ; rain water fresh fallen in gutters, and puddles, were covered by a green film in twenty-four hours. In happy contrast, all this is changed in 1878 ; even the ditches and drains in the low grounds around the town have remained free of all green coloring film in 1878.

The all-pervading and irresistible character of the poison, whatever that might be, in the epidemic of 1876, could not fail to be noted. During the month of September, not a household escaped illness, and generally two, three, five or more were sick at one time. The uniform character of the attacks was remarkable. In all cases, whether of malarial or of the malignant type, the illness was invariably fever, fever, and yet no class of diseases are so varied and protean as the malarial.

THE MALARIAL CHARACTER OF THE EPIDEMIC.

It is an error to term this epidemic "a yellow fever epidemic." The unvarying testimony thus far given by both professional and non-professional observers, defines it as a most extensive and fatal epidemic of malarial fevers, merging, by undefined lines, into yellow fever. For one case of yellow fever there occurred a hundred cases of malarial intermittent and remittent. This feature of the epidemic of 1876, and of every other epidemic which has visited Savannah is of great importance in considering the question of importation, for malarial germs are not *portable,* whilst yellow fever germs are overwhelmingly proved to be *portable*. Remove the thousand cases of yellow fever from the epidemic of 1876, and you still have the ten thousand cases of malarial fever to constitute a formidable epidemic; and this is true of the epidemic of 1854 and 1820. It is safe, therefore, to say these essential and *greater* parts of the three epidemics were *not imported*, but were of local origin.

Opinions in confirmation of this view of the epidemic are here given :

Opinion of Dr. O. A. White, of New York, who came to Savannah and was present during the continuance of the epidemic. In the *New York Medical Journal*, March, 1877, Dr. White reports :

"An epidemic of a similar nature, however, to that which prevailed last summer in Savannah, with such destructive effect, is not without precedent in this country. The posted student of the literature of this subject cannot fail to recall the detailed experience of Dr. Lewis, of Alabama, in the hybrid epidemic, which he describes as having appeared in 1842, in Mobile. In that epidemic quite a number of cases were distinguished, marked by evident blending together of malarial with specific yellow fever poison, as 'congestive, simulating yellow fever ;' and M. Thomas, in his very interesting 'Traite sur la Fievre Jaune observee a New Orleans,' also affirms he had detected 'a remittent pyrexia' in several instances among the hosts of cases he so critically passed in review."

The reporter of the SAVANNAH MORNING NEWS interviewed Dr. White, and on September 26th, 1876, reported him as follows :

"Dr. White thinks that the present epidemic is different in very many essentials from yellow fever, as that fever has heretofore come under his medical observation. That it is mixed largely with the type of malarial fever, and assimilates to what was known years ago in Charleston as the neck fever.

"He is satisfied that the ordinary treatment for yellow fever cannot be pursued with effect in the fever now ravaging our city, and that the good results following the quinine treatment pursued generally by the profession, indicates that the malaria enters largely into the diagnosis of the disease. "

The Georgia State Board of Health, in their report of their investigation into the epidemic, (page 121 of Second Annual Report, 1876) say : "That an epidemic of malarial disorders of an exceedingly acute grade, was prevalent in the city of Savannah,

prior to and subsequent to the month of August, 1876, is shown
by the testimony of Dr. J. C. LeHardy and others, and the Board
is strongly of opinion," etc., etc.

Opinion of Dr. Wm. Duncan, of Savannah (page 17, appendix
to *idem.*) : "I have no doubt that the local conditions of the city
of Savannah were favorable to the spread of the disease, and I
think that the MALARIAL ELEMENT prevailed to a great extent during
the epidemic."   .

The identity of the epidemic of 1820 with this of 1876, as to
the malarial intermittent and remittent character, has been already
given in the words of Dr. Wm. R. Waring.

The record of deaths from this epidemic of 1876 is the best
evidence of its mixed character ; 922 are yellow fever, whilst the
the total of deaths is 1,591.   Thus one half the deaths are placed
to the credit of yellow fever, and the other half, being placed to
the credit of other diseases, is a mortality in itself sufficiently
great to constitute an epidemic.   It has never been claimed for
quinine that it is a remedy for yellow fever ; yet the indiscrimi-
nate resort to this remedy, and the benefits derived from its
use, as well even in convalescence from yellow fever, is evidence
of the universality of the malarial element in the epidemic.

THE CAUSES OF THE EPIDEMIC OF 1876.

THE DIRECT OR EXCITING CAUSE:

TWO HUNDRED ACRES OF SURFACE PUTREFACTIONS WITHIN THE CORPORATE LIMITS OF SAVANNAH.

The indirect or proximate causes (not in themselves capable of producing an epidemic) :

1st. Exceptional meteorological conditions.

2nd. *Exceptional neglect and decay* of the elaborate and expensive system of drainage, carried out in former years by the city authorities.

3d. *Exceptional neglect* of the canal known as the Bilbo Canal, the large open conduit which conducts all the sewage of the town to the river, and which flanks the entire eastern side of the town.

4th. The usual but objectionable condition of 3,360 (privy) vaults.

THE DIRECT CAUSE :

The low or rice lands of Springfield plantation, will be seen by reference to the "map of Savannah," to lie to the south of the Central Railroad embankments. These cover 143 acres. The eastern slopes to this tract, marked yellow, which were peculiarly wet and undrained preceding and during the epidemic, and covered with the scavenger's garbage and refuse, are twenty acres or more. The Vale Royal land, within the corporate limits, that is bounded on the west by Musgrove canal, is an area of sixty acres. The total acreage of this tract is therefore 223 acres. It had been thoroughly drained, dried and cultivated for *eight* years ; but a singularly unusual rainfall of sixteen and a half inches, occurring between the 11th and 18th June, resulted in the conversion of this tract into an inland lake, which was neglected and not properly drained until the following October. When these lands were undrained and covered with water-grasses, any extensive and accidental overflow of them, aggravated the ordinary malarial diseases and sporadic yellow fever of the first quarter of the century, as is evidenced by the fever record table we publish, and the report of Dr. Wm. R. Waring, in 1821, confirmed by Dr. Lemuel Kollock. But Vale Royal and Springfield lowlands had been *dry* for eight years, the soil was interlaced by the roots of plants, which must have and *did* die and rot when subjected to an overflow, whilst the surface was covered with luxuriant crops, as oats, just harvested, whose stacks could never be removed, and rotted on the ground, growing corn, potatoes and pea-vines. These all died and became notoriously offensive, so much so that the officials of the railroad and citizens made complaint to the municipal authorities, and through the press, to the public.

Such *extensive putrefactions* within the corporate limits, must have been the result of a growth of bacteria, fungi and algæ, so great that the mind cannot possibly take in its myriads. The significance of such in the production of pestilence will be fully appreciated by any one reading the " Researches " of Ferdinand Cohn, which we publish, and the Twelfth and Seventeenth Reports of the Medical Officer of H. B. M.'s Privy Council

A stranger would suppose that the drainage of Springfield would be very simple ; but the formidable dangers to these low lands were well known to our fathers, and are well known to many of their children.

The first danger is the tremendous body of water accumulated in the great swamps of the Ogeechee, which occurs in the wonderful falls of rain to which we are occasionally subject in the summer months ; such as fell between the 9th and 18th of June, 1876, to the depth of sixteen and a half inches (see Signal Bureau reports which will appear farther on); and which rainfalls were alluded to in 1817, by Dr. Wm. R. Waring in the following language when advocating dry culture :

" There is a periodical recurrence of heavy rains in the months of July and August which may be emphatically entitled the rainy season, although the quantity of water is irregular, being much greater sometimes than it is at others.

" The amount of a single fall of water is frequently astonishing. The ground, after it, looks like a sea. It does not drop as in higher latitudes, but pours in torrents. This sometimes continues for ten or twelve days, as in 1820, without the interruption of an hour's clear sky. "

At these times the backwater dam and Springfield canal dam are liable to overflow and crevasse.

The second danger is the crossing of the Ogeechee canal midway of the natural drainage of Springfield at a level six feet above the level of the land. The outlet at the present time to the Springfield land was put in by the City Surveyor under my supervision, when an Alderman, in 1867, and is a syphon trunk under the canal, unfortunately unable to do the work as thoroughly as it ought. The Ogeechee canal is liable to great gluts of water in the great rains, and has frequently burst its banks and submerged Springfield. Moreover, the Springfield canal passes under the Ogeechee canal by two culverts, which are too small and not low enough for the drainage.

The third danger is the crossing of the embankment of the Central Railroad, and the unavoidable culvert under the embankment to let off the waters.

Springfield, when neglected, becomes a pestilential swamp great in size and close in proximity, and is the great danger to Savannah, enhanced by the prevalence of southwestern winds, and amongst many lesser causes, was the great potential cause of the epidemic of 1876. Could our forefathers rise from their graves they would affirm what I have just said, and their public acts spread upon the book of city ordinances point unerringly to this opinion.

The official report of John B. Hogg, City Surveyor, testifies to the correctness of the above facts:

CITY SURVEYOR'S OFFICE,
SAVANNAH, GA., December 11, 1878.

To the Honorable the Mayor and Aldermen of the City of Savannah:

GENTLEMEN: In accordance with the resolution of Council requiring an official statement of the condition of the western lowlands, known as Springfield and Vale Royal Plantations, during the epidemic of 1876, and the causes leading thereto, I respectfully report:

1st. That the condition of these lands during the months of June, July and August, 1876, preceding the epidemic and at its height was very exceptional as compared with previous years. 1st. Because during the years of the war, and also during 1865 and 1866, they were subject to a steady and continuous overflow, which

covered them with water grasses and water growth of every
description. 2d. Because subsequent to 1867 they were, with the
exception of a brief overflow in 1871, in continuous dry culture,
the soil covered with highland grasses and cultivated in high
land crops. 3d. Because from 1864 to 1876 certain portions of
the lands had been the depository of garbage and offal of the city,
but kept dry, and therefore harmless; and 4th. Because in the
year 1876, by providential causes, which are explained below,
these lands were overflowed in June, and, to a great extent,
reverted to their former bad condition, and were not drained off
effectually until October of that year. Decay of the growing
crops, weeds and grasses and garbage was the result, and an
offensiveness which was very noticeable.

In relation to the causes producing the overflow of these lands
a brief description of their character and location is necessary to
convey a correct idea to those unacquainted with them.

The Springfield plantation as a body consists of 960 acres of
land situated on the western side of the city. About 230 acres of
the tract are swamp land, of which 150 acres have been cleared,
and were formerly planted in rice. This portion had never been
embraced in the dry culture contract, and the object of the purchase of the Springfield property in 1850 by the city of Savannah
was to bring these lowlands under the conditions appertaining
to other dry culture lands. The 150 acres alluded to lie at the
base of the western slope of the city, and extend along the southern half of the western boundary. The low lands of the Vale
Royal plantation are a continuation of the same swamp and
occupy the northern half. They contain about —— acres.

All this lowland is of alluvial formation, and known as tide
lands. Were the tide admitted they would be covered to the
depth of one foot at high water. They are protected from inundation by embankments or levees along the river. This body of
land is two miles in length and about one-quarter of a mile in
width.

The uncleared portion of this swamp extends in a southerly
direction a distance of a mile and a quarter, where it unites with
a series of swamps having a fall toward the Ogeechee river, the
whole length of the portion draining into the Savannah being
three and one-quarter miles. The drainage originally was through
a natural channel or creek meandering through the land, but is
now conveyed to the river by means of a canal located on the

western margin, and known as the Springfield canal, and used only to carry off the waters of the uncleared swamp, a sewer commenced in 1860, but not completed until 1868, and known as the Springfield sewer, being the medium through which the cleared lands, both of Springfield and a large portion of Vale Royal, are drained. This sewer was a covered wooden box, rectangular in shape, but for some time previous to, and during the epidemic, the covering had, to a great extent, been removed. It extends from the river, through the Vale Royal tract, up to Springfield, the open ditches draining the Springfield lands connecting with and draining into it.

The extraordinary rainfall preceding the epidemic of 1876, which caused the inundation of these lands, commenced on the 11th of June and continued until the 20th, as follows: On the 11th, 2:47 inches; on the 12th, 3:34 inches; on the 13th, 0:42 inch; on the 14th, 4:16 inches; on the 15th, 2:04 inches; on the 16th, 0:37 inch; on the 17th, 1:37 inches; on the 20th, 2:54 inches; total, 17:74 inches. From the 20th to the end of the month the rainfall was one and one-half inches.

A word or two in relation to the system of draining the lands described is necessary to a clear understanding of the causes leading to the overflow which occurred during the prevalence of these rains.

The Springfield canal has an average width of about thirty feet, is two miles in length, and, as previously stated, is the outlet for the waters of the uncleared swamp lands lying above. To prevent the influx of tide water up this canal two trunks were placed in an embankment, closing up the canal at a point distant about three hundred miles from its mouth. The gates of these trunks are self-acting, opening riverwards when the tide is out, thereby giving vent to the waters of the swamp which have accumulated, and closing as soon as the returning tide has reached a level higher than the water in the canal. The canal, therefore, becomes a reservoir for the swamp waters, which can only escape when the tide has fallen to a lower level. The Springfield sewer operates in substantially the same manner, being provided with a similar trunk at the river end.

A short time previous to the setting in of the rains one of the trunks connected with the canal blew out, giving free ingress and egress to the tides. In order to prevent this, and at the same time give an opportunity of replacing the trunk, an embankment was thrown across the canal. This embankment had just been completed, and the work of replacing the trunk begun when the rain set in, as will be seen by reference to the rainfall above. Nearly six inches of rain fell on the first two days. The accumulation of water within the canal was therefore very great, and it became necessary on the third day (Tuesday) to cut away the embankment to permit this water to escape. On the fourth day (Wednesday) the rainfall amounted to 4.16 inches. Backed up twice every twenty-four hours by the incoming tide the accumulation of water became so great after this day's rain that the embankment of the canal next to the lowland was tapped in many places, more especially between the mouth of the canal and the Central railroad, which crosses it by an open bridge at a point about three-fourths of a mile above. This portion of the embankment was not in good order, and became quickly broken in several places. The bank once broken no impediment remained to prevent the constant overflow of the portion of the Vale Royal plantation adjoining, not only from the waters of the swamp, but during every high water from the river. The open Springfield sewer at once received and conducted these waters to the Springfield lowlands, inundating the greater portion.

I would here call attention to the want of capacity in the two culverts under the Savannah and Ogeechee canal, which crosses the Springfield canal a short distance above the point at which the Central railroad crosses, and to the effect produced thereby. During any heavy rainfall, even when the canal is in other respects in good working order, the water above these culverts is found at a higher level than below. The difference of level on the present occasion amounted to nearly two feet, and resulted in producing a slight overflow of the embankments next to Springfield, which here were in much better condition than next to the Vale Royal tract.

The condition of things described above continued during the whole period of the rains, which lasted until Monday, the 21st eight days, as also for nearly a week after they ceased. The amount of water which had accumulated in the swamps above was so great that no work could be done on the embankments, and the tide continued to ebb and flow over the lands. As soon as possible the banks were repaired and the tide shut out, but, in the meantime, an injury had been done to the drainage of these lands, which was not entirely relieved until the epidemic had nearly ceased. The extensive putrefaction of animal and vegetable matters caused an offensiveness noticeable and publicly commented on.

I remain, gentlemen, your obedient servant,
JOHN B. HOGG, City Surveyor.

The following paper was published in the Savannah *Morning News*, immediately after the close of the epidemic, December 20th, 1876. The paper herewith published, leaves little to change and little to add to the views then expressed :

THE EPIDEMIC OF SAVANNAH, 1876—ITS CAUSES—CONTRIBUTIONS TO THE STATE BOARD OF HEALTH—PAPER NO. 6.

The reasonable and unprejudiced man will always account for an *exceptional* epidemic of sickness in any country by seeking those conditions and circumstances which, *not existing before*, were in full force just before and during that *exceptional* epidemic. The man so reasonably inclined will be forcibly led to conclude that that epidemic, and those new and unusual conditions and circumstances, stand in the relation of effect and cause.

The causes of the late epidemic may be divided into meteorological, administrative and topographical.

METEOROLOGICAL CAUSES.

The exceptional meteorological causes will be seen at a glance in the following table of averages for the months of July, August and September, in 1873, 1874, 1875, 1876. Mean average temperature for June, July, August and September, condensed from Signal Bureau reports :

Year.	Temperature.		Rainfall.	Wind. June, July, Aug.	Wind. Sept.	Velocity.
	Highest.	Mid-night.				
1873	95.2	75.7	4.89	SW	NE	3.9
1874	94.0	75.4	7.61	SE	NE	4.4
1875	95.2	74.4	3.92	S	NE	4.4
1876	98.0	78.0	8.60	SW	SW	2.7

It will be seen that this summer has been hotter by day and hotter by night than for four years ; that the rainfall has been considerably greater ; indeed, that last June the rain fall during

3

ten days was greater than has been known for a half century, reaching the extraordinary amount of 16½ inches. It will be seen that for three years previously the northeast wind blew with *considerable force* in *September*, but that this year the sickliest possible wind—the southwest wind—blew *sluggishly* in the month of the deadly pestilence. Can we shut our eyes to the possible fact that this southwest wind had just force enough to lift the deadly miasms of Springfield upon the town and lay them there as a blanket or pall?

SIGNAL BUREAU REPORTS.

An extract from the Signal Service reports kindly furnished by Mr. Peter B. Finney, Acting Assistant Signal Officer at this place:

	Highest thermometer during month	Lowest thermometer during month	Monthly mean thermometer	Monthly mean humidity	Prevailing direction of wind for month	Total number of miles traveled	Total rainfall during month	Number of days on which rain fell
1873.								
June	95	62	78.8	74.8	SW	4.454	4.64	18
July	96	70	81.	75.	S	3.539	5.44	17
August	96	72	80.	78.	SW	3.420	5.45	16
September	94	65	76.4	81.9	NE	3.456	4.03	14
October	83	37	63.4	72.9	NW	4.492	1.09	6
1874.								
June	98	69	80.7	73.2	SE	5.050	4 85	14
July	94	71	78.95	78.83	SE	3.918	10.14	16
August	95	66	79.	74.25	NE	4.172	6.58	14
September	89	60	75.26	77.6	NE	4.540	8.89	14
October	84	46	66.3	71.	E	3.403	1.42	5
1875.								
June	97	65	79.38	71.4	S	4.173	4.10	6
July	100	78	84.75	65.	SW	5.082	1.51	3
August	91	68	78.4	74.9	S	4.160	6.14	13
September	93	58	74.67	78.	NE	4.242	3.95	7
October	83	45	63.5	69.8	NW	4.306	2.87	4
1876.								
June	99	65	80.56	71.20	SW	3.974	18.80	16
July	100	66	84.5	68.7	SW	2.997	6.11	13
August	97	70	82.1	72.6	S	1.963	6.88	14
September	96	55	78.	70.4	SW	2.184	2.63	12

ADMINISTRATIVE CAUSES.

"The exceptional administrative causes are now well known to the people of Savannah. Ten years ago a reform in the drainage and sewerage systems of the town was commenced, and vigorously pressed to a very fairly complete system. This system for eight years has been under the charge of Mr. J. K. Munnerlyn, the Dry Culture Inspector, and he has in each of these years, until this year, kept these systems of drains, canals and sewers in thorough order by constant and frequent workings, the Cedar Grove and Springfield lowlands and the Bilbo canal being constantly worked and the latter canal flowed and disinfected twice a week. This year not a drain has been touched nor the Bilbo canal flowed. The whole system upon which the people of Savannah had cheerfully spent such large sums was as unfit for the purposes intended as if it had never existed. Had this been a dry year and there had been no rains nothing would have happened ; but the floods came and the unusual heat prevailed and the sirocco blew from the southwest, with deadly result.

"Still another fact cannot be overlooked. The traps to our sewers, and the sewers themselves, were not supplied with water, watched carefully and properly washed out during June, July and August, and their offensiveness was notorious. At a later date, toward the end of August, the water was turned on and the evil remedied.

TOPOGRAPHICAL CAUSES.

"The topographical causes are the legitimate sequence of the meteorological and the administrative.

"The heavy rains of summer raised the water level upon the city plateau. Mr. Alfred Kent, the pump contractor, had found it difficult for several years to keep the pumps in order, and for several years his work has been severe in deepening the wells all over the town. But in 1876 not a well after June gave any trouble. The effect of this rise of water was to *keep all the privy vaults soaked and peculiarly offensive from their putrefaction,* a thing wholly different from former years.

"Lured into security by years of immunity from disease, the wise precautions of former years were neglected and exposed to the deadly result of a season of excessive rainfall, unusual heat and unfavorable winds. The consequent pestilential miasms were in some degree deadly and excessive beyond the record of years, and the animal putrefactions in our sewers, and in their great single outlet, were confessedly offensive and excessive.

"We all now confess and know the *exceptional* and *excessive* putrefactions of animal and vegetable matters in and around this town before and during our epidemic. These putrefactions could not exist at all without the plant growths and their spores, *the proven contagium or poison* of all forms of malarial diseases, fever, etc. And the *contagia* or *spores* or *germs* of the yellow fever of this epidemic of 1876 are to be found in the putrefaction ferments of the Bilbo canal, Springfield lowlands, the scavenger offal beds, the privy vaults and unclean sewers."

In few words, the epidemic of malignant malarial fever and genuine yellow fever in Savannah, 1876, has been caused by the EXCEPTIONALLY GREAT MASSES OF PUTREFACTION, AND THE INDISSOLUBLE AND ESSENTIAL CRYPTO-GAMIC FERMENT PLANT GROWTH, WHOSE SPORES WERE THE PUTREFACTIVE CONTAGIUM OF THE EPI-DEMIC.

LETTER FROM DR. WARING TO DR. McFARLAND.

THE SCAVENGER DEPOSITS OF OFFAL AND GARBAGE IN THE MOST DANGEROUS PART OF THE CITY.—OCTOBER 23, 1876.

Dr. J. T. McFarland, Health Officer and Chairman of Committee on Sanitary Measures :

DEAR SIR: I had occasion, on the 18th inst., to refer you to Alderman Douglass for information of a very serious nature affecting the health of Savannah. I asked you then if your committee had visited and inspected the slope of the hill stretching westward to Springfield plantation and extending from the Ark-wright Cotton Factory to the fence of Laural Grove Cemetery. The water springs out upon this slope at every point, making it intensely malarial. It is upon this slope, amid water, mud and maggots, that the City Scavenger has deposited the offal and gar-bage of Savannah, a feast for buzzards and a home for the yellow fever fiend. Trust me, I do not use too strong language. By reference to the Signal Bureau reports of prevailing winds it would appear that no more unfortunate spot could have been selected:

	1873.	1874.	1875.	1876.
June	S. W.	S. E.	S.	S. W.
July	S.	S. E.	S. W.	S. W.
August	S. W.	N. E.	S.	S.
September	N. E.	N. E.	N. E.	S. W.

It is to the windward of the town, on a western slope, soaking wet, and fully exposed to the hot western sun. This spot smells like a butcher pen; and throughout the last summer these putrescent exhalations have mingled with the rotting and stinking vegetation of neglected Springfield, only separated by a narrow drain full of water. All the conditions for yellow fever poison, it must be evident, are and have been since June 10th, the date of the overflow, in full force here, to be wafted steadily into and on this devoted town by the south and southwest winds. For this there can be no excuse. The President of the Central Railroad, I am credibly informed, as far back as July, complained to the authorities of the annoyance. I myself called on the Mayor on the 16th of September and told him I had driven off the buzzards and intercepted the carts at these heaps. He said he had sent a policeman to see about this matter. And yet, as I have before intimated to you, Alderman Douglass ordered these carts away on the 17th of October.

The slope for these deposits is well known to be a quarter of a mile within the city limits, and on the edge of a dense population of poor people. It seems to me a sad inconsistency that you close your report with these words: "In concluding, the committee would simply add that the city authorities and the officers have our entire confidence," &c., &c.

Though differing with you in relation to these public matters, I have the honor to assure you of my personal regard and respect.

Very truly yours,

JAMES J. WARING.

UPON QUARANTINE.

UPON THE POSSIBILITY OR PROBABILITY OF IMPORTATION OF YELLOW FEVER EPIDEMICS.

IF THESE EPIDEMICS ARE IMPORTED FROM HAVANA OR OTHER TOWNS OF CUBA, THEN THE ONLY PROTECTION IS NOT QUARANTINE, BUT A COMMERCIAL TREATY WITH SPAIN CREATING A JOINT SANITARY COMMISSION TO ENFORCE SANITARY LAWS, AND A REFORM OF STREETS, SCAVENGERING, VENTILATION, ETC., IN THAT ISLAND.

UPON QUARANTINE.

There seems to me to be much confusion in the minds of the various advocates of, on the one side the exotic or foreign origin of yellow fever, and on the other of the domestic or local origin. The facts of the history of epidemics are these:

1st. It has been the universal experience of human observation that pestilences, and amongst these eminently the plague and yellow fever, are filth or putrefaction diseases. Admitted. What is filth? What is putrefaction? Organic matters are *filth* so soon as putrefaction begins, not before. When they become offensive to the senses of sight and smell, they are filth. Now what is putrefaction? Putrefaction is one form of fermentation, and the fermentations are—

    1. Alcoholic,
    2. Acetic,
    3. Butyric or Lactic, and } Fermentation.
    4. Ammoniacal,
    5. Putrefactive,

And fermentation. What is fermentation? With the death of Liebig has passed away the chemical school with its catalytic, nassent and atomic theories, and it would be a bold scientist who would deny the crucial evidence of M. Pasteur (Ann. Chimie Phys,, 4th series, vol. 25, p. 145, 1872) that fermentation is a change of chemical composition, in organic compounds, brought about by a certain class of plants which deprived of the power of drawing the essential elements of their composition from the air, propagate themselves in the very substance of organic matters of all kinds by breaking up these matters and appropriating such elements as are necessary to their own growth. Chlorophyl (green coloring of plants) endows plants with the power to live on air. A certain class of plants—the fungi—having no chlorophyl cannot live on air, and, therefore, live on organic matters already brought into existence by higher orders of beings, whether animal or plant. Fermentation is, therefore, *"life without air,"* and science has advanced far enough to say: "This plant, *seen and plated*, invariably makes alcoholic fermentation; that plant, seen and plated, as in-

variably makes acetic vinegar fermentation, and the alcoholic ferment plant will not make vinegar fermentation, nor the vinegar ferment plant make alcoholic fermentation."

Further, all organic matters remain unchanged indefinitely, or
forever if unattacked by this class of plants. (See Pasteur's experiments.) And further, these plants attack *living organic matter* with as much vigor and power as dead organic matter. The
Isaria will destroy spiders, the Perinosporum Infestaws will destroy
potato vines, and the Spirochæte Obermeiri destroys man by appropriating into their bodies, and without air the very building material and elements of living structure. Further, these plants,
though living *without air*, can live *in the air*, and though able to
attack living beings, can nevertheless live on dead organic matter
and multiply illimitably, prepared at any moment to attack the
living.

Still further, these plants have in certain instances two forms ;
living in one form in or on one living structure, and its seeds or
germs developing into another form upon other living structure.
The Eurosium of the Barbury plant is the rust of wheat. Just as
the bitter almond is the sport or variety of the sweet almond, not
distinguishable to the eye, the one deadly and the other innocent,
so the Bacillus Anthracis is the sport or variety of the Bacillus
Subtilis, undistinguishable to the microscopic eye, one the innocent cause of decay in swamp water, the other the deadly poison
of living animals. This is polymorphism.

The atmosphere is at all times loaded with the seeds or spores
of these plants. Their botany is still in its infancy; nevertheless
this is elicited. The more elevated above the level of the sea is
the atmosphere, the freer is it of these seeds, or germs, or spores.
The atmosphere of the Jura was found destitute of spores by experiment. (See Tyndall.) So also atmospheres differ at times and
by circumstances in the amount of these spores, and atmospheres
otherwise loaded can be readily filtered of spores through cotton.
*Certain, the large majority of these fungi and their spores are cosmo-
politan, found everywhere, but certain well defined species are found
in certain localities—can readily be transplanted, but to develop or
propagate in other localities must be transported.*

But certain varieties, or sports, from innocent to deadly varieties, are more readily possible in these low forms of life than in
the higher. Here is a broad and reasonably possible field for the
polymorphism of cosmopolitan species.

If putrefactions are putrefactive fermentations, and hence are the result of the growth of living beings, how the mind is startled by the paradox, "decay is another form of life."

"Putrefaction is a corelative phenomenon, not of death, but of life." Ferdinand Cohn's Biologie der Pflanzen, vol. 2d.

Pasteur thus defines putrefaction. Comp. Rend., June, 1863:

"When, in a putrescible liquid, containing albuminoid organic matter, the dissolved oxygen has been absorbed, and has completely disappeared under the influence of the first infusoria developed, such as the *Monas crepusculum*, and the *Bacterum termo*, 'the *vibrio* ferments, which do not require this gas to sustain their life, begin to show themselves, and putrefaction is immediately set up. It is accelerated by degrees, following the progressive increase of the vibrios. As to the putridity, it becomes so intense, that the examination of a single drop of the liquid, under the microscope, is a very painful task.'

"It follows, from what has been said, that contact of air is by no means necessary for the development of putrefaction. On the contrary, if the oxygen dissolved in a putrescible liquid was not at once removed by the action of special organism, putrefaction would not take place ; the oxygen would destroy the vibrios which would try to develop at first."

If yellow fever and putrefaction, are closely related as cause and effect, then there is a similar indissoluble link between, or relation as cause and effect, between yellow fever and the Bacteria of Cohn (or vibrios of Pasteur) of putrefaction, etc.

All this being true and admitted, in what respect are the putrefaction bacteria of the West India Islands different from the putrefaction bacteria of the American coast, and does history and experience prove this difference ?

The violent assertion of the necessity of importation of the bacteria is as unreasonable as the equally violent assertion of the exclusively local origin of these bacteria on the American coast, are not these theories both right and both wrong ? It did not need the sad evidence of the epidemic up the Mississippi valley in 1878 to prove the possibility of the transplanting of these bacteria from one point to another, the common sense of all botany proved that long ago. That is not the question which presses home upon the people of Savannah. That other botanical question concerns them. Can innocent cosmopolitan varieties of bacteria be rapidly cultured into deadly *sports* or varieties ?

That is the tradition of this town ; *that* has been the belief of its ablest men, and its remarkable sanitary laws and sanitary efforts have been based upon *that* belief.

That other common sense result of all botanical experience that a plant will languish and die if it has not food to live on, is evidenced in the death of the late Wm. H. Tison. There cannot be a doubt that the bacteria which killed him lived through the hot months of the summer of 1877 in the house on Jones street, and were as effective for propagation as any *imported bacteria*, and yet no one was alarmed and no *spread* or *epidemic* resulted through the hot months of 1877.

In this connection the language of Dr. Cunningham, the Sanitary Commissioner with the government of India, is reasonable upon the irrational methods of quarantine.—*Journal of the Society of Arts*, April 28, 1876, p. 528. "The year 1872 was an epidemic year in India of cholera." * * * "This outbreak was carefully studied by Dr. Cunningham." * * * * * *

"In respect to the effect of quarantine in stopping the progress of cholera in this epidemic, Dr. Cunningham states that quarantine was tried in the hope of protecting a number of the cantonments in Upper India, that in many of them it signally failed, and that in no single instance is there any ground for believing that it was productive of any good; and he further observes that the direct evils of quarantine in stopping commerce and intercourse are great in themselves, but many indirect evils arise from it, and among these by no means the least is, that so long as men believe that they can escape from cholera by such means, they will never be fully alive to the importance of the greatest safeguard, sanitary improvement; and he adds that whatever opinion may be held on theoretrical questions, the great work to be done is to perfect and extend sanitary improvements among the population."

At a meeting of the India section of the Society of Arts, Edwin Chadwick, C. B., in the chair. * * The Chairman said: * * *

"A reactionary course, that has threatened interference with the course of sanitation in India, has been in directing attention to personal contagion as the chief means of preventing the spread of disease, by the re-enforcement of quarantines, the working of which we had examined, and upon that examination had declared them to be useless and mischievous, even upon the hypothesis on which they were maintained. In the illustration of the different doctrines and of the courses of action upon them, I may mention,

that on my first sanitary inquiries, on occasions of severe visitations of typhus fever in towns and villages, I found people—medical men as well as others—overlooking the stagnant marshes and
cesspools, and disregarding the evolution of the foul gases amidst
which they were living, maintaining positively that the disease
had been imported by tramps—for had not the first outbreak been
in the common lodging house?—which was true; but it was also
true that the common lodging house was more overcrowded and
in a worse sanitary condition than ordinary dwellings, and was
just the place in which, on current sanitary principles, any such
pestilence might be expected to appear. The remedy, however,
then held to be was just the same as in the plague, and now in the
cholera a *cordon sanitaire* against the beggars, "stamping" out
the disease by burning the clothes of the infected, and so on.
Now, by the sanitary course taken under Lord Shaftesbury's Act,
when properly executed, the "stamping" out has been effective
by the drainage of the common lodging houses, by the introduction
of pure supplies of water, by the introduction of the water closet,
for the immediate removal of all fouled waste water and excreta,
by ventilation, and by the prevention of overcrowding, and by
cleaned bedding. By these means, common lodging houses instead of being the first, are the last to be attacked, and are in a
sanitary condition and exemption from epidemic visitations, which
contrast strongly with the conditions of the wage classes and
their dwellings. The like has been the course in India, where it
has been held to be an undoubted fact there, as well as here, that
epidemics, and especially the cholera, were carried solely by
human communications, as by pilgrims. Is not its first development displayed at the great fairs in India where they assemble?
Truly so. But those vast fairs are fairs of vast filth, of vast overcrowding, of bad feeding, of depression, and susceptibility, from
weakness from these causes. The operations first conducted
against these causes at a great fair at Congeum, by Mr. Robert
Ellis, of Madras, were by the enforcement of cleanliness, by supplies of pure water, by pure and sufficient supplies of food, by the
prevention of overcrowding, by separation. By such means the
regular outbreaks of cholera, then and since, have been "stamped
out" at those fairs, and the people now hold them with the same
immunity from such epidemics that the tramps have here in well
regulated common lodging houses—the disease continuing its

ravages on the unregulated and ill-conditioned dwellings of the stationary wage classes of the population."

It is certainly true that the bacteria of yellow fever, propagated year after year in Havana, can be transplanted to the American coast, and are transplanted, though hard to prove. The rational method of relief from this quarter is not quarantine, but a commercial treaty with Spain, which would enable commissioners to enforce and remodel the Spanish towns, and enforce, through an effective police, sanitary laws. Havana is only another Indian fair, and only needs similar treatment for final relief.

"The Indian Government has placed these assemblies under strict sanitary supervision. Before the assembling of the multitudes the encampment is marked out, the water supplies are protected from pollution, surface cleanliness is enforced, and arrangements made for deposit in safe places of all refuse. The good results of these arrangements were illustrated in a fair at Manickpur in Oudh, attended by 125,000 persons, accompanied by at least 40,000 bullocks; cholera was prevalent in the district at the time, but there was an entire absence of cholera at the fair."— *Journal of the Society of Arts*, p. 529.

Whilst the evidence of transportation from town to town is overwhelming in this country, it is equally remarkable that in Savannah the importation from abroad stands entirely unproven. See the testimony of Dr. Wm. R. Waring in 1820, John E. Ward, Mayor, in 1854, and Edward C. Anderson, Mayor, and Dr. Mc-Farland, Health Officer, 1876. On the contrary, Dr. Wm. R. Waring testifies, in 1820, and is corroborated by Dr. Lemuel Kolloch, as his experience since 1780, that the yellow fever occurred continuously in all these years up to 1820, *without importation*. The history of the fever record placed side by side with the sanitary efforts of the town corroborates this view. See comparative table on page 23.

DIRECT EVIDENCE OF NON-IMPORTATION.

1. The testimony of Mayor E. C. Anderson before State Board of Health, 1876. (See appendix, p. v., of report of State Board of Health.) "No cases of yellow fever on vessels arriving here were brought to my official notice; the quarantine was in force and vessels from infected ports were kept in quarantine. Some were

detained so long that the Spanish Consul became impatient and made complaint about the delay."

2. The testimony before same, 1876, of Dr. J. T. McFarland, Health Officer, page viii., idem: "Don't believe yellow fever was brought here at all."

3. The letter of Consul General Henry C. Hall, upon the impossibility of importation, dated October 21st, 1876, and on file in the custom house at Savannah:

* * * "Its (the yellow fever) prevalence in Havana has been to no greater extent than during other years. It prevailed also in other places, but to a very limited extent. At Matanzas there were a few cases; at Cardenas no cases; at Cienfuegos, Trinidad, and Santiago de Cuba there were several cases. In all of these places yellow fever has prevailed in other years to as great extent, proportionately, as in Havana."

4. The following letter is also significant. It was addressed to Thomas Gadsden, Cashier of the Merchants' National Bank, by LeBaron & Son, of Pensacola, and dated October 7, 1876:

"DEAR SIR: * * * I am desirous of knowing how the yellow fever got to Savannah.

"The enclosed slip says it was taken there by vessels from Havana. We have had a number of vessels here from Havana and have had no sickness on board of any of them, and though we have a quarantine it is stupidly managed. This city has been and continues remarkably healthy."

5. The arrival and record of Spanish vessels. In the report of Dr. G. H. Stone to the United States Marine Hospital Service Department, Washington, will be found the following, well authenticated:

First case—A sailor named Schull, of schooner Severs, from New York, perfectly well on arrival, taken sick July 26, fourteen days after; admitted to hospital July 28, died July 30.

Second case—Thomas Cleary; date of attack August 6.

Third case—Patrick Cleary; date of attack August 17.

Fourth case—Child of John Lynch, attended by Dr. Read; date of attack and death only one day later.

By the records of quarantine and custom house all vessels arriving after June 1st had clean bills of health, excepting the Maria Carlina, which arrived at Tybee August 2nd; came up to city August 16th. Her record reads thus: One man died on the voyage; Captain is familiar with yellow fever; says it was not yellow fever ; the man was old ; did not turn yellow after death ; did not have black vomit ; the vessel was in quarantine till August 15th ; one man was taken sick at quarantine, not with yellow fever ; had yellow fever in hospital four weeks afterward. The Maria Carlina arriving as late as the 16th could not have produced the disease in either one of the four first cases reported. The Olympia arrivrd September 27.

THE INDIRECT EVIDENCE.

1st. The importation of the epidemics of 1820-1854 are formally denied in the official reports of Dr. Wm. R. Waring for 1820 and Mayor John E. Ward for 1854.

Report to Council, 1820, by Dr. Wm. R. Waring:

* * * *"It was said by some individuals to have been brought from the coast of Africa* in a brig called the Raminez, which had on board a cargo of new negroes. Unfortunately, however, for this hypothesis the Raminez did not only arrive with a healthy crew and entire freedom from any malignant disease, but she arrived some time after the fever had grown into considerable extent and severity. I have already stated that some rapid and insidious cases occurred in June, and that fourteen deaths took place in that month. I have stated that Mr. Patrick Stanton even died of black vomit on the 16th July. The Raminez came into port on the 22d. It was not, and could not be, an African disease. From the 23d of May to the 20th of July there came five vessels from the West Indies and one from New Orleans. I have not been able to learn of any others. On the 23d of May brig Rover, Captain James, from Havana; on 2d of June schooner Phantom, Havana; on the 13th of June schooner Charles, New Orleans; on the 24th of June sloop Darien, St. Domingo; on the 27th of June schooner Isabella, Matanzas; and on July 20th a vessel to Green & Lippit, from St. Domingo.

"It appears from inquiry, as to the state of these vessels, that the crews were healthy, and there was nothing in relation to them which could authorize a belief of their either having severe disease on board, or the power of propagating any disease whatever." * * *

Mayor Ward, report 1854, says:

* * * "Various causes have been assigned by different individuals for the existence of the disease during the past season. I

have felt it my duty to carefully investigate them. The first cause assigned was the introduction of the fever into our city from the brig Charlotte Hague, which put into Cockspur Roads about the 29th of June. She was a Danish brig, bound from Havana to Copenhagen. She was visited on the 30th by the Port Physician, Dr. Mackall, who reported two slight cases of sickness on board. It having been asserted that some of the men brought from her to the city died of the yellow fever, I have used every effort to obtain evidence to prove the fact, but I have found no proof to satisfy my own mind that there was any case of yellow fever brought up to the city from that vessel, and I herewith submit for your consideration a letter from Dr. Mackall and one from Dr. Wragg, the attending physicians of the Savannah Infirmary, to which all the men were carried. Dr. Chartres being absent I have been unable to obtain an answer from him."

The nature of the poison of yellow fever is such, nevertheless, that it can be imported if the views of the germ theory of disease be admitted in explanation.

2d. The deposit of certain stone ballast at the Atlantic and Gulf railroad wharf from Spanish vessels has been charged with being the medium of importation, just as the deposit of dredge mud in this very neighborhood in 1854 was also believed to have been a cause of production. This ballast was used to macadamize the roadways of the wharf, and came from a locality southwest of Regla and about two miles from the harbor. See Woodhull's report, *The American Journal of Medical Sciences*, page 37:

* * * "At that place are low ('little') hills which are dry, and in no way subject to drainage from human habitations, of which there are few in that neighborhood, the nearest being a fourth of a mile distant. The ballast is dug from these hills, and is carried from the quarries to the ships, by which it is bought as needed. Regla, the nearest town, is thought to be healthier than Havana, and in summer many families move to the neighborhood of the hills from that city. This is entirely confirmed by Dr. Belot, who says: 'The gray ballast referred to is a native rock taken from the side of a hill in West Regla, about forty feet above the level of the sea,' and that it does not contain any debris or organic matter whatever. That excellent authority further says: 'I do not believe that the fresh ballast referred to will, of itself, in any way influence the development of yellow fever. If such

4

were the case the disease would manifest itself as soon as the ballast is taken in.'"

3d. Yellow fever existed in Savannah every year of the first quarter of the present century ; see table of Mortuary Fever record, taken from the records in the Clerk's office of the city council.

The bitter controversies which existed in the first half of the last century upon the question of importation of yellow fever from the East Indies to the West Indies, is certainly significant, and suggests doubt as to the probability of importation when filth and nastiness prevail in towns. [A treatise on Plague and Yellow Fever, by James Tytler, compiler of the Medical Part of Encyclopædia Britannica, 1779 ; pages 372, 373, 374.]

* * * "When Columbus first visited the West India islands, we hear nothing of his having found such a disease exisiting there ; nor does it appear that it was known among the many Spanish adventurers who succeeded him, and who subdued such immense tracts on the southern continent. Soon after the settlement of some of the West India islands, however, by other European nations, this disease began to make its appearance, though at what time is still uncertain. Dr. Hillary says, that " as we have no accounts of this disease in the ancients, nor even in the Arabian writers, who lived and practiced in the hot climate, we must give it *some name ;* " and he calls it the *putrid bilious fever*. "From the best and most authentic account, (adds he) that I can obtain, and also from the nature and symptoms of the disease, it appears to be a disease that is indigenous [naturally belonging to the climate] to the West India islands and the continent of America, which is situated between the tropics, and most probably to all other countries within the torrid zone. But I cannot conceive what were the motives which induced Dr. Warren to think that this fever was first brought from Palestine to Marseilles, and from thence to Martinique, and so to Barbadoes, about thirty-seven years since (1721 or 1722). A better inquiry would have informed him, that this fever had frequently appeared in this and other West India islands, many years before ; for several judicious practioners, who were then, and are now living here, whose business was visiting the sick the greater part of their life time, some of them almost eighty years of age, remember to have seen this fever frequently in this island, not only many years before that time, but many years before that learned gentleman came to it.

"To the same purpose Dr. Mosely says, "Warren, though he lived at Barbadoes in 1739, supposes it never appeared in that island till about the year 1721, and that it was then brought from Martinique in the Lynn, man-of-war. He says the second appearance of it there was in 1733, and that it then came also from Martinique. He undertakes to show, that it is a disease of Asiatic extract; and says that a *Provencale* fleet arrived at Port St. Pierre, in Martinique, from Marseilles, on board which were several bales of Levant goods which were taken in at Marseilles from a ship just arrived from St. Jean D'Acre (probably the Ptolemais of the ancients). Upon opening these bales of goods at Port St. Pierre, this distemper immediately shewed itself; many of the people were instantly seized, some died almost suddenly, others in a few days, and some lingered longer; and the contagion, still spreading, made great havoc at the beginning. He says he had this account from Mr. Nelson, an English surgeon, who was seized with the disease at Martinique, and died of it a few days after his arrival at Barbadoes. He says it is very probable that the same fever, or one of very near resemblance and affinity, may first have been carried among the American Spaniards (among whom it is now endemic) in somewhat a like manner; and that possibly some peculiar qualities in the air and climate might have fostered and maintained it there ever since."

Dr. Mosely at once concludes the whole of this account to be *fabulous*, but whether fabricated by Dr. Warren or the surgeon, he does not say. He then appeals to Dr. Towne, who wrote before Warren, in 1776, but takes no notice of this *chimerical* origin of the yellow fever, but considers it as an endemical disease in the West Indies Hillary's opinion already given is also quoted.

"The next evidence is that of Mr. Hughes, who, though not a medical man, has written on the first appearance of the yellow fever in Barbadoes in the following terms: Dr. Gamble remembers that it was very fatal here in the year 1691, and that it was called the *new distemper*, and afterwards *Kendal's fever*, the *pestilential fever*, and the *bilious fever*. The same symptoms did not always appear in all patients, nor alike in every year when it visited us. It is most commonly rife and fatal in May, June, July and August, and then mostly among strangers; though a great many of the inhabitants, in the year 1696, died of it; and a great many at different periods since."

"As to the first appearance of the disease in the West India islands we have no accounts which have been deemed sufficiently authentic, though indeed it must be confessed that the doubts seem to be derived as much from an attachment to theory as to the investigation of truth. "The *endemical causus*, or *yellow fever* (says Dr. Mosely) which is the terror of Europeans newly arrived in the West Indies, is called by the French *la maladie de Siam.* Monsieur Pouppe Desportes, who practiced physic at *St. Dominique* from 1732 to 1748, and who had more experience, and has written from better information on the diseases of that colony, than any of his countrymen, says that this fever was so called from its being first taken notice of in the island of Martinique at a time when some vessels were there from Siam. This account, though probably true enough as to the time of its being first observed in the French colonies, is extremely incorrect in other respects ; for M. Desportes has not only admitted a supposition that the disease originated among these East Indian mariners, but calls it pestilential, and says that the Europeans are almost the only victims to it. "

HISTORY

OF THE

DISCOVERY AND TRUE NATURE

OF

PATHOGENIC BACTERIA,

THE GERM THEORY OF DISEASE.

TWELFTH REPORT

—OF THE—

MEDICAL OFFICER OF HER MAJESTY'S PRIVY COUNCIL

FOR 1869.—Page 243

INTRODUCTORY REPORT BY DR. BOURD N SANDERSON ON THE INTIMATE
PATHOLOGY OF CONTAGIUM.

There are two obvious objections which stand in the way of
the acceptance of any *chemical* explanation of the phenomena of
contagium. The first is that the multiplication of contagium is a
process which cannot be compared to any which is brought about
by chemical agencies independently of organic development.
The second is, that all contagia possess the power of retaining
their latent virulence for long periods (often resisting the most
unfavorable chemical and physical conditions) and only show
themselves to be what they are when they are brought into contact with living organisms. Outside of the body the contagious
material withstands all those changes to which, on chemical
grounds, we should expect it to be liable while in the body it
manifests a degree of activity, and gives rise to an amount of
molecular disturbance which is quite as unaccountable.

Neither of these difficulties stand in the way, if we suppose
that the contagious process is connected with the unfolding of
organic forms.   *   *   *   •   •   •

SEVENTEENTH REPORT

—OF—

THE MEDICAL OFFICER OF THE PRIVY COUNCIL TO HER MAJESTY'S GOVERNMENT.

1874.—P. 5.

Ten years ago we had not even a beginning of any true insight into the respective contagia which excite diseases. * * * *

I think the fact noteworthy that the first of such studies were instituted, and the first steps of discovery made with reference to a contagious fever of horned cattle. I refer to the researches which were made under Her Majesty's Government in 1865, in aid of the Cattle Plague Commission, when Dr. Lionel Beale, working at the microscopy of the disease, drew attention to the swarms of extremely minute particles which he found invariably present in the texture and juices of the animals, and which he believed to be the contagium of the disease ; and when Dr. Bourdon Sanderson, working at the matter from a different point of view, succeeded in showing, experimentally, that the true contagium admits of being physically distinguished in the animal juices which contain it, and of being so separated from them as to leave them without infective power. In the next succeeding years the writings of Dr. Hallier, Professor of Botany in Jena, brought under animated discussion, as a branch of micro-phytology the nature and mode of origin of contagium particles in a great variety of diseases, human and brute ; new experimental knowledge of several contagia was set forth in the writings of Professor Chauveau, of the Veterinary Schools of Lyons ; and in 1870 I had the honor of presenting Dr. Sanderson's first report of researches made in the matter under your Lordship's direction.

At that time these general conclusions already seemed justified ; first, that the characteristic shaped elements which the microscope had shown abounding in various infective products, are self-multiplying organic forms, not congeneric with the animal body in which they are found, but apparently of the lowest vegetable kind ; and, secondly, that such living organisms are probably the essence, or an inseparable part of the essence, of all contagia of disease. The study of morbid contagia was thus brought into seeming affinity with that which had for some years before been made by Professor Schroder and M. Pasteur, in the ordinary processes of fermentation and putrefaction; and then began to become faintly visible to us a vast destructive laboratory of nature, wherein the diseases, which are most fatal to animal life and the changes to which dead organic matter is passively liable, appear bound together by what must at least be called a very close analogy of causation. This view of the matter has since then become greatly more distinct in consequence of investigations made under your Lordships by Dr. Sanderson, practically, in 1871 and 1872, with reference to the common septic contagia or ferment, for in that ferment, particulate as above described, there seems now to be identified a force which, acting disintegratively upon organic matter alike, whether dead or living, can on the one hand initiate putrefaction of what is dead, and on the other hand initiate febrile and inflammatory processes in what is living.

Research of Dr. Bourdon Sanderson :

Report of the medical officer of the Privy Council, page 30.

There are four contagious diseases, in respect of which the presence in the contagious liquids of forms of vegetation differing from those met with either after death in the normal tissues or liquids of the body, or during life in the products of primary or secondary inflammation, has been established. These are small-pox, sheep-pox, splenic fever and relapsing fever.

The first statement as to the existence of organisms in the lymph of cow-pox and small-pox were made by Dr. Keber, of Dantzic, 1868.

*   *   *   *   *   *   *   *   *

In my first paper on pathology of contagion, published in 1870, I gave an account, accompanied by a wood cut, of certain bodies, to which I assigned the name of microzyms, the presence of which I found it was usually possible to demonstrate in vaccine liquid.

NOTE.—In the twelfth report of the medical officer of Her Majesty's Privy Council, 1870, page —, Dr. Bourdon Sanderson's experiments upon the physical properties of vaccine virus, demonstrated that the contagious particles of the vaccine lymph settled to the bottom when put into water, and separated into two parts, one of which could not reproduce the pustule, whilst the other did do so. On the contrary, the same lymph shaken up sharply in water was so diluted as to produce pustules in two out of twenty trials, whilst the lymph which had settle to the bottom, in water, produced pustules in sixteen out of twenty-two trials."

NOTE.—1870, page 233.—"With this view I diffused liquids known to be infecting, derived from plague-stricken animals, by the ordinary method, i. e.: through parchment paper, and found that while the diffusate was wholly innocuous, the liquid that remained behind retained its activity.

1871, page 62.—*   *   *   "So that we may conclude that the contamination of water by apparently dry surfaces happens only in those cases in which *desiccation* is incomplete. It thus appears that fully formed bacteria are deprived of their power of farther development by thorough desiccation."   *   *   *

Page 31.—Some months before the appearance of the paper from which the above description is quoted, Dr. C. Weigert, of Breslau, published a short communication, founded on the microscopical examination of the skin in persons who had died of small-pox, in which he stated that he had found the lymphatic vessels of the cutis plugged with a granular mass, which exhibited all the characters of the micrococci."   *   *   *

Page 33.—"These communications led to Dr. Klein's being requested to undertake the investigation, of which the results are embodied in his paper on the pathology of sheep-pox. It will probably be admitted by most readers that even if the problem has not been completely solved, the investigation has yielded results of the highest pathological value.   *   *   *

(Page 33, *idem*). "The first infective disease, in respect of which it could be asserted with anything like probability, that a specific organism was present, either in the blood or the tissues, was splenic fever. The peculiar staff, or rod-shaped bodies which are always contained in the liquor sanguinis in this disease, was discovered in 1855, or perhaps earlier.   *   *   *

(Page 35, *idem*). The discovery that, in the blood of animals affected with splenic fever, rod-like bodies are found in the liquor sanguinis, was first, I believe, made by Pollander, who in the year 1855, described them as fine, apparently solid, straight, unbranched objects, $\frac{1}{100}$ to $\frac{1}{300}$ of a line in length and $\frac{1}{3000}$ of a line in width. He noted they possessed no motion, differing in that respect from ordinary bacteria. (Note.—The spirilla of splenic fever will be given below from Cohn). A year or two after Brauell published the first of his very extensive series of researches on the contagium of splenic fever, in which he not only confirmed Pollander's discovery, but by experiments in which he communicated the disease to animals under a great variety of conditions,, acquired for pathologists the greater part of the accurate knowledge they now possess on the subject. * * *

(Page 36, *idem*). "The following are the most important facts relating to the contagion of splenic fever, which have been ascertained either as the result of clinical or experimental inquiry :

1st. "The disease may be communicated by any means which involves the transference of a portion of the blood of a diseased animal, to the living tissue of an animal previously healthy. It is not known that it can be propagated in any other way, for animals kept in the closest proximity to diseased ones, and placed under the most favorable conditions for infection through the air, are not infected.

2nd. "Although the blood of animals affected with splenic fever always contain the staff-shaped bodies, if it be examined at a sufficiently advanced period, the disease can be communicated by the inoculation of blood in which these bodies are either not present, or at all events not in such numbers as to admit of their being made out microscopically. * * *

(Page 37). "There are facts relating to splenic fever which show on the one hand that the contagious property, as it exists in the circulating blood, is very transient, and on the other, that there must be a form or state of the contagium in which it is remarkably persistent. * * *

(Page 39.) "The common ubiquitous bacteria, those which are concerned in putrefaction changes are known to be in their ordinary active state, easily destroyed. That they are unable to survive complete desiccation or a temperature higher than 80 deg. C. On the other hand, it is equally well ascertained that masses containing bacteria are not deprived of the power of originating new generations of these organisms by heat, unless they are either subjected to a temperature considerably higher than that of ebullition, or boiled for a very long period. The reason of the apparent discrepancy is to be found in the fact that the bacteria have two modes of existence, the one characterized by permanence and resistance, the other by rapid development and short duration ; thus in all bacteria masses, there exists, in addition to the ordinary forms of readily killed bacteria, other living particles of more stable structure.

"The properties of such bodies to which Professor Cohn assigns the name of lasting spores (Darosporen) are only just now beginning to occupy the attention of mycologists. * * * (Page 33, *idem.*) The most striking feature of the disease (splenic fever in cattle) is its externally rapid progress. In the most rapid cases, those to which all writers refer as "apoplectic," the disease runs its course in a few hours at most. In the ordinary cases as they occur among cattle, it lasts a day or two. * * * * * * * *

"Professor Buhl, at Munich, in 1868, discovered a rapidly fatal disease affecting the human subject which presents the characteristic of splenic fever, and turns out on investigation to be identical with it. The first case occurred in a man aged thirty-two years. Shortly after, two other cases were recorded by Professor Waldeger, now of Strasbourg, and all doubts of the matter was removed by Dr. Munch, of Moscow, who, at the Workman's Hospital, discovered that in all men who died from infection from diseased animals, there existed all the characteristic internal changes and lesions of splenic fever.

Relapsing fever, page 41.) "In the epidemic of relapsing fever, which prevailed in Berlin from November, 1867, to May, 1868, Dr. Obermeier, whose attention had been called to the question of the relation between specific organic forms and contagium, by the publications of Professor Hallier, investigated the blood microscopically in eighty-two cases. In general, the results were negative. In some cases, however, he noted appearances, of which he did not fail at the time to understand the full significance."

When relapsing fever again appeared in Berlin in 1872, the inquiry was resumed. In the very first case which was investigated, the bodies to be referred to in the following paragraphs as "spirilla," were discovered. On the 26th of March Dr. Obermeier published a second series of observations. Twenty new cases were investigated in veins of which the blood had been examined daily. The result of these examinations showed that the presence of the organisms in the blood was associated with the morbid processes so closely that as soon as the pyrexia disappeared they disappear with it, reappearing when the patient was again found in the relapse.

Soon after the death of Dr. Obermeier, in August, 1873, a third series of observations were communicated by Dr. Engel to the *Berlin Medical Weekly Journal.*

During the same year the epidemic prevalence of relapsing fever in Breslau afforded additional opportunities for investigating the subject.

The morphological and botanical characters of the organisms were subsequently determined by Professor Ferdinand Cohn.

Dr. Litten gave the history of the disease. It was infectious eminently from person to person in limited foci. Thus, in a hamlet called Wilhelmsruhe, fourteen persons, belonging to four families, *all of which inhabited the same room*, were attacked. Breslau was peculiarly exposed to overcrowding in that year. All the other inhabitants of the hamlet, although some of them occupied rooms in the same building, remained free from the disease. Twenty-one persons were attacked in the hospital. Poverty and want did not give rise to the disease.

Dr. Litten further gives the following summary of his observations:

"The spirilla of Obermeier are found only in the blood of persons affected with the disease, and present themselves invariably during the paroxisms. The following is the course of relapsing fever: Six to seven days, fever; eight days, remission; five days, second fever; nine days after, rarely fever returns."

Obermeier found in the blood of the sick very delicate, long, very rapidly moving spiral threads, seen only in the stage of fever paroxysm, not in the remission, nor in the period shortly before or after the crisis. Cohn saw them himself at Breslau, in "All Saints" Hospital. These threads are found exclusively in the blood, being never found in the secretions nor organs. They are found twenty-four hours, and leave two or three days after increase of temperature. On account of their delicacy of structure and rapid motion, they are easily overlooked The observer first detects them by the motion they give to the blood corpuscles. These threads or spirilla are never found in the dead body. Their number is various. They probably diminish toward the end of the paroxysm, and completely disappear before the crisis.

The number of spirilla varies considerably. They can be best kept alive out of the body in serum. As soon as the temperature of 60 deg. C. was passed, the movements became languid; no effect to this degree. By the time 65 deg. was reached, they had entirely ceased. No effect was observed on cooling the prepara-

tion to the temperature of freezing, but its continuance caused
the movements to cease. Sometimes they are found in small
numbers, and in others very abundant in the field of the microscope. According to Engel their number must be reckoned by
millions. This fever was seen at Breslau in 1868. It came on in
temporary and local epidemics, which probably were imported.
As a rule, it attacked all the occupants of a room, one after
another, and obviously was spread by personal infection.

FORMS AND CLASSIFICATION OF BACTERIAS—1870,
PAGE 244.

The organic forms which are met with in contagious fluids are,
according to Hallier, analogous. They are included by him under
the general term hafe, *scum or dregs*. By Hallier it is understood
to mean a form of *fungus*, which consists of minute single cells,
which reproduce themselves with extraordinary rapidity, exist in
all substances undergoing *putrefaction* or *fermentation*, and grow
and multiply at the expense of these substances. As they never
lose their unicellular character they cannot be said either to have
spores or mycelium, each individual cell being alike an organ of
growth and an organ of reproduction. Some of these organisms
are already well known, especially those which belong to the true
fermentations, as e. g.: The arborescent ferment plant, which
exists in most hormiscium, consisting of branching series of globules joined end to end; or the necklace-like ferment of common
yeast (torula); or the still more remarkable sarcina ventriculi, in
which the globules are set together in squares. These organisms
may be divided into two groups; one comprising the ferment
plants already mentioned, which have no direct relation to our
present inquiry; the other contains those forms which are associated with the commencement of decomposition of nitrogenous
compounds, of which putrefaction is the continuation. The
spheroidal particles which are observed under these conditions
are much smaller than those which occur in fermenting liquid,
and do not, in general, exceed $\frac{1}{7000}$ of an inch in diameter. They
are known to be living organisms, and thereby distinguished from
mere particles of protoplasm by the observed fact that they tend,
under conditions which will hereafter be fully discussed, to elongate into rod-like bodies, endowed with a peculiar progressive
and oscillatory movement. So long as they are still spheroids

they are called by Hallier micrococci, by others microspores.
After they have become staff-shaped they are usually called bacteria or bacteridia.

(Page 245, *idem*, 1868.) "Du Barry's description of these living
organisms: They consist of cells, each of which is roundish, or of
the form of a short cylinder, and multiply by continuous division
into two. They either occur isolated or are united into rows or
small masses, which grow equally at all points by cell division.
They include, adds Du Barry, forms of extreme minuteness, as
yet insufficiently known as regards their organization, which are
represented by the generic names vibrio, bacterium, zoogloa,
(Cohn), nozema, (Nagelé), sarcina, &c., &c.   1868.

(1871, report, *idem*.) "When common microzyms grow on moist
surfaces they, with their intervening jelly, form viscous masses of
sufficient size to be cognizable by the unaided senses, these consisting of a material similar to scum which forms on the surface
of liquids.

(Page 50, *idem*.) "As regards their action on liquids, the
most important facts are these: 1st. That their growth is attended with absorption of oxygen and discharge of carbonic
acid; 2d. That they are remarkably independent of the chemical
constitution of the medium, provided they are supplied with oxygen; and 3d. That they take nitrogen from almost any source
which contains it, and use it for the building up of their own protoplasm.

(*Nature—Page* 328—*August* 16, 1877.)

"In conclusion, Dr. Roberts pointed to the fact that there exists
a remarkable morphological identity between the organism of
certain infective diseases and other quite harmless saprophytes.

"Thus bacillus anthracis of splenic fever only differs from bacillus
subtilis in the fact that the rods are motionless, while the spirilla
of relapsing fever are identical in form and botanical characters with
spirochæte plicatilis of Ehrenberg. May not these coincidences,
he suggests, point to a natural explanation of the origin of contagia? May not the harmful organisms be merely variations, or
sports from the harmless saprophytes resembling them, just as
the bitter almond is a sport from the sweet, and the nectarine
from the peach? May not typhoid fever, for example, be explained
as due to a variation from some common saprophyte of our stagnant pools or sewers, which, under certain conditions within the
human body, acquires a parasitic hold?

(Journal of the Royal Microscopical Society, Page 87—Bacteria as Parasites in Splenic Disease—May, 1878.)

M. H. Toussaint has communicated fresh remarks on this subject to the French Academy, his object being to show that those who have attributed the disease to a virus, and not to the bacteria, are in error. Referring to a previous paper, he states that a rabbit, dying after inoculation with blood containing the bacteria, dies in consequence of the obliteration of the capillaries of essential organs, such as lungs and brain. Most of the flexuous capillaries of the economy are filled with bacteria at the moment of death. This effect is most readily observed in the choroid and retina of albin rabbits. He claims to have demonstrated that when fresh bacteria blood is received into tubes and preserved from contact with air and from putrefaction, it loses its contagious properties in six or eight days, or sooner, if kept at a temperature of 38 deg. to 40 deg., C. *A virus does not behave in this way.* Such a method would be adopted to preserve it. Filtration of bacteria blood, fresh and defibrinized, through a filter composed of eight sheets of paper, suffices to deprive it of its contagious element. This filter allows the granulations, and even some white corpuscles, to pass, but it retains all the bacteria. Such a filtration allows a considerable quantity of virus elements to pass, but completely deprives bacteria blood of its contagious properties.

The time elapsing between bacterium inoculation and the death of an animal, may be regulated by the quantity injected, though the incubation period may be suppressed.

* * * * * * * * *

He describes many experiments, all confirming the belief that death is produced by the multiplication of the bacteria organisms and their obstructing the capillaries. In one animal was injected $1\frac{1}{2}$ cubic contents of the infected blood, containing fifteen hundred millions of bacteria, in another seventy-five millions, and in a third fifteen hundred, the blood being diluted with water. The first died in seven hours, the second died in twelve or thirteen hours, and the third died in thirty-six hours.

Nature—Page 327.—Dr. William Roberts, F. R. S., on Subject of Spontaneous Generation and the Doctrine of Contagium Vivum—August 16th, 1877.

After alluding to the analogy, which may possibly be real, between contagious fever and the action, say of yeast in fermen-

5

tation, he proceeded to consider two propositions. The first proposition is : That organic matter has no inherent power of generating bacteria, and no inherent power of passing into decomposition. To substantiate this, he exhibited specimens of decomposable organic fluids, which, having been sterilized, had remained in his possession, undecomposed, for many months, or even years. Sterilization had been effeccted in three ways :

1st. By prolonged boiling, the exclusion of germs being afterward secured by plugs of cotton wool. 2d. By filtration through unglazed earthenware, previously heated to redness, into flasks, sterilized by the heat of boiling water. 3d. By transferring the organic decomposable fluid, such as blood, urine, pus, etc., directly from the interior of the body to well sterilized flasks, and subsequently defending them from germs by plugs of cotton wool.

The second proposition is : That bacteria are the actual agents of decomposition. This Dr. Roberts considers to be proved by the following considerations :

a. That which originates decomposition comes from the air, since removal of the plugs in any of the above cases is infallibly followed by decomposition.

b. That which originates decomposition consists of solid particles floating in the air, since filtration of the air, as above, is able to prevent decomposition, and air, which is optically pure, (Tyndall) has no fermentating power.

c. That which originates decomposition has not the nature of a soluble ferment, since decomposable fluids, in which *putrefaction has* already set in, yield filtrates through earthenware, which do not decompose, while pepsin, diastase, etc., readily pass through the same medium.

But it is, nevertheless, true, that certain liquids, as neutralized living infusions, and milk, often produce bacteria, even after they have been boiled for two or three hours, and when there is no possibility of subsequent infection ; and it is equally true that bacteria are invariably killed by exposure to a temperature of 140 deg. F., or more. Are not these facts strong evidence of abrogenesis ? No; and for the following reasons :

1st. Although bacteria invariably die at the above named temterpature, their spores may not ; and this is more than probable, since Dollinger and Drysdale have demonstrated that while certain monads are destroyed by heating to 140 deg. F., their spores survive a heat of 300 deg. F.

2d Cohn has examined the organisms which arise under the conditious named, viz.: in boiled living infusions, and he has demonstrated that they are not a new creation, as might have been expected, but invariably the well known bacterium, bacillus subtilis. Is it possible to believe, in the face of the whole theory of evolution, that abrogenesis is able, at one stroke, and within seventy hours, to produce such a specialized organism as this ?

A CLASSIFICATION OF PATHOGENIC BACTERIA,

BY

DR. FERDINAND COHN,

Beitrage zur Biologie der Pflanzen—Part 2, 1872, p. 100.

GENERA.

1st. Globular bacteria, (sphero-bacteria.)
2d. Rod bacteria, (micro-bacteria.)
3d. Thread bacteria, (desmo-bacteria.)
4th. Spiro bacteria.

SPECIES.

1st Genus.
- 1st. Micrococcus vaccinia; pock-bacteria.
- 2d. Micrococcus diphtherica; of diphtheria.
- 3d. Micrococcus septicus; pyæmia septicæria.
- 4th. Micrococcus bombycis; mycosis intestinitis of silk worms.

SPECIES.

2d Genus.
- 1st. Bacterium termo; of ordinary putrefaction.
- 2d. Bacterium tincola; of stagnant water.

SPECIES.

3d Genus.
- 1st. Threads straight; bacillus.
- 2d. Threads undulatory; vibrios.

Bacillus.
- a. Bacillus subtilis; of butyric acid fermentation.
- b. Bacillus anthracis; of splenic fever.

Vibrio.
- a. Vibrio rugula; diarrhœa and on mucus of teeth.
- b. Vibrio serpens.

SPECIES.

4th Genus.
- 1st. Spirochæte. { Flexible, moving rapidly, close wound thread of a screw.
- 2d. Spirillum. { Non-flexible, motionless, short, open wound thread of a screw.

Spirochæte.
- a. Spirochæte plicatilis, 1872. { Rotting swamp water, mucus of teeth.
- b. Spirochæte Obermeiri, 1873. { Febris recurrens Breslau. Obermeier commenced his observations in 1868.

Spirillum.
- a. Spirillum tenue.
- b. Spirillum undula.
- c. Spirillum volutans. { In water containing decaying fresh water snails.

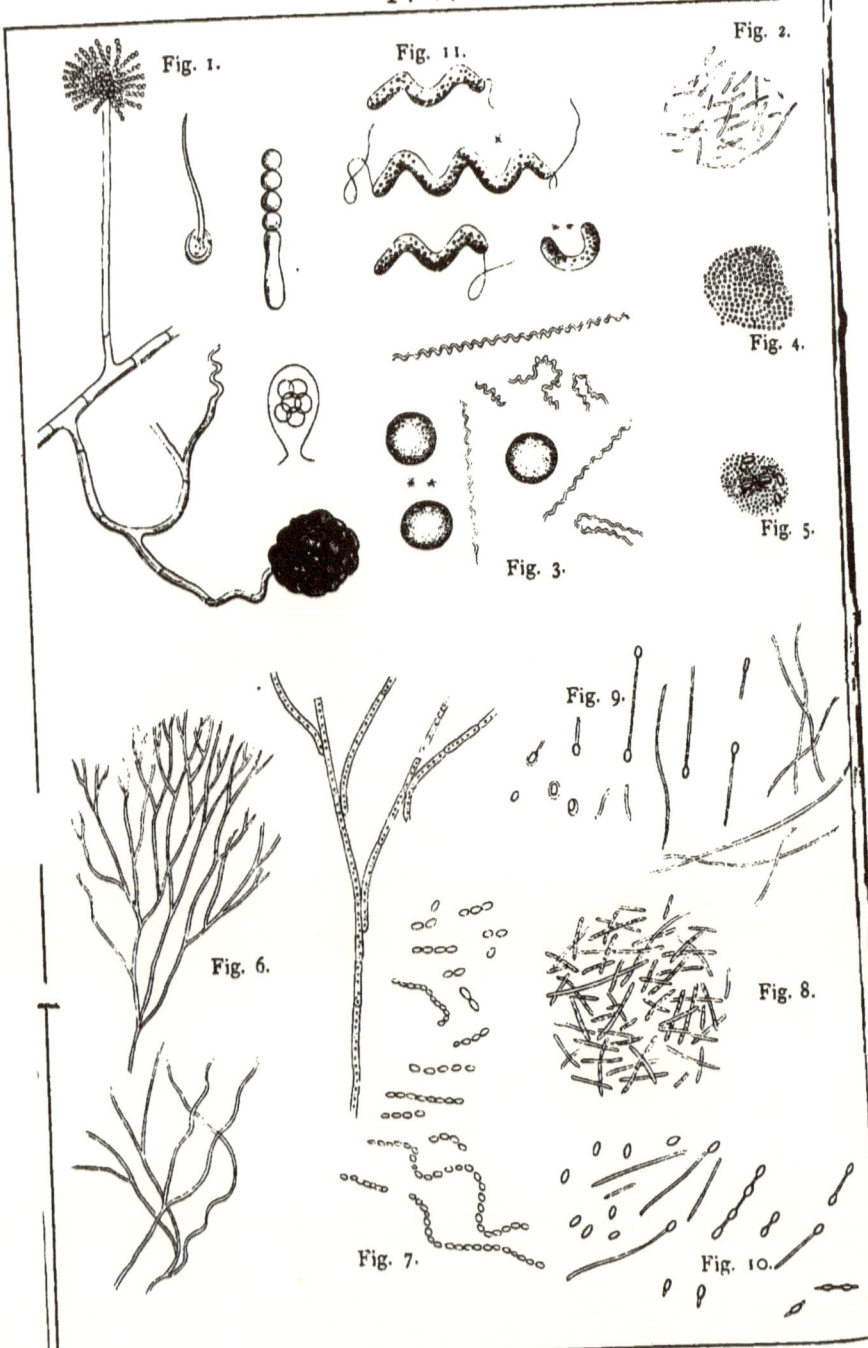

Fig. 1.

Fig. 11.

Fig. 2.

Fig. 4.

Fig. 5.

Fig. 3.

Fig. 9.

Fig. 6.

Fig. 8.

Fig. 7.

Fig. 10.

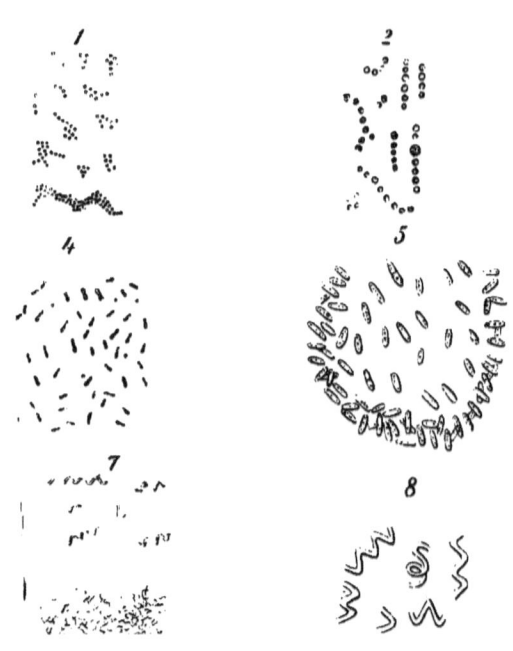

INDEX TO PLATES V. AND VI.

RESEARCHES

UPON

BACTERIA,

BY

FERDINAND COHN.

FROM THE GERMAN:
BIOLOGIE DER PFLANZEN.
BRESLAU, 1872.

TRANSLATED BY
JAMES J. WARING, M. D., AND ERNST DETMOLD

SAVANNAH, GA.:
1879.

RESEARCHES UPON BACTERIA.

When, twenty years ago, I made public my first investigations of bacteria [see history of the development of microscopic algæ and fungi,] there arose certain very important questions upon the morphology and development of these smallest of all organic things, which of late years have brought the development of bacteria into close connection with the most important problems of *Universal Natural Science.*

There are two men above all others whose labors, although of different value, have alike excited the interest of a large number in bacteria.

Pasteur described bacteria incidentally. The inferior accuracy of his microscopical observations, however, injured his work so far as they referred to these organisms, though not impairing the value of his investigations of the ferments ; nevertheless, all later investigations must be built upon his as a foundation. On the other hand, Hallier deserves the credit of having first called attention to the relation of these bacteria to contagia and ferments. He made this the subject, for many years, of close microscopical study and investigation, and we deeply regret that the later investigators, among them those in England and Germany, excited by him to these studies, were unable to avail themselves of his researches because his method was so poor.

For a number of years I have labored carefully with my friend Dr. Schroder, renewing our inquiries into bacteria with, in the meantime, more perfected opitical means of help, and have also, after Dr. Schroder left the Botanical Institute, in the summer of 1870, continued the work alone. I have thus endeavored to arrive at some independent conclusions as to the biological relations of bacteria and the classification of their species. I have also tried to determine, by experiment, their *ferment power.* I communicated some of the results of my labors to the Schlæssiche Society, on February 10, 1871 ; to the Medical Section, on August 4 ; also to the Natural History Section on February 10, 1872 ; also to the *Journal of Botany,* of M. DuBarry, dated December 22, 1871 ; Virchow's Archives of Pathological Anatomy, vol. 55, March, 1872.

Although my researches have as yet led me to no satisfactory conclusions, still I deem it worth while to give here a detailed statement of my labors.

To what organisms do bacteria belong? What genera, what species are there? I have directed my first efforts to answer these questions. Of late years, any reader will observe a great chaos in the nomenclature of bacteria. Each investigator has given his own names to forms, without regard to the names given by his predecessors.

The difficulties of nomenclature and classification is inconceivably great. Ehrenberg and Dujardin have alone taken the trouble to put into clear order the whole line of bacteria and divide them into genera and species. Their labors must therefore be considered the starting point; though their system of classification may be criticised from their magnifying powers being defective. Nevertheless it is a matter of great surprise and of great merit that Ehrenberg showed us structures which we find it difficult to make out at this day.

Though possessing the strongest magnifying powers, we are compelled to acknowledge that most of the bacteria are beyond the powers of our microscopes, for we are unable to observe the organization of their contents and their propagation satisfactorily. The existence of the smallest forms would escape us but for the enormous masses in which they generally appear.

Their classification is difficult because of their slight differences of form. Whilst in other organisms classification is based upon differences of propagation, bacteria cannot be so classified, because up to the present time their method of propagation has not been determined. Their external forms, as far as we can see, exhibit no varieties in their structure—no marked peculiarities of form and contents. It is their size and method of grouping, and their interlacement into colonies which show varieties. It is, however, impossible to determine how far they belong to originally different kinds; how far they are moulded by external influences, and how far they belong to different varieties of one kind, or how far they are only the same beings in various stages of development.

Although Lewenhoek recognized bacteria in the seventeenth century, and O. F. Müller saw and described the most important forms, yet the scientific method of classification commences with Ehrenberg. He gave us in 1830 the family of vibrios, which he ranks between the Volvocæ and Clausterias. To these he added the forms of thread-like structure, which were endowed with self-movement and segmentation. The segmental thread forms are based upon self-partition, in which both halves remain connected together, as Bury de St. Vincent showed in 1838. Ehrenberg, in his work on Infusoria, in 1838, gave four genera, which he classes in the following way:

EHRENBERG'S CLASSIFICATION.

1. Threads—straight, motionless—Bacteria.
2. Threads—straight, with serpentine motion—Vibrios.
3. Threads—spiral, with motion—Spirochæte.
4. Threads—spiral, motionless—Spirilla.

Of Bacteria he gave 3 species.
Of Vibrios he gave 9 species.
Of Spirochœta he gave 1 specie.
Of Spirilla he gave 3 species.

Dujardin, in his Natural History of 1841, has taken Ehrenberg's genus vibrios as the first and lowest form of infusoria. He also adopted the same genera and the same method of classification.

The bacteria, straight and with slow and little motion, he distinguishes from the vibrioes, which are straight, or sometimes bent and move quickly, with serpentine movement, and from the spirilla, which are always screw-like, with threads turning upon a common axis. The genus spirochæte Dujardin does not distinguish from the spirilla, which he says are not stiff and motionless, and therefore only differ from spirochæte by the larger or smaller screw threads, or the number of the turns of the screw.

Though the classification of bacteria, vibrioes and spirilla by Ehrenberg is very clear, it is by no means easy to determine them practically. We do find stiff, staff-like forms which are, no doubt, bacteria, and we find motionless spirals, which we just as truly call spirilla, and we find those eel-like and lightning moving forms, which Ehrenberg and Dujardin called vibrioes. The snail-like or serpentine motion of these vibrioes, conveying the impression of undulation, that is a partial flexion or stretching out of a flexible body, is really only an optical illusion, caused by the quick revolving spirals of an unchanging form of a more or less open screw turning on its own axis. I am convinced that the wave and screw-like motion of vibrios and spirilla are unchanging forms which are not capable of a stretching and bending, and therefore have no serpentine motion. Hence, there are no vibrioes which answer to Ehrenberg's definition; and, therefore, this genus must be classified according to other properties.

All those who have studied bacteria in the last thirty years have either taken Ehrenberg's and Dujardin's classifications, or have given new, and sometimes arbitrary, names to the forms they have observed. This, especially, applies to Pasteur, who at one time talks of animalcules, fungi, infusoria, torulæ, bacteria, vibriones and monads without giving any method of telling them apart, and at other times calls the same forms mocrozyms, mucors, mucedines or ferments.

We are now ready to put the question, whether there are really genera among bacteria the same as among the higher organisms. One who does not believe in the doctrine of metamorphoses, which begets anything out of anything, will feel troubled to make a natural classification of these innumerable bodies of every possible form. It appears as if these various forms were one and the same, being in different states of development; still I am convinced that bacteria have different genera and species, just as well as other low plants and animals, and that the way of telling them apart, in many cases, is rendered impossible to our powers of observation of to-day by their extraordinary small size and by the living together of different species. I base this idea upon the fact that the large bacteria are always to be found with the same forms under every possible condition and in innumerable quantity, without intermediate forms of development. This is especially true of spirilla, which are different in their species from the staff bacteria, just as truly as they differ from genuine algæ or infusoria.

Pasteur, who remarks that the nature of an organized ferment cannot be certainly determined by the microscopic form, but only by the physiological functions, calls particular attention to the extraordinary similarity of milk and vinegar ferments, and the ammonio-urine ferment to the jelly-like ferment of wine. The bacteria which produce red, yellow, orange, blue and other pigments may hardly be told apart, and yet plant them and they will always give the same pigments. The bacteria which are found in the different contagia are the same in their form sometimes with those found in the urine or butyric acid ferment; sometimes with those of the pigments. Shall we now call every kind which may be found in a certain medium, or have the same ferment power, a *special species,* even though they cannot be distinguished by the microscope? In this way we would only distinguish them into physiological species, which cannot be based upon their different forms. I believe that the time has not arrived to answer this question. We can find, probably, among the bacteria which do not differ externally, but which exhibit different chemical and physiological effects, both varieties and species, which, in the beginning came from the same spore, and which by constant natural or artificial culture, under the same circumstances, and on the same soil, produce the same results. As all bacteria multiply in the unsexual way, by budding or partition, it is easily understood that the peculiarities of their species may grow constant or fixed. Rees proved the formation of species in the various ferments by artificial culture. Just as summer corn cannot be used for winter seed, although both plants are of the same origin, and by constant culture may be converted one into the other, so the High ferment cannot be used as the ferment for Bavarian beer, and, in fact, each wine and beer has its own kind of ferment, yet it is probable that many of these alcoholic ferments belong to one and the same kind of species, though become numerous culture varieties. I think, also, that amongst the bacteria which act as ferments in different chemical and pathological processes, and consist only of a small number of independent species, there may be found a much larger quantity of natural and culture varieties, which, however, keep with great tenacity their individual peculiarities, because they multiply only in the unsexual way.

THE ORGANIZATION AND DEVELOPMENT OF BACTERIA.

The following description defines the structure and organization of bacteria :

"Bacteria are non-chlorophyl cells, globular, round, oval, cylindrical or twisted, which multiply by fissation and which vegetate either singly or in groups."

Bacteria cells contain carbonic acid and a usually colorless protoplasm, having a higher refraction than water, with slimy, oily granules. This protoplasm is flexible or contractible, as I have proved in the oscillaria ; the coloring of bacteria is due to pigments in the protoplasm. The refractive powers of the protoplasm differs from water, and hence bacteria in large quantity make water appear cloudy and milky. The larger the quantity of the bacteria, the more marked is this cloudiness. Pasteur attributes this cloudiness to the movements of the bacteria.

Generally, liquids filled with bacteria, appear milky, with a bluish tint and in thicker layers appear orange colored or smoky by transmitted light. As a rule, the degree of dimness in a clear liquid is a measure of the quantity of the bacteria. This is not true of thicker liquids, as serum and lymph, in which they are invisible to the naked eye; further, a small quantity of them do not cause any change of color in the liquid; therefore, we should not fail to make microscopic examinations in doubtful cases. With pigment bacteria, the water is colored.

That bacteria have a cell membrane, is proven by their behavior when exposed to chemical reagents. They are not disturbed by potash, ammonia, or acids. This is attributable not to the free and exposed condition of the protoplasm, but to the cell membrane. In like manner this cell membrane resists putrefaction for an extraordinary long time, and agrees in this also with the cellulose membrane of cellular plants. With a strong microscope, one can plainly distinguish the cell membrane of bacteria; for with a certain focus, the plasma appears somewhat black, bounded by a wide, yellow glistening ring. In some species, the membrane is tender, easy to bend, with a flexible protoplasm, in others it is stiff, retaining one form, and cannot be bent, so much so that Ehrenberg compared it to a *siliceous* coating, although he was well aware of the absence of any silicic acid. The stiff species undergo certain bendings when dead.

The multiplication of bacteria is by partition, and in this wise.

The cells elongate to nearly double their length, the plasma divides itself into two halves, and is permanently separated by a cell wall. Thus, two bodies are formed which adhere together for a longer or shorter period, or by the immediate decrease of the mother cell and splitting of the partition, part, one from the other. Immediately thereupon the daughter cells begin another division, and thus their number increases to an almost incredible extent. I believe that all the partitions which form bacteria cells, with the resulting subdivisions, run in parallel lines, consequently only one row of cell-chains can be found.

A formation of branches, as Dujardin and Hoffman describe and picture for vibrios and bacteria, is entirely incorrect, according to my observations; also a crosswise partitioning which would make the cells stand perpendicularly is never to be seen among true bacteria. This proves that the celebrated sarcina ventricate which have been found in the gastric fluids by Goods and by others, must be another kind of schyzomycetes. In smaller quantity this sarcina has been found in different organs, as (brain, lungs, etc.,) and outside the human organism, as for instance, on boiled potatoes, in dry yellow heaps. I myself saw a light yellow, dry speck of sarcina on a cooked white of an egg, on the 25th November, 1871, and even on the surface of a chemical solution (on the 2nd April, 1872,) in which orange colored bacteria were growing, appearing as a yellow floating film.

Pasteur found traces of sarcina on the sides of a vessel containing yeast water exposed to the air but a short time. This shows that the spores of sarcina often exist in the air, and propagate themselves under different circumstances and methods. Lately Losdorfer has discovered sarcina in the blood of both healthy and sick people, and I can substantiate this, as I saw, on the 19th of March, 1871, in a microscopic preparation of the blood of a healthy man of four days' standing, traces of sarcina, which were in groups of four, growing among the blood corpuscles. Although true bacteria may appear like sarcina at the separating point of any four-fold layers of their threads, I cannot find sarcina in this relation, and will not touch on this subject again. As already mentioned, the divisions of a bacteria cell (the daughter cells) sometimes may separate entirely, forming single, so-called, globular bacteria, or they may remain bound together in longer or shorter threads, as thread bacteria.

In the first case, class or group, we find the single bacteria, during their division in pairs, in the shape of a figure 8. The number of the cells connected in a thread is, however, various, and depends partly on their specific nature, partly on their outside surroundings, consequently the lengths of the threads differ, sometimes appearing in two, four or eight divisions. The threads of bacillus subtilis are sometimes very long, and are then described as a special kind, under the name of leptothrix. It is not to be understood from this that all kinds of leptothrix (which are usually of a green color) are bacteria, or grow out of bacteria; but on the contrary, this is not proven of that kind of leptothrix which contain phyco-chromate; only the colorless fungus species of leptothrix belong to the class of thread bacteria. On such the divisions are hard to discern; in other cases the divisions are marked by slight indentations, and as the threads break very easily, the irregular ends appear ziz-zag when the divisions are torn apart.

Most of the new discoverers are inclined to adopt the view that all bacteria are alike in their method of thread forming. Yet I am convinced to-day, as I was twenty years ago, that this is not the case, but that the bacteria are divided into two groups, which also, in their further development, show difference. For this reason the distinction of their generation must be observed. The daughter cells of the round rod-like bacteria separate themselves according to their partitioning; and, therefore, in a free position, appear single or in pairs, with now and then exceptional double-paired cells. But under certain circumstances the cell generations remain wrapt up in each other so that their cell membranes swell up to a jelly-like, refracting, intercellular substance, and through that bind themselves into larger elastic jelly masses. I have already called attention to this jelly mass in my essay on bacteria, in the year 1853, as a form of zooglea. These, swimming on the water, or spread out on a stand, formed irregularly round, clustered or skimlike jelly masses, in which the bacteria cells were more or less completely imbedded. In this zooglea jelly the bacteria continue to propagate by partition; and when the increase is very large, the young cells are extraordinarily crowded one on the other, while the intercellular substance is very little developed. In this form they appear as small, compactly filled jelly balls, of about ten mikrometres, and sometimes less than that. Later on, the cells soften and separate, and are imbedded in larger spaces. One can see with the naked eye that these jelly masses are colorless, swimming in flakes in the water, settling on the surface of the sides or bottom of a vessel. If the water contains iron in solution, the latter will unite with the jelly as iron oxybydrate, in which case the jelly will be stained red-brown. Should there be pure sulphate in such water, the rust-brown zooglea jelly will become blackened. These are found in the dregs of foul pump water, or in ditches—black zooglea. In a group of globular bacteria the form of the zooglea is somewhat soft; the more so that they prove in the air to be dregs of interstitial substance in the vessels, or prove to be a covering for little infusoria.

The bacteria cells which are imbedded in the jelly are not dead, as they in this condition not only freely multiply, but, through solution, are very easily freed from the jelly, and can then float upon the water.

The second group of thread and spiral bacteria are never seen in jelly masses, as I have already said in my first essay, but spring up either freely strewn or in swarms. It is necessary to watch the forming of a swarm in all bacteria, both of the rod and spiral kind, when they gather in innumerable masses in the midst of a fluid in search of richer food, or on the surface of the same, hungering for acids. Already has Lewenhoek and O. F. Müller, and, later, Threnbey, shown us the wonderful appearance of a bacteria swarm, which often gathers under the microscope, around a small crumb. The bacteria swarm differs from the zooglea in that the cells of the latter are knitted together by an immeasurable amount of intercellular substance. Therefore the zooglea jelly forms, in water, a sharp, well defined lined border, because the bacteria cells are imbedded in a thicker layer at the edge of the jelly mass than in the middle of it. On the other hand, the thread swarms are composed of only free movable cells, often so pressed together that they touch, and therefore form a slimy mass. In moving water, the single cells divide themselves without any other assistance, as they are not bound together by any other substance. The swarm forming of bacteria is best seen in a sea acquarium, when a dead animal decays at the bottom of the water. It is soon covered by a white bacteria mist, which becomes wider from day to day, and is plainly seen by its contrast to the crystal clear water, and spreads in currents as a smoke cloud in the water. In still water, the bacteria propagate by partition more equally, because their food is more evenly distributed. In this case, one generally finds the bacteria swarms near the surface of the water, often a centimeter in thickness, like an oily stratum, which is distinguishable from the deeper and thinner fluid on which it floats. It is plain that a craving for acids gather the bacteria here. Pasteur designates this form of bacteria as *mucor*.

On the surface of fluids in which bacteria multiply, there swims generally a very thin iridescent film, in which innumerable bacteria are arranged straight or entwined crosswise, or following each other in parallel lines. These films are called, by Pasteur, mycoderma, and are distinguished from zooglea, for in the latter the cells are bound together in round masses by an intercellular substance, while in the films there exists one single stratum without an intercellular substance.

6

Another form in which bacteria appear is that of pulverized sediment. As soon as the nourishment of a liquid is exhausted in which bacteria are developing, this ceases and the little bodies settle on the bottom of the vessel. The fluid clears day by day, so that the surface first clears like the settling of very light powders. At the bottom of the vessel the bacteria heap themselves up into a white, always thickening, stratum, which appears to the naked eye like a sediment of fine, slimy clay. The bacteria sediment is diffused by shaking the fluid, and gradually dissolve until the fluid becomes clear again. The number of the bacteria is proportioned to the amount of food in the liquid, and it is not difficult to get in a reagent cylinder containing ten grammes of food— a settlement of five centimeters. Indeed, it would be no hard matter to get bacteria sediment by the pound. In this sediment are all kinds of species mixed together, which are not altogether dead, for by seeding them in a fresh liquid containing their nourishment, these kinds of bacteria multiply very quickly, like yeast cells. It is therefore possible that in all waters these kind of bacteria are found, which begin to develop as soon as food is offered them. This change of specific gravity of bacteria is very strange, because so long as they are movable in the water they must have the same specific gravity as water. Perhaps the cause of their gathering on the surface is that they are lighter than water. It is the opposite, however, when the transition is to a quiet form. They then become heavier than water when possibly they have formed the lasting cells (Daurosporen) and a thickened plasma. In sweet liquids prepared after Pasteur, the bacteria form and settle very slowly. I have sometimes found the fluid remain milky after six months. In the sediment, of course, are dead bacteria, which one detects by the decaying of the plasma and the absence of oil granules. A rottenness of bacteria, which destroys their bodies, very seldom happens, for the bacteria sediment will remain unchanged for many months, perhaps for an indefinite length of time, which is evidence of the presence of a hard cell membrane, and is entirely different from infusoria, which, in decaying, entirely dissolve.

Bory remarked, in 1824, that dead " *vibrio bacillus*," in thousands, kept themselves unchanged for years in a corked bottle. Ehrenberg is mistaken in doubting this.

Most bacteria have an active and a motionless state. Their movement is a rotation on the longitudinal axis, and is accompanied with active and passive bendings and stretchings in the length of the thread, but is never serpentine. All the different movements are governed by this law. Bacteria can, through a simple change of rotation, move backwards and forwards. No morphological distinction of front and rear can be determined. Bacteria have no special movement organs, and none have yet been discovered. The motion of bacteria is not more or less wonderful than their entire analogy to oscillaria. Of the movement organs of spirillum, recently discovered by me, I will speak later. The movement of bacteria seems to depend on the presence of acids. When acids are absent bacteria go over to the motionless state. But without recognizable cause rest and motion change at short intervals. The active condition is lasting when the bacteria are bound in jelly-like masses or films. The movement is never noticed with round bacteria and certain thread bacteria.

It is doubtful whether bacteria form spores or conidia. In the stillness of sediment or slime masses we sometimes find bacteria cells which have a strongly glittering, oily substance in them, and seem to be "CELLS OF DURATION." Perhaps those wonderful bacteria, which are said by some to possess a tail and head, are nothing more than "duration cells." I found them in 1851 in great quantity in an infusion of dead flies; also in spoiled paste, white of an egg and other spoiled liquids. Numerous round or oval bodies, with a strong, oily appearance, are sometimes found among them, such as expand into short, tender threads. They swim like bacillus subtilis, of which they remind one.

These are the only developing conditions in bacteria that I have been able to discover. After mature study, reviewing their classification, I do not intend to settle on the difference between natural species, form species and physiological species, or to give a complete enumeration of all existing species. I rather intend to revise and classify a number of forms which appear to me to have a right of recognition, because they deserve a more special study. I shall submit a critical revision of those species which appear oftenest and have been noticed by many, and I shall attempt to show their difference in a much stronger light than has been done before. I hope such an effort will not be useless. In the midst of the chaos and confusion of other descriptions I have also tried to picture and engrave certain species, always using the same magnifying power. Works about bacteria and similar organisms, unaccompanied by plates and pictures, I consider useless, because they cannot fix the forms, while the characteristic but unfinished plates of Leweuhoek and O. F. Müller make these forms recognizable.

I classify bacteria into four (4) groups, of which each consists of one or more specie. Not to confuse the nomenclature, I have kept throughout the old names of the species, though I have classified them distinctly according to other principles.

1st Genus.—Sphero bacteria, (globular bacteria.) Species—micrococcus.

2d Genus.—Micro bacteria; rod bacteria. Species—bacteria.

3d Group.—Desmo bacteria, (thread bacteria.) Species—bacillus. Species—vibrio.

4th Group.—Spiro bacteria. Species—spirillus. Species—spirochæte.

3. GLOBULAR BACTERIA.

Globular bacteria can be classed according to the shape of the cells as globular or oval. They are of a minute size, less than 1 micrometer. Granular contents are not noticed, but a double outline membrane. In consequence of their method of partition the cells are connected in couples, and are narrowed at the point of partition.

When the partitioning continues there occurs short chains of three to four, or eight or more links, which are either straight or crooked, and in consequence of their being drawn in show the form of rosaries.

These chains, therefore, differ from the leptothrix forms of thread bacteria, which has no hour-glass contraction on their links, just as the thread of the nostoc species differ from those of the oscillaria.

Hallier has proposed the name of micothrix for the rosary forms of the globular bacteria; I call them torulaform.

The globular bacteria may be found in two stages of development beside the rosary form. The cells which form a chain are subject to a displacement, because, no doubt, the intercellular substance which connects the links is soft; therefore, the chains appear irregular, bent zig-zag, and single links lay themselves the other way, and thereby, when the partitioning continues, there occurs a confused mass, bags and colonies of cells which consist of a large number of cells, and show in irregular ranks. You would hardly think the origin of such colonies to be a single

little globule, if you did not see the different stages of development of the globular bacteria in small-pox lymph, though it may
be also found in different kinds.

It is often the case that these daughter cells, which occur
from the partition, place themselves close to the mother cells,
without adhering in chains, and connect themselves with these
through their intercellular substance without adhering in chains.
In this way there occur heaps of innumerable globular cells,
which form jelly-like sheen masses, which are often exceedingly
tenacious, extensive threads drop-like, or membranous. This
sheen formation may be especially observed with the pigment
bacteria, which grow in the open air ; but it is also the usual
form of those species occurring in pathological processes which
overgrow in thick layers the sick organs, or which encamp in the
interstices of the lymph vessels and other tissues. This construction corresponds with the zooglea form of rod bacteria, but as a rule
differs by the smaller development of their intercellular substance,
in consequence of which the globular cells are close pressed on
top of each other, and show under the microscope a very characteristic, closely dotted and finely granulated appearance.

Pasteur gives the globular bacteria different names. Those
with single or double cells he calls monas; the gelatinous masses
he calls mycoderma; the rosary threads he calls torulacæ. Under
the latter name Van Tiegben gives them the name of torulacæ.
Ehrenberg calls the globular bacteria, monads. The infusoria,
without color, he calls monas crepusculus. Those which produce
a red pigment he call monas prodigiosus. Hoffman also calls
globular bacteria by the same name and plates them. The
globular bacteria cannot be called monads for the following reasons: The species monas includes, in its present grouping, two
different beings ; on the one hand, zoospores of water fungi,
myxomycites and others, which are mouthless, and on the other
hand infusorias, which, with a mouth, take food particles. Both
forms are either globular or oval, and colorless, moving by the
aid of a tail end. But there is no tail end to the globular bacteria as far as I can see. They have no spontaneous motion, and
they only show some molecular motion, which may be very swift
with these small and light bodies and easily mistaken for a spontaneous motion, especially if true monads involve the globular
cells in their motions.

On account of the want of spontaneous motion, Schrœder gave

the globular bacteria, which produced pigments, the same names given by Darwin to the motionless rod bacteria of splenic fever blood. Splenic fever bacteridie differ from globular bacteria entirely, either in rod or thread forms. They cannot, therefore, be classed with globular bacteria merely because they are wanting in motion. It is not improbable that Hallier understood by his micrococcus, the same organisms, which I call globular bacteria. But Hallier's description of the micrococcus, as proved by Hoffman and Du Barry, is so filled with false ideas and uncritical hypotheses, that it is almost impossible to pick out his correct observations.

Setting aside forms and motions, the globular bacteria differ from the staff bacteria by their functions. "*Bacteria termo*" is the ferment of putrefaction, globular bacteria are also ferments, but do not produce putrefaction, only a decomposition of another kind. As a rule, they struggle for their existence on the same ground with the putrefaction bacteria, and if they succumb their products, are destroyed by the latter.

As it is difficult to class the species micrococcus by the form and size of their cells, but easy to class them by their physiological functions, I give here the following *three* groups, chromo gene, zymogene, and pathogene or pigment, fermentation and contagium generators.

Globular bacteria, which occur in a colored gelatinous mass, I call pigment bacteria. All pigment bacteria vegetate in the zooglea form : that is, they form a slimy mass, which, in consequence of the enormously quick multiplication of their cells upon the surface of their sometimes fluid, sometimes solid organic food substance, envelope themselves in a colored slime. The pigment is brought out by contact with the air, and appears first on the surface, and by and by gets more and more embedded in the depth of the water.

All pigment bacteria give an alkaline reaction ; some of the mixtures in which they multiply have been originally acid or neutral. Alkaline reaction will arise as soon as color is produced. According to Schroeder, the production of acid precedes alkaline reaction, and by overgrowth of the alkaline material the pigment is destroyed.

Boiled potato slices, are an inexhaustible source of pigment bacteria when left exposed to damp air. After a short while a slimy colored mass forms upon these potato slices; hence we suggest the air carries the spores of pigment bacteria.

According as the pigment is soluble in water or not, pigment bacteria fall into *two* groups. In the second group the pigment consists of protoplasm and intercellular substance (zooglea). In the first group it develops in the medium in which it vegetates.

The first class have yellow and red pigment.

The second class have orange, green and blue. Of some colors we are not yet certain.

INDISSOLUBLE PIGMENT.

1. Micrococcus prodigiosus.
2. Micrococcus luteus.

SOLUBLE PIGMENT.

1. Micrococcus aurantiacus. ***
2. Micrococcus chlorinus. ***
3. Micrococcus cyaneus. ***
4. Micrococcus violaceus. ***
5. Micrococcus ureæ, ammonia ferment.

It is known that fresh, normal urine is clear and a little acid; that in getting cold it precipitates a sediment of urate of soda and other sediment, and at the same time it becomes non-acid. After four or five days, and sometimes sooner, according to circumstances, it becomes alkaline, and is subject to a fermentation, in which the urine decomposes and produces carbonate of ammonia. It was supposed long ago that a ferment was the cause of the alkaline fermentation, but Pasteur gave us the proof that this was an organism and communicated from the air, as boiled urine protected from the dust remains unchanged and acid after months, and, as Pasteur has lately shown, after many years. He also showed different organisms in the alkaline urine, as mould fungi and bacteria. There is one structure, however, he shows with great probability to be the especial ferment of alkaline urine, by which the urine is changed into carbonate of ammonia, and in consequence the alkaline urates and phosphates of ammonia and magnesia are produced. This ferment is, according to Pasteur, torulaceæ formed globular cells, in rosary shape, of $1\frac{1}{2}$ micrometer diameter. Van Tieghen proves by experiment that Pasteur's idea was correct, by showing that in urine diluted with a ferment water, in which was some of the rosary-formed urine ferment, which he also calls torulaceæ, urea and uric acid disappear in thirty-six hours, and are changed into carbonate of ammonia. Other ferment organisms do not produce ammoniacal fermentations. For instance, beer ferment put into urine produces alcoholic fermentation. Van Tieghen also found that hippuric acid was changed into benzoic acid and glycollamine by urine ferment, probably identical with torulaceœ.

Pasteur gives us a new and better plate of urine ferment. He thinks it is identical with the one he has shown in slimy thread forming wine, whose rosary threads consist of globular cells of 2-10 micrometer.

My own observations corroborate his discoveries. Fresh acid urine, after having stood open for two days at a temperature of 30 deg. centigrade, shows a discoloring and a development of globular bacteria, which swim about singly as globular or oval cells, or are attached to each other in chains of two, four or eight links, torulaceœ-form. With the chains of four or eight links, I could see a somewhat larger interval between every two cells. The reason for this is that each two spring from a mother cell. The cells do not always lie in straight lines, but shifting zig-zag or crosswise form groups. The diameter of the single rather large globules, I determined to be $1\frac{1}{4}$ to 2 micrometers. They show molecular motion only, whilst rod and thread bacteria, show a quick, rolling rotation motion. A few days later they generally have become motionless, though they continue to multiply just as fast.

PATHOGENIC GLOBULAR BACTERIA.

Pathogenic globular bacteria develop another series of physiological functions, which we consider to be the ferments of contagia. It is not my intention to specially mention every case in which, during the last four months, bacteria have been found in quite different pathological processes of contagious nature. I will only point out those which I know myself, or about which observations of scientific importance have been published.

MICROCOCCUS VACCINIÆ—SMALL-POX BACTERIA.

In my essay on the organisms of small-pox lymph in 1872, I gave a detailed description of these little bodies, which, minute globular and connected in pairs, are found in perfectly clear and fresh vaccine virus ; also in the lymph of variola pustules in excessively large quantities, and also have been observed before now with more or less accuracy, especially by Keber, Hallier and Zinn.

By enclosing fresh lymph between an object and cover glass, which have been very carefully cleaned, and at once sealed by asphaltic wax, the lymph was protected from contact with foreign germs. In such a preparation of vaccine lymph, placed in a crucible heated to 35 deg. centigrade, after a few hours, the single globular cells have multiplied into rosary cells of two to eight links. By.shiftirg of the single members and the continued partitioning, irregular groups of all imaginable combinations occur. In the course of several days irregular cell heaps of colonies of 16 to 32 and more globules were found of 10 micrometers, or even more, in diameter. Micrococcus cells of pock are in all cases motionless. I could not find a permanent difference between those of the vaccinia and variola, and therefore would call them different culture races of one and the same genus. I could not measure the size of the globules, still I put them at $\frac{1}{2}$ a micrometer and less

C. Weigert, in 1871, before my researches, discovered in the . dead bodies of small-pox patients the capillaries of the skin filled with very small globular bodies, which adhere close together, and which I do not hesitate to consider identical with the micrococcus of the lymph, according to the preparations which he has shown me. It seems as if the pock bodies get out of the lymphatics into the lymph of the pustules. If you preserve pock lymph in sealed glass tubes, it keeps its activity longer. Large flakes form, visible to the naked eye, which are considered the principal effective ingredient of the lymph, and was produced by the multiplication of the pock bodies, by adhering and sticking together. The occurrence of large globular cells, with oily contents, seems to show a formation of permanent cells.

MICROCOCCUS DIPTHERICUS—DIPTHERITIC BACTERIA.

I shall base what I have to say upon the important observations, microscopical, chemical and experimental, made by Oertel, in 1871. As early as in 1868, Buhl, Hunter, and Oertel saw a massy, fungus vegetation in diphtheritic membranes, which Oertel calls micrococcus. In his newer work, he proves the enormous spread of this micrococcus, which appears without exception, in all cases of diphtheritic sickness, upon the mucous membranes of larynx and trachea, equally also in the

lymphatic vessels and in the capillaries which surround the
lymphatics, between the meshes of the fibrous connective tissue,
also in the fat cells in the kidneys, in the muscular tissue, and
also in the blood itself. The micrococcus of diptheria, consists
of oval shaped granular formed cells of $\frac{3.5}{1000}$ up to $1\frac{1}{10}$ micrometer, which are sometimes single or cling together in couples
or rosary chains of four to six links, and are also found in immense multiplication like colonies on the surface and interstices
of the tissues of the sick organs, forming globular masses,
cylindrical or in nests.

The plates which Oertel has added to his work leaves no doubt
that these fungi belong to the globular bacteria. Oertel mentions
a second movable state of his micrococcus, which he calls micrococcus *rocket like*. He says that the round shaped bodies single
or in couples, or in torula chains, rotate or move like screws and
have partly single or double fly-thread. In the blood of such
people, Oertel found an innumerable quantity of moving bodies,
really rod bacterias, by their shape. The principal and most
important part of Oertel's observations lies in the proof that the
micrococcus colonies degenerate and destroy all the tissues and
muscular fibres around which they entwine themselves and pene-
trate. The fungus growth spreads especially upon the mucous
membrane. They besiege the cells, enter into the young exudation cells, and cause a slow disintegration. They fill the capillaries and lymphatics, and cause, in a mechanical way, the arrest
of the circulating fluids, which must lead to a serious exudation,
as they choke up the capillaries and produce arrest of the blood
circulation, thus producing a destruction of the material of the
walls of the capillaries and even a tearing of the same. In very
violent sickness, enormous quantities of fungi in the uriniferous
tubules and Malpighian corpuscles of the kidneys are accumulated,
which causes a general diseased condition of these organs. The
urine is exceedingly full of these fungi, which are excreted from
the organs. It is evident that diphtheria, as a rule, is found in
the mucous membrane of the trachea, as these are exposed to the
attack of the micrococcus germs, which no doubt, are conveyed
by the air. But the experiments of Oertel upon animals, have
shown that by vaccinating the exudation infected with micrococcus heaps subcutaneously or upon open wounds of the different
parts of the body diphtheritic sickness is invariably caused.
Diptherica is not a local pathological process, though it may

commence with it ; it is a general sickness by infection, which spreads, radiating over the whole body, starting from the focus of infection which bears all proof of blood poisoning. If the poison commences from a contagium, its bearer, as vaccinating trials have shown, is the micrococcus cells. The effects of these organisms are specifically different from the general putrefaction ferments, as vaccinations with putrifying material has never been able to cause an attack of diphtheria. Inflammation of the wind-pipe can be also caused by administering a few drops of ammonia. In this case those fearful distructions do not occur which characterize the diphtheritic infection sickness, and which belongs to the power of the micrococcus. By eliminating the micrococcus cells in the urine a slow process of recuperation is introduced.

MICROCOCCUS SEPTICUS.

Under this name globular bacteria have been proved in the last two years, especially by Leyden, Jaffi, Buhl, Traube and others to be present in different putrid sicknesses of men. The influence of these organisms is the cause of pyæmia and septicoemia, as also the form of sickness called mycosis intestinalis. Klebs, found in the secretions of wounds small globular cells of ½ micrometer, motionless, close together, in heaps or connected into rosary chain threads. The same organisms of zooglea form, inhabiting the granulating surfaces of ulcerating cartilages, (On Gunshot Wounds, 1872) he calls *microsporon septicum*. These structures entering the plasma cells of the tissues cause inflammation and suppuration of the bone. In traumatic osteomyeletis entering into the vessels, they fill the same and get into the blood, and are deposited in places where the circulation is slower. All around they cause inflammation, suppuration and abscess formation. They cause by their vegetation, or by a ferment which they have, a chemical change in the wound fluids, or in the blood, whose product the fever-creating power differs very much from common putrefaction. Experiments corroborate the contagious effects of these organisms. The wound fluids, if filtered through clay cylinders, lose their poisoning effects. The same organisms Klebs also found in septic processes. Observations by Richinghausin of the million fostering poison of pyæmia, typhus and other sicknesses, which are caused by bacteria, agree with this. Klebs, besides movable globular cells, mentions the presence of staff-like bodies

of oscillating motion, connected to long threads and motionless.
But Orth denies that putrefactive or rod bacteria are accom-
plices of the septicoemic processes, and refers them to the pathogenic effect of the micrococcus spores, which doubtless belong to
the globular bacteria.

MICROCOCCUS BOMBYCIS.

Regarding these little bodies I am compelled to refer to
Pasteur's researches, as I have not studied them myself. Pasteur
shows in a series of essays published since 1868, in the transactions of the Academy of Paris, that a very severe epidemic took
place during recent years among silk worms in the south of France.
This epidemic is entirely different from the Muscardine or Gattine,
and these animals dying of this sickness were designated as morts
plats and morts blancs.

The cause of this sickness is a ferment " en chapelet," or neck-
lace, similar to the one found also in other fermentations,
consisting of little globules bound together in two, three, four or
five links of one micrometer diameter, which, together with monads,
vibrios and bacteria, are found in great quantity, especially in the
intestinal tract of the sick worms, but which cannot be found in
the healthy ones. Although a closer investigation might yet be
desirable, there can be no doubt that these corpuscles " en chapelet" are the torula form of a pathogenic species of globular
bacteria.

GENERAL CONCLUSIONS.

In reviewing these observations which I have made upon
the micrococcus or globular bacteria, it will be found that these
little organisms are of great importance, both in a chemico-
physiological and a pathological point of view. The latter would
appear of greater value if the material of investigation would
permit in all cases the distinguishing of globular bacteria from
rod bacteria. I refer particularly to observations about the
existence of bacteria in pyelo-nephritis, typhus, cholera, scarlatina, measles, tuberculosis, farcy, rinderpest, etc., etc. But I must
particularly call attention again to the observations of Pollander,
Brauell, Davaine, and more recently of Bollanger, who state that
in the highest states of contagious sicknesses amongst animals
in the splenic fever and pustule maligne of men, not globular
bacteria, but motionless thread bacteria are the cause. We are
therefore, not safe in regarding all pathogenic bacteria as globular bacteria.

MICRO-BACTERIA—ROD BACTERIA.

The second group of bacteria I have called micro-bacteria or rod bacteria. They are similar to globular bacteria in the smallness of their cells, and their union into gelatinous or slimy masses. But they differ without regard to their physiological functions by their short cylindrical shape and the spontaneous motion of their cells. In this genus I only recognize one species, which I call bacterium in the most limited sense. The organisms belonging to this species consist of short cylindrical or elliptical cells, which hang together in couples during their partition. After the partitioning is completed, the daughter cells separate, while sometimes they still adhere to each other at an angle. Rarely the daughter cells commence to partition themselves before they have isolated themselves, and then we may see four cells in one line. Under favorable conditions of sufficient food and carbonic acid, they have a vivid spontaneous motion, but in such a way that states of rest are succeeded suddenly by states of motion. They form no chains nor threads, therefore they never appear in leptothrix nor torula form, but in vegetating unite into gelatinous masses, which differ, as said before, from the slimy films and heaps of the globular bacteria by the much more plentifully developed and firmer intercellular substance, and, therefore, they do not show the fine granulated appearance of the slimy masses of micrococcus. The rod bacteria may easily be confounded with free globular bacteria on account of their minute size, or with single individuals of thread bacteria; still I am convinced that they are independent organisms, which do not originate from these last, nor do they develop into them. It is very difficult to distinguish apart the different kinds of rod bacteria, and the number of the species is very large. On boiled potato slices there vegetate also slimy masses of rod bacteria of characteristic spindle-formed shape. Ehrenberg, in his work on infusoria (1838), gives us three kinds of bacteria; eight kinds, which he formerly named, he abandoned; even still the three kinds which he retained cannot now be recognized. Two of them, bacterium puncturm and bacterium enchelys, have been found only in Russia, and marked with ? by Ehrenberg himself, and the third one, bacterium triloculare, been observed in the oasis of Ammon and in Berlin.

I have made two species, to-wit : Bacterium Termo and Bacterium Lineola.

1 B. Termo : Ehrenberg in 1830. We may thank Dujardin for
a more accurate description of these bacteria, whose character he
gives as follows : Form, cylindical ; length, two to three micrometers ; thickness, $\frac{1}{2}$ to 1-5th of this size ; often connected in
couples with a trembling motion. This species Dujardin calls the
smallest of all infusoria. It appears, as he says, very often in
infusions of animal and vegetable matter, at the commencement
of putrefaction as innumerable, forming swarms, and before other
kinds multiply, to which they form the food. Again, they are
found in abundance as soon as the infusion commences to smell
to such a degree that no other kinds can live in it. In the transactions of the Berlin Academy, Ehrenberg, in 1830, first called
attention to what he called Bacterium Termo, which he found in
infusions of hay, of blood, or other substances In his large work
on infusoria, in 1838, he gave them the name of Vibrio lineola,
because it is capable of slower snake-like motions. Dujardin
declares that his Bacteria Termo is also identical with the one O.
F. Müller found in an offensive infusion after twenty-four hours,
and which he called monas termo, whilst Ehrenberg understands
by monas termo a true monad. The description and plate of
Bacterium termo which Dujardin particularly gave us, is so characteristic that this kind can be easily found anywhere, although
their sizes vary very much. In my essay of 1853, I have treated
of the history of their development, and especially of their grape-
like, globular, gelatinous, zooglea form, to which Perty calls
attention in his book entitled "The Smallest Organisms," 1852.
The motion of the bacterium termo does not vary much from the
motion of other bacteria. The cells turn about their long axis,
swim forward, and, without turning, swim back again, or go
through the water in a curve ; usually, not quickly, but trembling
and tottering, shooting with a quick jump, like a rocket ;
sometimes rotate on their short axis, like the handle of a gimlet ;
sometimes as quick as lightning, like a top ; then again resting
for a while and then run away altogether, suddenly. If one
infusorium swallows swarms of bacteria termo, you may see them
moving about vigorously in his stomach. The cells of bacteria
termo are short, cylindical and oblong, the contents according to
thé medium, being bright or dark. The cell membrane is com-
paratively thick with a common medium ; they appear like very
tender, dark lines, bound by a bright margin. We almost always
find them with their partitioning more or less advanced or

connected as couples. They are only 1½ micrometer long and only ½ or ⅓ as wide. The double cells are of course twice as long. In innumerable myriads they fill the water as soon as putrefaction has begun, sometimes so thickly that the water will become a living jelly. They multiply generally as long as the putrefaction proceeds, and disappear as soon as putrefaction is passed. From my own experience, and the observations of others, I have come to the conclusion that bacterium termo is the ferment of putrefaction ; that, indeed, no putrefaction can commence without bacterium termo, or can proceed without their multiplication. I even suppose that other bacteria, although they might take part in the putrefaction processes, take only a secondary part while bacterium termo is the excitor of putrefaction—the true saprogene ferment.

BACTERIUM LINEOLA—VIBRIO LINEOLA OF EHRENBERG.

Under this designation I understand those rod bacteria, which are similar in all regards to the B. termo, but are much larger, and not only longer, but also, in comparison, wider, for which reason, I do not consider them a development form of the B. termo. I find them in swill water and in stagnant water, even though no putrefaction has been noticed, and also in slimy heaps on the surface of potatoes, and in infusions of different kinds. The cells are clearly cylindrical, about four times as long as they are wide, occasionally crooked, and possessed of strong, translucent, soft contents, filled with fatty granules, and therefore dark punctated. Their length is 3.8 up to 5¼ micrometer; their width is 1½ micrometer. They are found singly or hanging together in couples, sometimes forming crooked double rods ; exceptionally, also, two double pairs, but never forming longer threads. They move like B. termo, but stronger, trembling with the one end as if they had a tail, or swimming about in curved lines forwards and backwards; then they jump a little, and again continue their circles, or rotate around one fixed point, like the arm of a lever. B. lineola forms zooglea jelly of a similar kind to B. termo, as I have stated in 1853. I observed in such zooglea that the motionless little rods, being imbedded in the water-like jelly, suddenly commence to turn, make with one end a motion like a gimlet, and swim away. Double rods, being in the state of partition, came out of the jelly and moved away. If the single rods are somewhat bent, or the double rods have knees, they make, in rotating, a snakey motion, which caused Ehrenberg to put these senseless cells amongst his vibrios. Ehrenberg at first called them bacteria; later on vibrio tremulens, and gives the size as $\frac{1}{288}$ of a line, that is, 7 to 8 micrometer; but the size of the vibrio lineola is put at $\frac{1}{300}$ to $\frac{1}{1000}$ of a line, that is, 6 to 2 micrometers, so that he seems to mix together the smaller forms of the bacteria termo with the larger B. lineola. I have, therefore, with Dujardin, kept the name of lineola for the larger form, but called it a special kind of the genus bacteria. It is possible, however, that I shall include several species in the bacteria lineola, and that especially a large and elliptical form may be designated bacteria tremulens. Whether the bacterium lineola is a specific ferment I cannot say.

To the true bacteria belong, also, according to the opinion of Hoffman and others, the ferment of lactic acid. Pasteur, the discoverer of the milk ferment, describes this as champignon, short, slightly drawn in about the middle, as if two points had been connected together. The plate shows the bacterium termo, and also chains of four links are found, which show a globular bacteria form. My observations about the ferment of lactic acid have not yet been brought to a close. If you observe with the microscope the souring of milk, butter globules of all sizes and pseudo bacteria, obstruct every clear view. Soon, besides other organisms, globular B. and B. termo appear, later on, also oidium lactis. If sugar of milk is exposed to the air, with a warm temperature, in a few days it becomes dissolved and sour, innumerable bacteria form, which after awhile make a thick chalk-like sediment. It must be left to later observations which of these organisms is the true ferment and which are only secondary companions. As in the souring of milk a large number of different processes occur, the fermentation of each ferment is difficult to state. I myself found in the souring of milk globular cells similar to those in urine ferment, like those with rosary chains, hanging in torulæ form, of two, four or eight cells. A solution of sugar of milk on the 20th of February was discolored, on the 24th was sour, on the 27th its sediment consisted of globular beer ferment of rosary chains, $1\frac{1}{2}$ to 2 micrometers diameter. Pasteur says that the souring of milk is caused by the lactic acid, which is formed from milk sugar. But alkaline and neutral milk gets sour also if it comes in contact with vibrios, which show an active power analogous to the lob upon caseine. These vibrios, which cannot be killed by boiling, but die at 105 deg. centigrade,

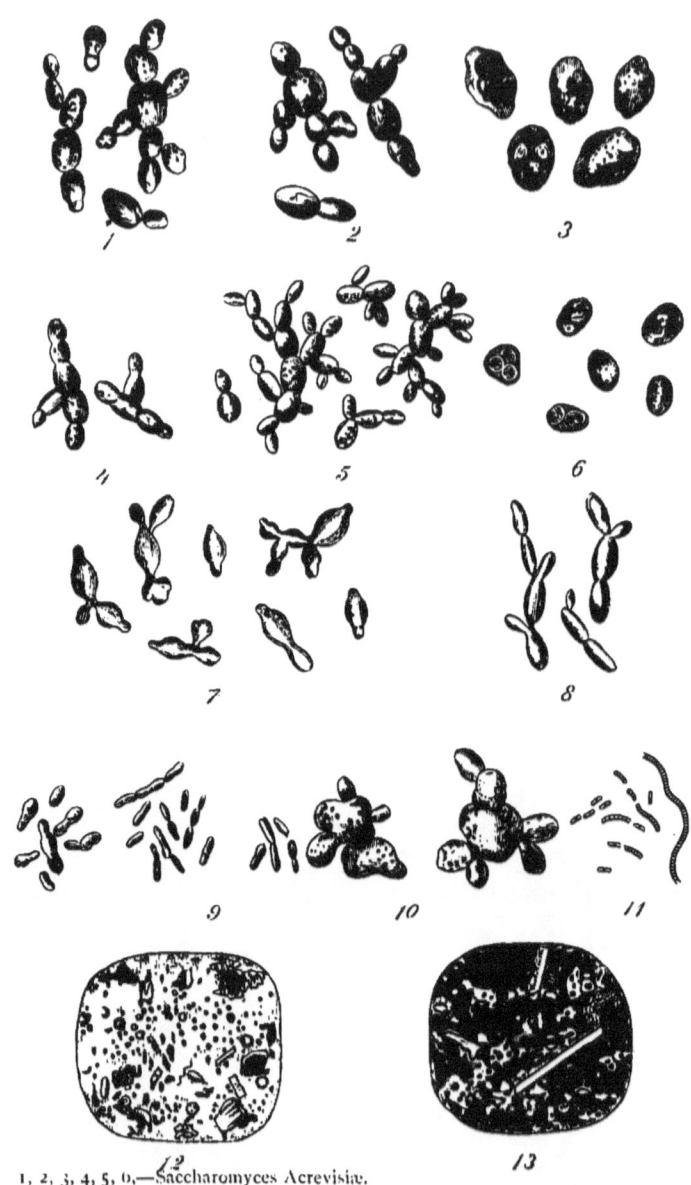

1, 2, 3, 4, 5, 6,—Saccharomyces Acrevisiæ.
9—Saccharomyces Mycoderma.—Pasteur.
10—Mucor Racemosa.
11—Mycoderma Aceti—Vinegar Ferment.
12, 13,—Organic Corpuscles of dust found by Pasteur in ordinary atmosphere mixed with amorphous particles.

"ON FERMENTATION," BY P. SCHUTZENBERGER.

are the bacteria of butyric acid. The name is bacterium subtilis. If milk which is sour becomes alkaline after a long time from putrefaction, ægile bacteria form, according to Hoffman.

The true ferment of acetic acid has never been determined, botanically. Former observers, for instance Kützing, describe the mother of vinegar as algous jelly, in which an enormous quantity of globular cells are imbedded. Pasteur describes acetic acid ferment as mycoderma aceti. It consists, according to him, of short constructed members of 1½ micrometer, twice as long as wide, in rosary shape, often extended into long chains, forming a thin film on the surface. According to Pasteur, acetic acid ferment is similar to lactic acid ferment, perhaps identical with it. The members of lactic acid ferment are, however, longer and constructed less regularly. Generally we call this peculiar form of ferment fungi—vinegar ferment (atrococcus), whose true-like cells are oblong or cylindrical, and swim on the surface of alcoholic liquids which have become sour, especially beer. Pasteur plates this atrococcus as a wine ferment, which he calls mycoderma vini. He says that this mycoderma has no part in the formation of vinegar. It rather antagonizes the development of vinegar ferments and develops *bouquet* of the wine. Rees, also, who describes and plates this ferment as an especial kind, under the name of saccharomyces mycoderma, thinks that they have no part in the formation of vinegar.

Vinegar and lactic acid ferments need further investigation. I find that beer which has become sour, is discolored throughout and covered with a film, whose discoloring consists of oval saccharomyces and elliptical mycoderma, and an enormous multiplication of moving elliptical bacteria, similar to the bacteria termo but somewhat larger than the usual form, hanging together generally in couples, rarely in four if two just parted cells are again parting. Their motion is sometimes trembling, sometimes gliding, sometimes moving, screw-like, sometimes spinning like a top. If the acetic acid ferment multiplies, they lose their spontaneous motion and only show molecular motion. These rod bacteria fill the whole fluid ; and I find rarely bacillus threads ranged into lepthothrix threads. The film on the surface is formed of the same bacteria in motionless, parallel, straight and crooked lines, and this form Pasteur has placed under the name of mycoderma aceti. We also find globular, zooglea

7

masses, thickly filled with elliptical bacteria, partly belonging to
a micrococcus species, and formed of round dots.

Certain rod bacteria seem to act as chromogene ferments.
The pigment of yellow and blue milk are added since Ehrenberg's
time to the physiological functions of bacteria (vibrios). Schroeder describes these as bacterium xanthimum, being the bacteria
which produce the blueish green pigment of pus.

7—THREAD BACTERIA—DESMO-BACTERIA.

This third genus of the bacteria comprises two species; the
first of which having straight threads I call Baccillus, the
second with curled threads, I call vibrios, which old name however, is to be taken in a new sense.

All thread bacteria consist of long cylindrical members, which
if they are isolated, are similar to bacterium lineola, but multiplied by partition, form longer or shorter threads. These threads
are not constructed at their points of junction like the rosary
chains of globular bacteria, but are throughout round, like our
long-jointed stick, as the oscillaria. In this state they are called leptothrix threads. Thread bacteria often form swarms, but never
zooglea jelly mass. as I asserted in my essay in 1853. States of
motion and rest alternate with them, according to the presence or
absence of oxygen, or the reaction of the medium or other circumstances. Certain species seem to be without motion.

It is difficult to separate the different varieties of thread bacteria. The differences which we do observe are mostly due to the
strength of their threads, which vary from the finest hair, which
cannot be measured up to the thickness of 1½ micrometer, and also
to the length of their threads, which depends on the number of
members connected in a chain. They have more or less flaccidity,
which is entirely missing in some forms and very evident in others,
similarly to the flexile beggiatoa. They have either straight lines
or a wave-like curve to their rigid threads. The wave-like threads
often deceive in their rotations, simulating an undulating or snake-
like motion, and thereby have caused Ehrenberg to call these
germs vibrio, when this motion is really only an optical illusion.
The real motion, which is observed only in long threads, is partly
passive, partly spontaneous, but only like oscillarium threads,
turning in irregular chains—turning the whole thread and stretching it, but never changing the unyielding waves.

There are two genera.

a.—STRAIGHT THREADS GENUS BACILLUS.

Threads very thin with motion : Bacillus subtilis. Threads thicker and stiff: Bacillus ulna. To this also belong the bacteridia of splenic fever, called bacillus anthracis, which must be classed with bacillus subtilis, according to its morphological construction, but must be classed as an independent variety, on account count of its pathogenic importance.

b.—THREADS CURVED IN WAVE FORM GENUS VIBRIO.

Threads thicker, with simple motion, vibrio rugula.

Threads thin with complicated wave motion, vibrio serpens.

a.—GENUS BACILLUS.

1. Bacillus subtilis. (Vibrio Subtilis Ehrenberg.) (Butyric acid Ferment of Pasteur.

Ehrenberg found this variety to be stiff and straight when at rest; to be swimming in straight lines, and trembling when in motion; but without a serpent-like movement, which he thinks is caused by the shifting of the cellular membrane of the thread. They measure $\frac{1}{30}$ ''' (60 micrometers) in length, their thickness is $\frac{1}{2000}$ ''', but the plate also shows little rods of only $\frac{1}{2}$ or $\frac{1}{4}$ of this length. Dujardin ranks the vibrio subtilis amongst the doubtful species, which he does not consider animals but oscillaria.

I find that Ehrenberg's form is a widely disseminated species found in infusions together with the bacteria termo and other bacteria ; it is present also in butyric acid fermentation and in other conditions where the bacteria form is not found.

The threads are very thin and minute, so that the joints of union of the cell members cannot be recognized, except that you can see when the segments separate, that these segments are as a rule six micrometers in length. These segments we find sometimes isolated, in which case they are distinguished with difficulty from the bacteria lineola. Generally they are found in pairs of twelve micrometer lengths or in triplets, and then sixty micrometers in length or in longer extensions. I have measured threads of twenty-six, forty, sixty-six, and even one hundred and thirty-two micrometers; the latter may have consisted of more than twenty lengths.

The thickness of the threads cannot be measured easily, it is so to say of gossamer delicacy. The contents show no granules. The threads are very active, or flexibly passive, which lends to their motions a peculiar character.

They swim in straight lines with alternate restings, with a certain clumsiness; sometimes quick and active, as if trying to find their way through obstacles like a fish trying to find his way through water grasses; then they remain quiet for a little while, suddenly the thread trembles and swims backwards without turning, and will soon swim again straight ahead. It is very difficult to prove that they turn constantly on their long axis; it is only to be noticed by a certain trembling of the threads; if one of the links in the act of partition is somewhat bent, this motion on the long axis becomes clearly visible.

As a rule, the threads have a pendulum motion at a varying point of beginning. When the pendulum motion is very quick the flexible threads are passively and actively bent by the resistance of the water; longer threads show spontaneous flexible curves. The two ends approach each other like the ends of a bow, then the bow bends to the opposite extreme. Again, it stretches itself straight; if the threads are very long, several curves follow each other like waves; *a true, short, serpentine motion is not found.* Observing the thread for sometime under a cover glass the motion becomes slower and the intervals of rest lengthen, though the motion does not cease altogether.

I have expressed the opinion that this kind might form only cells or gonidia, and that these globular, or oval gonidia, might be developed when germinating into movable tailed forms just as I have shown on my plates.

Pasteur describes the ferment of butyric acid fermentation which he described as long, thin movable vibrios, which are able to bend their bodies. His plate of 1864 shows distinctly our bacillus subtilis. Before I ever saw the plate of Pasteur, I knew that this species took an active part in the Butyric acid fermentation, from the fact that beans and peas which were put into distilled water in a closed glass retort and heated to eighty degrees centigrade, by which bacteria termo are generally killed, on account of want of air changed into butyric acid. This fermentation developed only bacillus subtilis, and no bacteria termo, as I shall prove later on.

Pasteur says in his essay on spontaneous generation of 1862, that boiled milk gets filled with small vibrios after a few days, which he designates as bacteria lineola, but which, according to the plate, must be our bacillus subtilis, and they were only killed by a temperature of 105 deg. centigrade.

Rheinfleish, in his essay on lower organisms, gives us bacteria whose long threads, he thinks, are caused by the mixing together of several separated members. These also I consider to be bacillus subtilis. Hoffman gives us the same species without separating them from the bacteria termo.

2.—BACILLUS ANTHRACIS.

I have never investigated the bacteria of splenic fever. Davaine's and Bollanger's observations, however, show that they differ only from the bacillus subtilis in the place of their existence and in their ferment function. Davaine describes them as stiff threads of 4 to 12 to 50 micrometers length and of very minute width, rarely bent or crooked. Bollanger says that if fresh they have no links and are homogeneous, but that with careful examination there can be seen plasma and cell envelope with the segmentation of the little rods into short cylindrical cells. The latter are also found isolated, and are the germs of bacteria. They differ from other bacteria by their regularity of form and by their having no motion. This, however, is also found in the bacillus subtilis for short periods, and occasionally, according to circumstances, for long periods.

I attach to this a plate of the bacteria found in splenic fever, from a preparation which Koebner gave me, taken from recently dead cattle. These specimens of bacillus do not differ from the butyric acid ferment bacillus subtilis, but, as a rule, are stronger, shorter and show less motion. Bollanger says that the bacteria of splenic fever blood were discovered by Pollander in 1849 even, before Davaine in 1863, and that Brauell made very important researches into this matter in 1857. He says the rods are straight cylindrical, 7 to 12 micrometers long, 8-10 to 1 micrometer thick. In the fresh state they are homogeneous. When they are in water, or in a state of putrefaction, they show a jointed structure of short cylindrical cells, each one containing a darker plasma in the transparent cell envelope. They break up soon into single globules,

Bollanger considers the rods of splenic fever as the torula form of globular bacteria, and thinks that the globular bacteria which are also found isolated, may multiply by partition and be joined together by links. I have never found in splenic fever rosary chains, but without intending to compare my observations with Bollanger's very careful observations, I must adhere to my former opinion that splenic fever bacteria are a bacillus species, and cannot believe in their relationship to globular bacteria.

3. BACILLUS ULNA.

This name I give to stiff and thick chain threads which, by their dense and finely granulated plasma, rank close to the oscillaria species, and can only be distinguished by the short and rod-like threads, readily breaking up into shorter members. I observed such members, remarkable for their thickness, distributed amongst other species, sometimes predominating over, or to the exclusion of, all other. Water which had been poured on boiled white of egg, and boiled with this once more, and left exposed, became discolored after two days. This discoloration was caused by innumerable little rods which moved strongly and actively, but were stiff and little flexible by themselves. I could observe a distinct membrane and a thick protoplasm with dark granules. The single membranes were 10 micrometers long and 2 micrometers wide. They formed straight or zig-zag-like broken chains of two or four members. The chains of four links had, therefore, a length of 42 micrometers, and showed very queer motions. Not only the whole thread rotated, but also the single links, as if they wanted to separate, making diverging motions. Five days later they were all dead, and lay in heaps on the bottom. Little drops showed themselves on their decaying threads, and in their place bacillus subtilis appeared in the water. Other glasses filled with boiled white of egg also developed bacteria, but none of this large bacillus form.

Ehrenberg says that the rods of vibrio bacillus have a sliding motion without being serpent-like, sometimes having an undulating motion. I think this is impossible. Ehrenberg estimates them at $\frac{1}{24}'''$ in length, and $\frac{1}{1440}.'''$ in thickness. Dujardin gives but half this size.

6. GENUS VIBRIO.

The two species of this genus are characterized by the wavy motion of their threads, and they form, therefore, a transition into the screw bacteria or spirilla.

1. VIBRIO RUGULA.

The threads of this species are eight to sixteen micrometers in length, have finely granulated contents, and a soft and thick protoplasm. They are twice as thick as the bacillus subtilis and especially distinguish themselves by being like an *italic s.* When the thread rotates slowly on its long axis it looks like a gimlet in motion. If it turns very quick, it is easily confounded with bacillus subtilis. The smaller species of this vibrio have but very little curve. I have measured them as of 8, 9.6, 10.4, 14.4, 17.6 micrometers. Longer ones are not to be found, but shorter ones, which turn like a gimlet or swim like an eel and are shaped like an S. Vibrio rugula form large swarms like swarms of bees; the decaying rods form films. Lewenhoek discovered them on the mucus, or tartar, of the teeth and in the faces of diarrhœa. Ehrenberg says they can be easily confounded with bacillus. He places their size at $\frac{1}{96}$ to $\frac{1}{48}$ ′′′.

2. VIBRIO SERPENS.

I distinguish this form from that of vibrio rugula in this, that the latter have in each link only one or one-and-a-half curve, while the threads of vibrio serpens have only half the thickness, are not flexible, and have several regular wave curves; in rotating, they show three or four undulations, the shortest members have also a double curve, still there are also chains of two to four bent pieces, which show a greater length and many curves. I measured such threads of 11.5, 13.1, 15.6, 19.5, 20.8 rnd 25.7 micrometers. The distance between two curves is five to six micrometers.

The motion is the same as the subtilis, the undulation excepted. A peculiar sight is the swarms which grow into each other and form long strings, in which innumerable trembling staffs lay parallel to each other.

8. SPIRO BACTERIA—SCREW BACTERIA.

The fourth group of screw bacteria is closely related to the vibrio serpens. It might even be better to put both in the same group. An evident difference from the genus vibrio is the more close and narrow spiral thread of the screw; and here too it may be added that I have observed an organization in the flexible whip in a species of spirilla volutans, which has not been seen in other bacteria, and which makes a special class necessary for the species having such organs of motion. I have seen these whips only in the largest kinds of spirilla, but it must be also looked for in other similar kinds. Future observations will prove whether other species of bacteria have also this whip, as Ehrenberg has always asserted.

The four species of screw bacteria into which Ehrenberg and I have classified this group are very easily distinguished. They are generally found together, but I do not believe that they are either varieties or stages of development of one and the same species. I think that the spirilla do not exist in artificial infusoria, but only in those prepared with river water, so that their genus are spread, not by the air, but by water. According to Ehrenberg we have two genera of screw bacteria:

a.—Spirochæte, having a flexible, long, closely wound screw.

b.—Spirillum, having rigid, shorter, and open wound screw.

a.—GENUS SPIROCHÆTE.

This genus has only one species—spirochæte plicatilis, of which I wrote at length in 1853. Of all spirilla, this species has the quickest rotation and most flexible motion. It is rather rare. Lately, I have found the spirochæte in the mucous of the teeth. The opinion that the spirochæte plicatilis is only a spiral in the atheromatous degeneration of the minute blood vessels is not correct.

SPIROCHÆTE—OBERMEIERI.

The most important fact with which in recent times our knowledge of the existence of ferment organisms in infectious diseases has been enriched, is the discovery by Otto Obermeier of spirilla in the blood of patients sick with recurrent fever, which he made in 1868, but published in 1873. Typhus recurrens has a fever paroxysm of six to seven days; then follows a remission of eight days; then a fever paroxysm of five days; and occasionally afterwards a third, fourth or fifth paroxysm of fever after a remission of nine days. Obermeier discovered in the blood of persons suffering with recurrent fever very long and thin screw threads moving rapidly, but only in the time of the paroxysm, not during the remission, nor shortly before or after the crisis. This discovery has been confirmed by later observers. On March 15th, 1873, Carl Weigert showed me in the "All Saints Hospital," at Breslau, where, in consequence of an epidemic, there were a large number of cases of recurrent fever, spiral threads in the blood of the patient. Here I will remark that these do not belong to the species spirilla, but to the species spirochæte, which differ from spirilla by their flexile screw threads capable of a circular and snail motion. Of the genus spirochæte but one species was known, which Ehrenberg found in stagnant water near Berlin and I near Breslau.

As their very characteristic shape and motion admits of no mistaking them for other species, we can say with certainty that the spirochæte plicatilis is not common in putrid water, but only found in exceptional cases.

The spirochæte which is found in the blood of recurrent fever, is the same size, and shape, and motion as the spirochæte found in swarms, still we must consider it as a specifically different class by the peculiar home of their existence and physiological power and effects. I call it, in rememberance of Obermeier, who discovered it, and who died in the cholera epidemic of 1873, spirochæte Obermeieri.

The most important facts relating to the spirochæte of febris recurrens have been discovered by Obermeier, Engel, Bliesener, Weigert, Litten, Birch, Hirschfeldt and Laptschinsky, and besides such as have been above mentioned are the following:

The screw motion is constant in the different species, but not the length of the threads. Obermeier says they are one and a half to six times as large as the blood corpuscles. Engel says they are twenty-six times as large as blood corpuscles. Litten says they form long chains, too long for the field of the microscope without moving. The screw threads show an undulation, besides moving their position, which characterizes them as spirochæte. In the height of the fever the threads are stiffer or stretched out. Towards the end of the paroxysm the motion becomes slower and more like a pendulum. They have a circular motion. The wave motion continues longest, even after change of position has ceased. Spirochæte retain their active motion out of the body for upwards of twenty-four hours; in a solution of salt, one-half per cent. for several hours; in glycerine, mercury, salts and distilled water, their motion ceases at once. Potash dissolves the threads. The form remains the same in osmium salts. The temperature of sixty degress to sixty-five degrees centigrade destroys them, but they are not destroyed at zero centigrade freezing. This is upon the authority of Litten.

The sickness which is characterized by the spirochæte Obermeiri, has only been known since March, 1868, according to Lebert. This sickness is sporadic and endemic, and very probably is imported from a distance. Generally, all the occupants of one room are attacked; it is therefore spread by personal contact.

The part which the spirochæte plays in the pathological processes of febris recurrens is yet as obscure as the periodical appearance and reappearance of them in the blood of the sick. It is not known yet whether the spirochæte plicatilis of the swarms and the Sp. Obermeiri of recurrent bloods are specifically different, or whether they are the same organism, and the contagium of the first form is developed by the drinking of swamp water containing spirochæte. It is also uncertain whether the spirochæte threads which I found in April, 1872, in the mucus of teeth, is only an intermediate stage between the swamp water spirochæte and the blood spirochæte.

b.—SPECIES SPIRILLUM.

Spirillum Tenue.—The fineness of their threads is like the vibrio serpeus. Like these, the spirillum tenue forms lie closely in globular heaps, in which they grow together and have no motion. Ehrenberg, with his well-known keen eye, has noticed this species. Dujardin says that they are one and a half times as thick as the undula. Ehrenberg's plate and description show just the opposite. Dujardin connects, without reason, the spirillum tenue with the spirillum undula. His plate shows only the spirillum tenue. The characteristic screw motion of the spirilla of this minute species, which I have observed by the million in every drop of an infusion, is especially quick, like lightning, so that the observer is scarcely conscious of it. The height of the elegant screw threads is two to three micrometers, and the diameter is about the same. The thread has one and a half curve, and is in form of an S, or Greek omega. Threads of two, three, four and five curves or turns are more plentiful; the length is four to fifteen micrometers.

No. 2. Spirillum undula differs by their stronger threads and somewhat more open screw thread. Every turn has four to five micrometers in height and diameter; the members have generally but a half or one turn, seldom one and a half to three spiral turns. Longer ones are never seen. The enormously quick motion hardly permits a careful observation of a single spirillum. They move like meteors, sometimes like the sudden expansion of a loosened spiral spring, sometimes like a sling shot; then they sometimes screw themselves in one direction. When they turn somewhat slower it looks to me as if they had whips at each end, but I could not be certain.

O. F. Müller and Ehrenberg have given characteristic descriptions of this species. Ehrenberg's vibrio prolifer I could not distinguish from the Sp. undula.

3.—SPIRILLUM VOLUTANS.

The largest of the spirilla, the giant among the bacteria. Müller and Ehrenberg have also recognized them. The plate of the latter gives so characteristic a form that it can be recognized at first sight. Dujardin has not seen or observed this variety. He gives this name to a form which he has seen in sea water and infusions of insects and conifera. His plate, however, does not show the character of the large screw turn, but the very tender spirals of spirillum tenue. It is like most of Dujardin's plates of bacteria, worthless for recognition.

In July, of 1872, I saw Sp. volutans in an infusion of dead fresh water snails, in which this species, together with spirillum tenue, undula, vibrio serpens and rugula, multipled enormously, and by adding new food remained in constant multiplication, these species being distinctly recognized.

Spirillum volutans not only excels by the greater thickness of their threads and their darkly granulated contents, which Ehrenberg has also observed, but also by their regular corkscrew-like spiral, 13.2 micrometers in height, 6.6 micrometers diameter. One turn of sp. volutans is as large as three turns of spirillum undula. The screws are turned to the right. I have taken great pains to recognize the links as Ehrenberg states them, but in vain—their membrane can be distinguished from the contents. There are generally two and a half, three or three and a half turns. Double spirals of six and seven turns are rare. Sometimes a pair twists itself round each other.

Spirillum volutans lies sometimes very quiet, then suddenly commences to turn in a screw-like motion forwards and backwards; sometimes shooting with a lively energy, so that the screw motion can hardly be recognized.

Until opticians have given us microscopes with magnifying powers much greater than they now are, and, if possible, without immersion, in the kingdom of the bacteria, we shall be like a traveler in the dark in an unknown country, where he knows that in spite of all his watchful care he cannot keep from wandering into wrong paths.

ARE BACTERIA ANIMALS OR PLANTS?

Looking over the literature of this subject, it is seen that formerly bacteria were generally considered animals, but now are considered by most naturalists plants. Some call certain bacteria infusoria ; other species, or perhaps the same species in a different stage of developement, fungi. Pasteur even asserts that vibriones being animals, require oxygen, whilst the same organism, as far as he considers them plant-ferments, vegetate *without* oxygen, and that, indeed, to certain of these ferments oxygen is poison. Upon this question, I make the same remark made by me in 1853. "Bacteria (vibriones) appear to belong to the vegetable kingdom, because they show a close and direct relation to the true algæ. On the other hand, bacteria have no true relations to animals. The animal kingdom begins with the infusoria, most of which (infusoria ciliata) have a large number of moving ciliæ, whilst a small number, the most simple of them (infusoria flagellata) have a tail. Even the lowest of the infusoria ciliata have a mouth and œsophagus by which they take solid food. Many kinds of the flagellata have mouths, and thereby differ from all plants. A few species only which generally are found among the infusoria flagellatta, have no mouth. These can be classed among plants. Bacteria have just a little relation to the *rizopods*, which represent a very simple type of animal organization. Possibly a relation to the monads may be recognised. The globular and rod bacteria may be easily mistaken for the globular or elliptical monads. Should the tails I have discovered in the spirillum belong to the true bacteria as Ehrenberg supposes, then the mouthless species of the genus monas would have to be classed with the tail bacteria.

Most writers who class bacteria among plants, consider them fungi. This is true if we include all cell plants or thalophytes among fungi, which are deprived of chlorophyl or an equivalent pigment, and therefore cannot assimilate carbonic acid. Bacteria have no relation to typical fungi, which develope a thread like mycelium and propagate by bassidia spores or asci spores. But they agree in their entire morphological and developing behavior with the phycochromaceæ, whose cells are filled with phycochrome, that is a mixture of green pigment, (chlorophyl) with a blue (phycochrome) and therefore are colored of an oxidized green. The phycochromaceæ differ from bacteria only in their power to assimilate carbonic acid, for which reason they are classed among the algæ. Bacteria are the beginnings of phy-cochromaceæ life. They are probably one of the oldest phases of organic life and combine as a primordial form, different charac-ters belonging to various families of the phycochromaceæ. Globu-lar and rod bacteria are related to the chrocococcaceæ, this being a division of the phycochromaceæ, whose cells vegetate singly or in families connected to the palmella jelly by a slimy intercellular substance. The chrocococcaceæ differ from palmel-laceæ by their contents of phycochrome.

Our genus micrococcus bacterium is related to chrocococcaceæ, in which the cell partition extends in but one direction, while sarcina belongs to the chrocococcaceæ with a crosswise partition. Rod bacteria are similar to the genus syne-coccaceæ, whose species form a blue green coating, on humid rocks, and agree in shape with the bacteria ; micrococccus differs from chrocococcaceæ by their small and colorless cells ; zooglea jelly and slimy masses we find in the chrocococceæ in very similar way.

Thread bacteria are closely related to oscillaria, that is, with their sub-genus beggiota and lepthothrix. Excepting in the short-ness of the thread, there is hardly any difference between them. The straight bacillus is similar to the normal form of oscillaria. The wavy rods of vibrio can be seen also in oscillaria terebriformis and similar species.

The species spirochæte is closely related to the smaller spirillinæ. The spirilla are only shorter forms of the same type. The dis-covery of whips in the spirillum volutans, which makes it similar to the flagellata, makes the natural positions of these organisms rather doubtful, as no oscillaria have whips.

The principal reason which made it difficult for most observers to classify bacteria, as plants was their voluntary motion. This, however, is only an illusion. Will, sensation and reflex-action are such complicated physical functions that they cannot be detected in these organisms, which have a kind of spontaneous motion. We don't know what is the nature of the power of spon-taneous motion which turn bacteria about their long axis, causing, at the same time, a changing of position, but we are convinced that it does not belong to the kingdom of will and reflexaction, but to the kingdom of involuntary action.

There is no relation between bacteria and mould fungi. When I commenced these observations I made it a main object to find out whether bacteria come from germs *suigeneris,* or are developed from other fungi. The results are in refutation of the latter view.

It is easy to cultivate pennicillium and other mycelia in a fluid without developing any bacteria. It is easier still, if you put in a reagent glass germs of bacteria without fungi spores or mycelium spores, and cover the glass with cotton ; the bacteria will multiply immeasurably, but no mycelium will develop. I have made hundreds of observations, and they show me that bacteria will only bring bacteria, mould fungi only mould fungi, and that no modification from one organism into another can exist.

All this shows that bacteria are a group of organisms having no connection with yeast or mould fungi as regards development. They are, or may be called fungi in consequence of their parasitic way of living. But they very much differ from typical fungi by the want of mycelia, and bassidia or asci spores. They therefore are, with justice, called an independent part—schyzomycetes. Bacteria and schyzomycetes are closely connected with the algæ phycochromaceæ in their morphology and development. In trying to get all these into a natural system, I have classed the bacteria and the other schyzomycetes, together with the family of phycochromaceæ, into one natural order, under the name of schyzosporen.

THE BEHAVIOR OF BACTERIA

UNDER DIFFERENT TEMPERATURES.

It seems clear that bacteria cannot survive the boiling point, and it is uncertain, from experiment, at what temperature below 100 deg. centigrade they cease to live. Experiments show very uncertain results, for so very reliable an observer as Schwann says that a temperature above the boiling point does not always prevent the development of bacteria. Pasteur says that the utmost power of resistance of bacteria in sour milk reaches the point of 105 deg. centigrade. I say nothing of Wyman, Crace, Calvert, etc., who give a much higher temperature. In June, 1871, I made some experiments, aided by Mr. Stud. Troschke. We boiled a pea in a glass test-tube with five grammes of distilled water, and then cooled it ; a bacteria drop being then added. The retort was then placed in water at different temperatures from a quarter to a half hour ; the neck of the retort was stuffed with cotton. The results were as follows :

Putrefaction came on after three days with a heat of 45 deg., 55 deg., or 60 deg. centigrade. At 65 deg. c. no change took place for a time. Putrefaction set in later. August 7th, the pea was dissolved into a yellow, dirty brown paste. At 75 deg. c. the pea did not putrefy, but the water did not remain clear, it became opalescent, and a little bacteria sediment was found. At 80 deg. centigrade, the pea did not putrefy, and the water remained clear ; in a second experiment, after heating for a half hour, a white mycellium appeared, but neither Pennicillium nor putrefaction; in a third experiment, in spite of a heating for three-quarters of an hour, putrefaction set in; and in a fourth experiment, after a half hour's heating, a little discoloring and sediment appeared, but no putrefaction. Temperature above 80 deg. c. showed no development of bacteria nor putrefaction. Whilst our experiments have shown that in an artificial fluid bacteria have been deprived of their power of development at 60 deg. centigrade, we cannot explain why in other cases bacteria have shown a development in organic structures after being heated up to boiling points.

8

The setting in of cold weather delays putrefaction, which is evidence therefore that it suspends the vital powers of bacteria and prevents their increase, while an increase of temperature increases their development. Everybody knows that meat does not putrefy so soon and milk and beer sour so quickly as in summer; the dead body of a mammoth, kept unchanged in Siberian ice through thousands of years, and was destroyed by putrefaction in the shortest time after the ice had melted away and the temperature had risen. Here is evidence that the ferment function of putrefaction bacteria does not exist below zero c. It is, therefore, quite important to prove whether bacteria are killed by freezing just as they are by heating up to 60 deg. centigrade. The experiments made by Dr. Horwath proved the opposite, for they show that these organisms can stand a severe cold without being killed. The experiments were made as follows:

A reagent cylinder was filled with a breeding fluid on June 6th, 1872, and closed with a cork, through which a thermometer had been passed which reached down to the bottom of the fluid. The whole cylinder was placed into a freezing mixture, as also a little retort filled with the same mixture and the end sealed by melting the end of the tube.

The temperature in the reagent cylinder was as follows:

12 h., 30 seconds,	temperature	....	0 deg. c.
1 h., 30 "	"	....	16 deg. c.
1 h., 45 "	"	....	17 deg. c.
3 h., 30 "	"	....	18 deg. c.
4 h., 30 "	"	....	18 deg. c.
5 h., —	"	....	17 deg. 5c.
6 h., —	"	....	14 deg. c.
7 h., 30 "	"	....	9 deg. c.

The following day the tubes were taken out—the temperature was 15 deg. c. On the 8th of June, after freezing more than seven hours, an increase of bacteria was evident by the discoloring of the fluid. A second series of experiments with closed retorts, treated in the same way, and frozen to 7 deg. below zero c. for 18 hours, resulted in an increase of bacteria, clearly visible after the thawing of the mixture.

From these experiments we see that bacteria are not killed by a very low temperature, even though lasting for several hours, but at zero c., or probably a somewhat higher temperature, they fall into a torpor from the cold. Their motion, their propagation, and, therefore, their ferment power ceases, but not their power of recommencing their *propagation* in higher temperatures. While the thawing of a fluid was going on, into which a Sp. Volutans had been frozen, we could observe, under the microscope, that the screw threads remained motionless for some time and simulated death ; but under increasing temperature their vital activity was restored, and they returned to life. *Euglenen*, however, which were frozen in this fluid were killed altogether, just as higher infusoria, with the exception of encysted vorticella, whose contractile vacuoles evidenced the continuance of life.

REPORT

—TO THE—

CITY COUNCIL OF SAVANNAH

—ON THE—

EPIDEMIC DISEASE OF 1820,

BY WILLIAM R. WARING.

REPORT.

In compliance with the appointment of the Council, I have composed a memoir concerning the causes, character, and treatment of the late epidemic. It is not very brief, in the place of a common report, but it has been contracted into as narrow bounds as could possibly comport with the nature of the subject. The disease made its appearance in May. A death occurred on the 7th, another on the 10th, and another on the 30th of that month. In June, the mortality was augmented to a death on every second day, and the whole sum, at the end of the month, amounted to 14. In July, the number of deaths ran up to 39, being an advance to more than double the devastation of June. In August, it amounted to 111 ; in September, to 241 ; in October, to 268 ; in November, to 50, and in December to 3. The degree of mortality, on the surface of this statement, appears to have undergone a gradual reduction after the month of September. But when it is considered that, in the course of this period, the population had been greatly diminished by absence and death, it becomes evident that, so far from having sustained any diminution, it was really increased throughout the month of October. The whole aggregate of deaths resulting from the epidemic, from its commencement in May to its conclusion in December, is thus estimated at 666. The yellow fever of 1793, in Philadelphia, destroyed near 5,000 people, so that, reckoning the inhabitants of that city at 50,000, the mortality would amount to the proportion of one in ten. When the late epidemic first appeared in May, the population of Savannah may be computed at 5,000 whites. In June, and beginning of July, it was probably reduced, from emigration, to 2,500 ; and, on the 14th of September, when the Mayor's proclamation was published, the number was still further reduced, and could not have exceeded 1,500. The medial population, therefore, of white inhabitants may be fairly estimated at 3,000 for the whole season, which would constitute a sum of mortality amounting to one in five, and just doubling that of Philadelphia in 1793. Such an enormous sweep of human life has scarcely a parallel in the medicine of Europe or America. The epidemic of the present year commenced

unusually early, in a comparison with others of a date prior to
1817. In former times, and antecedent to this period, the season,
commonly denominated the sickly season, was not expected until
the latter part of July, or beginning of August. The month of
July, 1816, was, I believe, the most prominent for its health and
pleasantness in that year ; and the late Dr. John Grimes informed
me then, that it was not a casualty, but a general and expected
occurrence. In 1817, some vicissitude seems to have been established, for the epidemic began to develop itself very early, and
before the expiration of July, had been propagated widely and
fatally. The epidemic of 1818 scarcely deserves to be called so.
For, although bilious fever did in some instances take place, and
was the genuine product of the period, yet it was mild, sporadi-
cal, and the bare testimony of its annual return. Such as it was,
however, it commenced to declare itself even in spring, and, in a
few cases, terminated in death. The epidemic of 1819 made its
appearance under a distinct shape, in the latter part of June, and
went on increasing in extent and destructiveness, until the frost
came and ended it. I make these remarks in regard to the anticipated birth of those epidemics, because I shall place that cir-
comstance among the co-operating causes which have produced
the disease of 1820, when I come particularly to discuss its origin.
Throughout the months of June and July, the late epidemic was
bilious and remittent in its general complexion. It was the ordinary malady of other seasons, featured with the wonted symptoms,
and pursuing the common course. But there was a grade and
form more violent and deadly, assumed at first in solitary instances
only, and always preserving some characteristic of alliance to the
ruling type, which grew, step by step, in extent, and finally spread
its dominion everywhere. This terrific contour of the disease
was distinguished by its unabating continuance, by its black
emissions from the stomach, and by its inflamed eye. It was
evidently the epidemic remittent, propelled into this aggravated
shape by the violence and consequent intercurrence of paroxysms.
In the first place, because the black ejections from the stomach,
which were incident to it, were frequently attendant on cases
accompanied with remissions. Second, because in many instances
where no remission could be distinguished, there was a total
absence of black evacuations, either from the stomach or lower
intestines. Third, because the majority of cases were connected,
in the first stage of their progress, with discharges of bile, which

were sometimes copious, although afterward they became suppressed entirely, as the disease rose to the summit of its strength. Fourth, because, in some cases, by the tendency of the attack, or by the imprudent administration of acrimonious substances, the remittent was excited into the continued form, and the character which was assumed, in the onset, became finally obliterated. Fifth, because, in some cases, which were genuinely continued until the force of the disease was in some measure exhausted, and the constitution beginning to triumph in a recovery, the remittent garb was gradually and eventually completely disclosed and established. Sixth, because the inflamed vascular membrane of the stomach was the source of the black ejections, and that inflammation was repeatedly ascertained, by the morbid dissection, to exist with profuse secretions of bile, and without the production of one particle of black matter. Seventh, because, in connection with this inflamed state of the stomach, and abundant secretion before death, and presence of bile after death, without any appearance of black matter, there was sometimes not a mere remittent, but the exhibition of a perfect intermittent form of fever, such as is ordinarily witnessed in every season. Eighth, because, it appeared, after death and dissection, in a case of remittent fever, that there was inflammation of the inner coat of the stomach, with small parcels of black matter upon its surface, while the cavity of the stomach was filled with green bile, and the *duodenum* with deep yellow bile ; thus evincing, in the most decisive manner, the unity of the bilious and black vomit forms of the epidemic. Ninth, because, at the winding up of the season, the intermittent and remittent forms of the disease became more numerous, while there was a corresponding diminution of the continued cases, which had been predominating. This fact could only be explained by the general mitigation of the epidemic, which the cool weather had effected, and which was the suitable result of a reduced state of the morbific causes. Tenth, because, in the same family, and under the same roof, all the varieties of intermittent, remittent, and continued fever, were sometimes simultaneous. In the family of Mr. T. V. Grey, there was one servant affected with common fever and ague, another with a severe remittent, and a third with a continued fever, ending in black vomit, at the same instant. Is it possible to conceive that there were three distinct atmospherical sources of disease in this narrow compass? If the case of black vomit be sundered from

the intermittent and remittent cases, and ascribed to a separate
agent, then the intermittent and remittent must consequently be
sundered from each other, and with equal propriety, he also
ascribed to separate agents. Eleventh, because, in all epidemical
diseases, there are mild as well as mortal cases. Now, the advocates in general, for the nosological distinction of the continued
form of fever, in combination with black vomit, have neglected to
point out and define the mild cases which eventuate in the re-
storation of the patient. I have yet to learn what they are. For,
in the season, which has just elapsed, there seemed to be very
little difference. The event was almost universally mortal, where
black matter was ejected from the stomach. Even the plague of
Canstantinople and Cairo does not destroy all. The natural small
pox presses with a heavy hand on some, but, in others it is kind,
and does not even disturb the tranquility of the general circulation. Influenza, in some cases, is nothing more than the slightest
catarrh; while, in others, it engorges the lungs, and prostrates
the strength, even to death. As those epidemics which are well
understood, seem to be governed according to the principle of
variety, in force, and grade, and features, none is positively and
inflexibly defined by fixed points and lines. It is not probable,
therefore, independently of other considerations, that the continued fever of black vomit is subject to the same principle also?
That it is not always fashioned by an unbending and deadly pat-
tern; but, in the same manner, varies its outline, and sometimes
invades the system with a part only of the ordinary violence?
This is rendered still more probable by its correspondence with a
general law, which governs the operations of the human body.
There is not an active substance of the *materia medica* which constantly preserves an uniform influence over every constitution.
Habit, predisposition and internal peculiarities of structure, are
as various as the external figure. Seldom are two frames suscep-
tible of similar movements, from the action of the same cause, and
nothing is more common than different depths of impression, not
only in different systems, but even in the same system, at different
junctures. All medicines, all articles of food and drink, are employed in practice, under the control of this law. All poisonous
remedies are subject to it; for it is as much a constituent part of
the physiological body, as any of the vital functions. It were
then indeed a strange circumstance, if a poison, which happens
to be diffused in the atmosphere, a miasma of bogs or foul heaps,

should be made of such a flexible material as to defeat the usual tendency of that law, and to adapt itself to all the differences of susceptibility, or arrangements of predisposition, in such manner as to produce always the same effect of grade and form. There is an accommodating power in the body, which gradually, but not promptly, and often unsuccessfully, tends to fit it to exigencies, and to the forces which are exercised by the agents which operate on it; but there is no such convenient power of compliance, in any degree, in agents to the various states of the body. Their character is immutable, so that it is not possible for them to raise up the same morbid affections in every instance. What, then, are the minor effects of that cause which produces continued fever and black vomit, if they be not the bilious remittent and intermittent forms of fevers? These have been the only forms of disease associated with them, and they have been the only obvious milder effects which it could have produced.

The epidemic began then as mild and manageable intermittent and remittent bilious fever. In the course of its march, it became a remittent, more severe and fatal; at another step, a continued fever, most ungovernable and destructive, at first of short, but afterwards, in some instances, of considerable duration; and, finally, concluded with a relapse into the primary intermittent and remittent types. I have said, that, almost from the moment of its declaration, certain causes were appareled in the continued dress. The first which came under my notice, occurred on the 26th of June, in Washington Ward, which is situated at the northeast point of the city. There was some appearance of a periodical remission it this case, but it was not very distinct or well marked, and the patient died on the third day. I have often seen examples, at a late period in other seasons, of cases running thus rapidly to a close, and was contented with accounting for its early occurrence by some extraordinary exposure or intemperance. On the 14th July, a mechanic was attacked with continued fever, in the same ward, and died on the fourth day, with hemorrhages from the nose and bowels, with a spongy state of the gums. About this time, Mr. Patrick Stanton, who occupied a store in the neighborhood, was also malignantly and insidiously seized with fever, which terminated in black vomit and death, on the 16th July. This was the first case, I believe, in which this terrible symptom appeared.

The epidemic had hitherto prevailed, with as much extent and mortality, in the western, as in the eastern flank of the city. But, towards the latter part of this month, and the beginning of August, it planted itself chiefly in Washington and other eastern wards. Its most prominent and fatal impression was felt there. The strongest features of the disease were exhibited there, while the ravages which had been made in Yamacraw, and the western sections, were proportionally moderated. The fact is worthy of notice ; for, on examining the register of deaths, it is perceived that, at this period, when Washington Ward became the great theatre of desolation, it was not the acquisition of a new disease, on the back of an ordinary bilious remittent, which had occupied the western, as well as the eastern districts of the city, but an apparent concentration of effect in the eastern districts, which had been divided between eastern and western districts.

The explanation of this singular transition is to be found in the character of the winds, and in the peculiar localities of these eastern departments, which will presently be rendered sufficiently obvious, by an inspection of the meteorological diagram which I have constructed. The fact, however it may be accounted for or solved, gives a correct warrant for the inference, that the cause had been divided, and was now condensed, in conformity with the effect. It was not a mere increase of the cause, but a concentration of it in one place ; and thus leads to the conclusion that it was general, and founded in some common constitution of the air and circumstances of the city. The consequences of this vicissitude, in the distribution of the morbific matter, were suitable to it. The mortality and devastation soon attracted universal notice, and appalled every man of consideration for his family or friends. The municipal authorities were specially convened to deliberate on measures for the health of the city. The Mayor addressed a letter of respect to the Medical Society, for information of the grounds of the peculiar destructiveness of disease in Washington Ward and other eastern departments. A committee of the corporation was also appointed to make further inquiry into the same subject ; and finally, a Board of Health was constituted, to ascertain means of preventing the further progress of the disease, or to mitigate it, by removing whatever might contribute to produce it. Notwithstanding every effort, however, the epidemic continued its career in the eastern wards, until death or flight, in a few weeks, had divested them of inhabitants. Tar was burnt in the open squares and was recommended to be burnt, also, in yards and dwellings. Every practicable mode was em-

ployed to remove the filth of streets and lots, and to extend the
system of purgation.   Committees of the Board of Health were
organized, to make frequent and regular visits of investigation
into every part of the city, and those committees did whatever
was in their power to do.   Still the epidemic rioted on, and continued to propagate death and dismay.   Exertions were inefficient, because it was impossible to reach either the general or
local root and source of the calamity.   It gradually penetrated
into all quarters of the city, except that part which is situated on
the south common, and to the westward of the new Presbyterian
church.   But its greatest ravages were spread along the streets
and lanes, which were crowded with old wood houses, in a state
of partial decadence, were badly ventilated, and over-tenanted
with non-residents, or strangers to the climate.   In such places,
the scene of sickness, misery, and ruin was awful, shocking, and
well fitted to inspire a melancholy sentiment of the shortness, uncertainty, and insignificance of life, and to humble all that pride
and self-greatness which is incident to health, strength and
pleasure.

Beyond the boundaries of the old town, there was no example
of continued fever or black vomit.   The ordinary intermittent
or remittent bilious fever were the prevailing forms of disease in
the country, and they corresponded, in every way, with what
might be called the sub-cases, or the intermittent and remittent
cases which were contemporary with them in the city.   There
seemed to be a link of association between these, which leads
strongly to the deduction, that the same species of agent constituted the foundation of all the cases which were co-existing within
and without the boundaries, notwithstanding every difference of
exterior appearance.   The continued form of fever, and the
symptom of black vomit, never passed the ancient and well settled positions of the city.   In the progress of the season, that
form came to predominate, and attained to such general supre-
macy as to constitute the common features of disease.   An epidemic was established, therefore, it may be admitted, under this
shape.   Was it specifically distinct from the intermittent and remittent epidemic of the country?   Was its origin distinct, not
only in degree, but chymically and in quality also?   Did they
come into actual contact at the precincts of the city, without tres-
passing on the soil and empire of each other ; so that, while one
was occupying an extensive adjacent country, the other was cir-

cumscribed and locked up within those precincts? The country was invested, for many miles, with an unsound and epidemic state of the atmosphere. The city was encompassed with it on every side. Was there a spell which repelled its further progress, or warded off the access which no natural obstacle could have prevented it from finding? Is it not much more probable—nay, is it 'not certain, that it did not only envelope the city, but penetrated also into every part of it—that it carried the same infection along with it into streets, lanes, houses and lots, and, being unchanged, scattered its baneful effects in the same manner as it had done in the country? This was an inevitable consequence, which there was nothing to obviate. There was no barrier to the inroad of the winds, and there was no cleansing power which could wash away the unwholesome materials which they carried. Could they be present, then, and inactive? What circumstances of the city was there possible, which could have so fortified the systems of men, as to make them invulnerable to that fell agent, which was holding strong influence everywhere else? What power was there which could so neutralize it, as to defeat it in that way? I know of none. It was there; and that it was inert, while there, is inconceivable. It must have operated on the body with as much certainty, as we have in the operation of arsenic, under every vicissitude of place—with as much certainty as we have in the competence of a cause to produce an effect, which has been uniformly produced by it before. Whatever, then, that effect was, it was at least founded, in some degree, in the general morbific constitution of the air, which was suspended over the town and country. That constitution of air must at least have contributed largely to produce it; and, indeed, if there be any truth in the technical rules which are commonly taught, in regard to the succession of epidemic diseases, and the exclusive sovereignty of one only at the same time, it must have acted, not only an important, but a chief part. It must have impressed its character on all cases, and must have turned to its own tendencies, whatever of impurities, from local sources, might have mingled and associated with it. It must, in fact, have formed the basis of one general disease, more violent and destructive in certain places, according to the greater abundance of local circumstances to aggravate and promote it—more pestilential in one situation than another, in consequence of greater fruitfulness in the furnishing of those pernicious substances, or miasmata, which are probably the product of putrid collections or marsh fermentations. I can easily imagine a compass of twenty miles, diversified in such a way as to exhibit a pond in one place, a simple quagmire in another, a bog in another, with all the complex festerings of city filth ; a fertile soil in another, without any standing waters, but rich with vegetables in decay, and dead insects ; a great assemblage of rotten corn, coffee, beef, or fish, in another ; an immense mass of wood, crumbling by putrefaction, in another ; a great number of wooden houses, crowded upon each other, and inhabited by a species of tenantry, careless, by poverty and habit, of the foul aggregations which take place around them, in another; and then I can imagine that an epidemic, produced by the operation of heat and humid air upon all this surface, to be identically and specifically the same, founded in the same general principle of putrid decomposition over all its parts, and diversified with various degrees of severity, according to this enumeration of circumstances. Such consequences would inevitably result from such causes. A fever, of different grades and features, but entirely of the same species, would be thus wrought into existence. An intermittent would form the general grade in one place—a remittent in another—an active continued fever in another—a fever attended with prostration of all the energies, in another—and, in another, with hemorrhages and perverted secretions. From such a multiform origin, there could not be any unity in the symptoms or the degree, although the remote and the proximate cause might be perfectly uniform. These must be subject to change, according to the diminished or accumulated forces which produce them. And thus it happens, that epidemics, which unquestionably arise from the same local circumstances, assume such various types, in different seasons. At one time, as in the summer and autumn of 1817, the muscular coat of the stomach is irritable, while the internal coat indicates very little disorder. At another, as in 1819, the stomach evinces a high degree of insensibility, so as to bear without nausea, the largest doses of medicine. At another, as in 1820, the internal coat is the great seat of action, while the muscular coat is comparitively passed by and untouched. What then ? Shall we attribute all the varieties of summer and autumnal fever to different agents ? Shall we have a new and distinct species for every year ? If such a principle of dividing diseases were once admitted, the catalogue would be unbounded, and we should have

as many fall epidemics as there are annual periods of sickness.
For, although an epidemic has occurred in this city, since my
residence in it, in connection with every return of the warm
months, I have not witnessed two which were parallel with one
another, at every point.   However nearly they have approximated
in outward character, there has always been left some chasm in
the similitude, or some inequality in the morbid excitement.   But
it would not merely tend to the indefinite multiplication of general diseases.   By a parity of reasoning, and by pushing such a
method of pathology a little further, it would become correct, and
equally consistent to divide each of those general diseases into as
many minute species as there might be different cases.   For
cases, during the prevalence of a general disease, are as variant
from each other, in a multitude of instances, as the general diseases themselves.   They are so much modified by moral and
physical circumstances—by the age or progress of the epidemic
season, that very often they take on peculiar dresses, and present
themselves to the spectator under novel and unsettled shapes.
At one point of the city, a drunkard dies of black vomit; at
another, an abstemious man dies of fever, combined with dysentery ; at another, a man of mental uneasiness dies with inflammation of the brain ; and at another, a painter dies with fever,
united to palsy of the limbs.   In the outset, the common type may
be remittent ; in the middle of the season, it may become continued, with a critical duration of six days; and at the conclusion,
that duration may be spun on to twenty days, and the skin ac-
quire a deep yellow complexion.   Thus, varieties are multiplied,
according to accidents, predispositions and the epidemic power.
Is it scientific to consider these cases as so many distinct diseases?   It would lead to confusion and embarrassment, without
effecting one useful purpose.   How, then, are epidemics to be
distinguished, and what mode is to be pursued, to ascertain the
cases which do or do not belong to them ?   It is evident that
symptoms and external signs are too fluctuating and mutable to
be relied on.   It is evident that, to receive their authority, is at
once to swell the list of diseases beyond all bounds.   The saga-
city of the most learned is baffled by them, and practical physicians acknowledge their insufficiency, by the constant references
which they make to other sources of information.   The first
process of the mind, in regard to an epidemic, as to ascertain its
existence ; and this is done, not so much by observing, in every

case, an unvarying uniformity of shape and feature, as by observing that many persons are seized with disease at the same time. The pneumonic fever, which prevailed in many parts of the United States a few years ago, sometimes affected the head with a *phrenitis*, while the pneumonic system entirely escaped ; and yet, such cases were ascribed to the common cause, as well as those which had given origin to its denomination. After coming, in this manner, to a knowledge of the positive prevalence of an epidemic, the next step is to find out its cause, not so much for the purpose of learning the philosophical nature, as of ascertaining the character of the disease which it has kindled. It is for the purpose of comprehending the grade and seat of the disease, by some former experience, and thus attaining to the true method of treating it. In this point of view, the cause bears no relation to exterior appearances, and an acquaintance with it cannot be considered, except with great uncertainty, as conducting to an acquaintance with them. They are to be considered as its casual and irregular products, not immediately, but mediately, through the proximate cause which it establishes. They are really the direct effects of the proximate cause, by the sympathy of parts ; and nothing can be more unsystematic than the operations of this unintelligible principle.

There is a general analogy between the conformation of one body and another, which, in a considerable number of the cases of an epidemic, tends to develop some uniform symptoms. But that analogy is not perfect enough, and, even if it were perfect, is not sufficient to counteract the accidents of predisposition and the sympathies, so as to demonstrate regular appearances. Hence, it seems that the symptoms of an epidemic are too vague and unsteady to constitute the foundation of its pathological distinction. They are not the fixed outlines which are always exhibited to denote and distinguish it. They have their place, and contribute to an understanding of the treatment of diseases: Thus far they are useful and indispensable, but to use them for the purpose of systematic arrangement is to found an edifice on a sand bank, which the very next wind is to scatter and carry away. When cases, then, differ in their external manifestations it is not reasonable to conclude that they differ in fact, and in their secret character also. When the eye is inflamed in one instance, is yellow in another, is clear in another; when the skin is at one time purple, at another deeply tinged with bile, and at another fair and

9

ruddy as nature ; when the stomach disgorges a black fluid at one moment, a yellow fluid at another, and no fluid whatever at another, it does not follow that any original diversity must necessarily exist among the morbid affections on which they are bottomed. Where, then, are the points of specific difference between the fever of the city and that of the circumjacent country ? Since the doctrine of symptoms is incapable of opening a way to a knowledge of them, what other resources have the advocates of that difference ? I know of none. The epidemic causes are of less avail than the doctrine of symptoms. What are those causes in the country ? The decomposition of various substances. What are they in the city ? The decomposition of substances again. The result of that decomposition we call miasma, which we understand only by its effects and by its connection with the dissolution of animal and vegetable matter under the influence of heat and moisture. It is an undivided cause, and has more power at one time, and in one place, than another, only by its quantity and degrees of condensation. If, therefore, any weight be allowed to the cause, the unity of the epidemic would be at once established. Notwithstanding the intermittent of the south common, which was the general grade and form in that place—the active remittent at Mr. John Eppinger's farm, five miles from town, the more prostrating remittent at White Bluff, nine miles distant, and the continued fever of the city—still the epidemic would be univerversally the same in regard to its real and not its apparent character.

But it is frequently observed, that the mortality has been unprecedented in the city—that so much black vomit has never occurred before, and in short, that the disease has no likeness to former epidemics. These have been admitted by some, as a sufficient warrant for believing it to be new and peculiar, and unexampled. The mortality has indeed been unprecedented ; but, if a pathological distinction is to be founded on different degrees of mortality, there would be no end to such distinctions ; it is of all modes the most preposterous. I recollect once to have heard a physician say, that an ulcer, which another had pronounced to be cancerous, was not a cancer, because it healed and the patient got well. A cancer, according to his surgery, was an ulcer, which always ended in the destruction of the subject of it. There is much of this cancerous philosophy in those who found their pathological dogmas on the mere issue of cases, and not a

little of it, even in those who found them on extreme severity
and forms. It is true, also, that there has been an uncommon
abundance of black vomit. This symptom has prevailed more
generally and extensively, in the character of the late epidemic,
than in any other which has gone before. But it is not a new
symptom. Scarcely a season has passed in which it has not made
its appearance. In 1817, the number of cases was considerable,
and Dr. Maxwell, who has been an attending surgeon at the City
Hospital, has informed me, that, for thirteen years, he has constantly met with occasional occurrences of this symptom. It
seems to be the highest and most inflammatory grade of the periodical fever, which requires the greatest virulence and plenti-
tude of the usual causes, to produce it. It seems to be an ex-
acerbation of a mere irritation of the stomach into the state of
rapid inflammation, which an increase of the causes of that irritation is fully adequate to accomplish. But, with regard to the
origin of the symptom of black vomit, I shall speak more particularly, when I come to discuss the pathology of the epidemic.
Hitherto, however, it has almost invariably happened, that cases
of fever, distinguished by black vomit, have occurred among foreigners, or persons estranged from the climate. What was common remittent in the native, in the strangers seemed to become
continued, and then assumed this fatal symptom. But the remittent was nevertheless a high state of fever, and not only frequently attacked, but very often, either broke down the constitution, or was mortal. And, notwithstanding the opinions entertained by some, in regard to the unusual destruction among the
native residents, by the epidemic in 1820, it is certainly far from
being new. It is not now, surely, that we have to learn, that the
periodical fevers of this city have been always fatal, in a greater
or less degree, to its permanent inhabitants ; and that, although
black vomiting has not been a conspicuous accompaniment of the
disease in former seasons, the devastation, from rapid and uncontrollable remittents, was extensive and melancholy. To speak
therefore, of the novelty of the fever, in consequence of the extent of its violence, and the redundance of one symptom, appears
to be unreasonable, or founded in a want of more general and
accurate information.

    I have now arrived at that part of the subject of this report,
which relates particularly to the causes of the epidemic, and more
especially to the causes of its aggravated character in the city. In

the first place, I shall describe the weather which preceded and
was contemporaneous with it; in the second place, the peculiar
circumstances of the city itself; and, last of all, I shall examine
the reasons which have induced a few to attribute our troubles to
the dry culture, and to importation. I hope that I shall be able
to make it appear, that in these are to be found ample causes for
the production of the severest grades of fever, without resorting
to additional whimsical, and groundless suppositions. By referring to the register of the heat, for the month of February, it will
be perceived, that, even in that month, the thermometer rose to
an extraordinary height—on one day, to 35 degrees; which ex-
ceeds the medial mid-day heat for the month of August. The
whole medial heat, at mid-day, was 73 degrees. In March,
the weather became cooler; but the thermometer rose to 80 degrees at mid-day, and the medial heat for the month, was 68 degrees. In April, the medial heat at mid-day, was 77 degrees, and
the thermometer rose as high as 92 degrees. May was somewhat
cooler than April; but the medial heat at mid-day, was not less
then 75, and the common heat increased to 90 degrees. From
this time, the heats of summer were established, and did not
begin to abate until the approach of September. But the following table will exhibit in a more lucid manner, the early and pre-
mature invasion of the summer temperatures, and the gradual,
though not entirely uniform, ascent of the mercury after the
month of January.

THE MEDIAL AND GREATEST COMMON HEAT AT MID-DAY, IN THE SHADE.

	Feb.	Mar.	April.	May.	June.	July.	Aug.	Sept.	Oct.	Nov.
MEDIAL..............	73	68	77	75	81	85	82	78	67	65
COMMON..........	85	80	92	90	92	96	90	85	85	75

From this it appears, not only that the summer commenced in
April, and converted the usual temperature of the spring into the
hot weather of that season, but that even through the months of
February and March, an uncommon warmth had been infused
into the climate. A lady, who has always been in the habit of
taking the cold both in summer, informed me that she began, this
year, in March, as a matter of comfort, her system of cold bath-
ing. The whole winter, indeed, of 1819-'20, was remarkably mild,
and did not wear the character which was suited to it. Beside
this unsalutary substitution of the genial spring, by heating suns,
there were considerable falls of rain. In the course of March,

April, and May, there was a deposit of nine inches of water. So that, what is denominated the rainy season, instead of making its entrance along with the summer months, as it commonly does, and as it does usually in years which are only of moderate inclemency, anticipated this period for ninety days. In the two months of June and July, the quantity of rain became more abundant, and as many inches were laid as in the three preceding months. Hitherto, the rains had been divided by considerable intervals, but, on the 2d of August, they set in, and continued incessantly for twelve days, and at the close of the month, the enormous depth of thirteen inches of water had fallen. It was during this spell of twelve days' rain, that the epidemic grew so destructive in Washington Ward, and cited the public alarm. This fact is very strong, in proof of its local origin and connection with excessive moisture. In September, there was a remission of the rains; but on the first of October, seven inches and a half of water fell in a single shower; and during the months of September, October, and November, there were fifteen inches of water deposited. Throughout the greater part of this time, the atmosphere was loaded with vapor, and was very oppressive. Notwithstanding all this long term of cloudy skies and heavy rains, there was almost a total absence of the electrical fluid. And, although I am unwilling to admit that this fluid is possessed of any direct agency in the preservation of health, or that it operates in its general diffusion throughout the atmosphere on the system, in any efficient or important manner, I think it exercises a useful function in sustaining the wholesome qualities of the air, by the condensation and removal of vapor. When there is much moisture, this fluid is always inconsiderable ; but it is always abundant, when there is little moisture; and when this fact is connected with the refreshing character of rains, which are accompanied with much thunder and lightning, together with the sultriness and oppressive tendency of those which are not thus characterized, it becomes probable that they serve to assist in the formation of clouds, and to desiccate the atmosphere to a proper state for respiration. The chemistry of rain is not perfectly understood. The production and accumulation of clouds are yet to be accounted for. Is it possible for positive and negative electricities, in the first place, to give origin to vapors, from the elementary gases, and then to attract them into masses? I have remarked, that sometimes the rain poured in greater torrents after a severe flash of lightning. Whether the electrical fluid was deficient, in consequence of redundant moisture, or moisture was redundant in consequence of the deficiency of the electrical fluid, it is, at all events, a strong testimonial of the extreme dampness which pervaded the atmosphere, throughout the season. Its uncommon absence, if produced by dampness, affords the strongest confirmation of the uncommon extent of that dampness. After vapors are taken from the earth into the atmosphere they are either decomposed or aggregated, by a power which does not appear to be known. If, by any means, that be withdrawn, then it is obvious, that neither the decomposition nor aggregation can take place, and an excess of atmospherical moisture must ensue. It was owing, perhaps, to this circumstance, whether it arose from a sparse state of the electrical fluid or not, that a constant sense of great oppression was produced by the heaviness and want of elasticity in the air. Profuse exhalations were incessantly going on, and the falls of rain were considerable ; but the formation of rain did not appear to equal the exhalations, and to remove the excess of moisture which they produced. These were the general causes of the epidemic, which were present with it, in its whole extent, over town and country. They were the common foundation of the miasma which engendered it. In regard to the city, however, there are many peculiar circumstances, not only because of its internal condition, but of its remarkable elevation, and exposure to the most concentrated operation of these general causes. Standing on a lofty bluff, and being entirely defenseless against the influence of extensive marshes on every side, except a point to the south, it affords an intercepting barrier and lodgment for the abundant fogs which are constantly raised from them. Not a wind comes—not a breeze blows from a north, east, or west direction, which is not laden with moisture to be deposited and retained by the city. Along the channel of the river, to the east and northeast, and to the west and southwest, the fogs and damps are raised by the winds to be condensed upon the high plateau of the town. Especially is this the case on the east and northeast, whence the winds bring their vapors loaded with *miasmata* to poison the atmosphere of Washington Ward.

It is interesting to compare the years 1818–'19 and '20 as regards the relative amounts of rainfall, calms, winds, and electricity. From such accumulated data I have been enabled to condense the following table of conclusions, averaging the number of days in each month for each series of observations :

FROM MAY UNTIL DECEMBER.

	N., and N. E. Winds.	Rains.	Calm.	Electricity.
1818 Healthy.........	20	25	33	29
1819 Sickly..........	25	37	34	17
1820 Very Sickly.....	24	40	20	5

This is an interesting epitome of the weather, and exhibits, in a strong light, the great connection which subsists between these natural phenomena and the degree of disease. The difference in the winds is not so remarkable as in the rain and electrical fluid. But there is still a difference of some magnitude; and when the circumstances of the atmosphere are included in the calculation, it becomes very important. The quantity of moisture being very minute in 1818, the winds could not act a prominent part; but, when that quantity was advanced so considerably as in 1819 and 1820, their influence rose immediately into the most serious consequences. They served to embank it on our lands, and particularly at frontier situations. Hence it happened, that such a peculiar and great accumulation took place in Washington Ward, and other places to the east of the town. Mr. Grey, whose residence was in that ward, informed me, that after having removed into the Baptist Church square, he felt as if he had been transported to New York. The deposit of dew in the evening was so profuse, as to drench the cover of my gig in a short time, while engaged in visits of business there. None but medical men, who make the daily circuit of the city, appear to be thoroughly aware of this fact, and the consequent various degrees of insalubrity, which appertain to the different departments. This moisture, which steeped the air of Washington Ward in such excess, was also, in more or less extraordinary profusion everywhere. The houses became damp and articles which were even locked in drawers or trunks grew mouldy and rotted. It penetrated into every crevice and private recess, however remote or protected. This untoward circumstance of extreme general moisture was still more aggravated by the shrubbery of unpruned trees, which are thickly studded along the streets and squares. The shade which they afforded shielded the heavy dews that fell in the night from the dispersing power of the sun during the day; and, in this way, sustained a constant soaked condition of everything that was not impenetrable to water. It will be perceived, by a reference to Raffle's History of the East Indies, that the same observation is

made in regard to large and umbrageous trees in Batavia. They
are enumerated among the causes of sickness in that place, by the
protection which they give to the foul vapors which are vomited
up by the neighboring marshes and canals and deposited in the
city. Some defence against the influence of the sun is necessary,
in a situation where it beams so intensely as it does in Savannah,
during the summer. It would, therefore, be proper to preserve
the trees, and to lop off all their great branches, so as to admit a
free circulation of air. In very dry seasons, as that of 1818, their
utmost luxuriance would not only be delightful, but innocent. In
rainy and wet seasons, however, which are very frequent in a latitude bordering on the torrid zone, it would, on the contrary, be
obviously productive of mischief, by fostering the seeds of disease, in accordance with the fact of the present year. Such an
abundant accumulation of the fogs, and *miasmata* of the swamps,
within the city, from the local causes of situation, the trees and
the winds, was of itself an evil of no common extent. It was a
concentration of the general epidemic composition of the atmosphere, and sufficiently calculated to produce a more violent and
unmanageable grade of fever, than that which commonly prevailed. But, besides these superficial causes of drawing together
and heaping up the product of the marshes, there seems to be an
attractive power, in lofty places, over clouds and vapors, which
was calculated to augment it. Baron Humboldt has made this
remark in regard to the Peak Teneriffe, without accounting for
the phenomenon. There can be no doubt, however, of such a
power and of its extensive influence in adding to the insalubrity
of all such places as fall into the vicinity of low grounds. It renders them even more intolerable than the low grounds themselves.
The fact is well and generally known, and this cause very well
explains it. The fever of Savannah has always exhibited more
severity and malignant excitement than that which prevails in the
country which embraces it ; and so, also, does the fever in all
situations under similar circumstances.

Thus inundated with moisture, it is not a matter of surprise
that wooden houses should go into a state of decay ; that even the
furniture which they contain and the filth or offal that was collected within or about them should enter upon the process of putrefaction. If vegetable decomposition be a source of *miasmata*,
then there cannot be a more prolific cause of disease than the
great number of old buildings of this kind. Every man who ob-

serves must have perceived that there is always over their surface a thick stratum, which is undergoing, or has already undergone, a dissolution. In a wet and warm season this operation is rapid and conspicuous, and even comes under the cognizance of the smell. I think it exercises a considerable agency in the unwholesome effect of our summers. Dr. Rush has said that, in the yellow fever of 1793, in Philadelphia, the greatest mortality took place in wooden houses ; and it is certainly very remarkable that the newly erected part of this city was almost exempt from the disease of the last season. Might it not be owing, in some measure, to the more general use of brick in the construction of their houses, that the mortality of fever has been diminished in our Northern cities ? And might it not have been a good deal in consequence of the greater abandonment of wooden materials, that London has been exempt from the plague since the fire of 1656 ? This is a subject well worthy of the serious attention of the corporation.

In addition to this great mass of vegetable decadence in our very bosoms, there was an unusual accumulation of various pernicious matters, still more formidable, perhaps. These were extremely and inordinately abundant, from the mixed, imprudent and destitute population which have flocked among us from every part of the civilized world. Whatever could have contributed, from ignorance of the climate, from poverty or neglect, to increase and to add to them was done. Since the conclusion of the late war the periodical epidemic, which has uniformly prevailed more or less in Savannah, seems to have been augmented in the violence of its character. The poverty and distress which have arisen from the superfluous population of Europe, and particularly of the English dominions, compelled great numbers, after that period, to emigrate to the United States. That poverty, distress and emigration were still further advanced when the general peace took place. The first enterprises of these unfortunate foreigners were made at the North; but finding that the rewards for labor were small, and that the inducements presented in the Southern cities were stronger, they launched a second time on the sea of adventure, and came in crowds to Southern ports. In consequence of this great accession of strangers, without acquaintance with that kind of economy of living which is adapted to an unwholesome latitude; without money and without conveniences; destitute of proper clothing, food or bedding; gathering in throngs of fifteen or twenty in narrow wooden buildings with small yards; without caution, and without that considerate industry which leads to the prompt removal of the daily products of filth which drop from their immediate persons, a source of pestilence has been established in addition to that which has ordinarily existed. If, in the most salubrious climes, a destructive disease has been engendered by the concomitant circumstances of poverty, it cannot be a cause for wonder that those circumstances, under the operation of heat and moisture, should give birth to deadly and uncontrollable fevers. I have already said that 1817 was the most severe that had ever been experienced in Savannah, and was attended with a greater number of cases of black vomit. In the course of the summer of 1819 fifty Irish emigrants arrived in the same ship, not one of whom survived till the frost. The year of 1820 has been tinged with a deeper and more melancholy gloom. Our older inhabitants look back and tell us that these are not former times. Then the fever was remittent, and analogous to that which now prevails outside the bounds of the city. Then there were deaths, but recoveries were not uncommon, and cases of the continued forms of fever were extremely rare. But I say that then the population had not advanced in growth more rapidly than the city; the number of the destitute and laboring had not been pressed into that narrow compass which was erected originally for the convenience of a few. Then the common labor was altogether done by the negroes, and white laborers collected in crowds in small houses were unknown. Then the population was thin, resident and composed of natives, or permanent inhabitants, whose constitutions, manners and customs, modes of living and comforts, fitted them, in the best way, to perceive the means of health and to preserve it. All this has been changed, and everything has been introduced which can render a spot unfriendly to the human constitution. All cities are esteemed to be more or less unsalutary. The open and unobstructed air of the country; its freedom from the noisome collections which are incident to people congregated into crowds, is much more congenial to the soundness and vigor of the frame. This observation is an old one, and is applicable to those which bring their population into the smallest compass, or to those parts of cities in which great numbers are forced by poverty into the narrowest space. The less the character of the country is preserved, and the more nearly men and residences are made to approach one another, the greater is the suffering of the system and the more is curtailed from the term of life. All sorts of putrid matter become accumulated and incorporated with the very soil, and, instead of pure sand or earth, which may have originally constituted the surface of the ground, species of compost is formed and an active fermentation is taken on whenever there is heat and moisture enough to produce it. This state of soil is insensibly brought, in the progress of time, to contain the utmost abundance of putrefiable materials, and, of course, to engender great quantities of poisonous gas, which compact buildings and walls do not permit to be dissipated. Hence it is that, all other circumstances being equal, large cities are more hostile to health than villages, and are found to have advanced, where their progress can be traced, from one step of insalubrity to another until, from having been visited by moderate diseases, they become the seat of typhus fever, yellow fever and the plague, acording to the climate in which they happen to be located. This progress has been very remarkable in many of the cities of the United States, and very well accounts for the grades of fever to which they have been such frequent victims in latter years. Such an event was to be expected from their growth in a climate so subject to heavy rains and epidemic constitutions of the air. It ought not, then, to be matter of wonder that in Savannah there should be an augmentation of violence in the diseases which visit it in proportion of its population since it has only recently arrived to that point which was attained some years before by New York, Philadelphia and Charleston. It evinces aggrandizement and increased importance, but at the same time the counterbalancing evils of greater force in disease and more inhospitality of climate. There have been, consequently, scenes of misery, wretchedness, filth and want, from these circumstances, in 1819-20, which are very extraordinary notwithstanding, for a country so rich in the facilities of subsistence, and which have a parallel only in the plagues of the world.

There is another cause of the disease which belongs to the city, and is entirely recent also. The fire of January exposed to the operation of the sun and rain a great number of vaults and cellars, which co-operated with other local impurities and added to the insalubrity of the climate. But they have not constituted the basis of the extreme severity of the epidemic as some had very erroneously imagined, since the first cases of black vomit and continued fever occurred at a considerable distance from the

situation of the fire, and, in some instances, among persons whose
occupation and residence were seated in such manner as to bring
them very seldom within its neighborhood. The principal mortality was for some time confined to the eastern wards, so that the
Mayor was, at one moment, induced to speak of the propriety of
drawing a cordon around that portion of the city and obstructing
its intercourse with the rest. If the origin of the disease had been
founded, even chiefly, in the consequences of the fire, it must certainly have broken out first and most destructively in the lots
which immediately surround them. I am disposed, however, to
attribute still, some share of the morbid effect to the vaults and
cellars and the *miasmata* which must have arisen from them,
remarking at the same time that they did not act, and could not
have acted, from their situation and condition, that very powerful
part which some have ascribed to them.

The epidemic was not the result of one source merely, but
many. It arose from *all the local and general sources which have
been enumerated.* And when all these have been brought into
view—when they are combined and made to operate together in
one point, the effects of that operation cannot be otherwise than
uncommonly efficient when all the local sources of *miasmata,*
which are somewhat new and unexperienced in this city, are
joined to the usual and prolific sources afforded by the marshes
which surround us—when they are joined to the general epidemic
agent, which was pervading the whole country for many leagues,
and which was poured in by the winds in such abundance—when
it is considered that the general cause was itself severe and fatal,
it becomes, at least probable that a compound so deleterious was
fully competent to produce a malady greater than any other of
former years.

It becomes an adequate cause for the superior virulence of the
epidemic within the borders of the town, and satisfactorily accounts
for it. Whether it be or not an adequate cause, it is yet unques-
tionable that the cause of the general disease was founded in the
local atmosphere. The general affection was drawn from general
circumstances, and the local affection from a composition of general and local circumstances. Such appears to be the most probable origin of the epidemic of 1820. But since it has been attributed by one class of persons to the imperfect state of the dry
culture, by another to importation from the West Indies, and
by another to importation from the coast of Africa, it becomes

proper, not because these sources are reasonable or much accredited by this community, to meet and refute such groundless imaginations. With regard to the dry culture, it is to be observed that this system has been only partially carried into operation, and at best comprehends but a small portion of the swamp lands which more or less extend their influence to the city. I have myself always viewed the original purchase as the commencement of an extensive plan of redeeming from pollution all these lands in the course of time, and as contributing, as far as it went, to reduce the unwholesomeness of the climate. I have never been so sanguine, nor have any of the intelligent supporters of the system of dry culture been so visionary as to anticipate more than an incomplete benefit from its present extent. A benefit, even such as it was calculated to procure, was, however, to be considered worth possessing, and was still more esteemed because it was contemplated as laying the ground-work of further benefits. It is impossible for any man who has any acquaintance with the former and present condition of these lands to feel other than the utmost confidence in the principles of that system. If dry soils have more salubrity than mud flats and quagmires, then it cannot be doubted, on an inspection of the grounds which have been properly managed, that, so far from having become more fitted to create disease, they have very much approximated to the innocuous circumstances of high situations ; and were it practicable to insulate them or defend them against the influences of the rice fields in the vicinity, I verily believe that as much health might be enjoyed upon them as upon any of the cotton or corn plantations in the lower country. What is there to prevent it? They can be as easily drained and can be preserved as free from collections of water. In relation to their present state the board has been already instructed by their inspector, whose investigations have been more minute than my own. But so far as I have been able to inform myself, it appears that, in some places, the ditches and canals have not been assiduously cleared of obstacles to the afflux of water, yet those ditches and canals are not in a more objectionable state than the margin of the river, or those ditches and canals on cultivated rice lands, where instances of black vomit are unknown. Such lands are very abundant along the coast of Georgia and South Carolina, and yet I believe an instance of yellow fever, or what is vulgarly called so, has seldom or never occurred. I was born on a rice plantation, and have spent a greater part of my early life in the midst of the cultivation of that plant without having on my mind the remembrance of a single instance. It seems to be totally the disease of uncleansed places or cities, conditioned very similarly to the manner in which I have represented this to have been, or operated upon by the same abstract cause. Generally the proprietors have not been negligent of the terms of their contracts, and these grounds, in many places, have been beautifully managed in the culture of corn, cotton, and the grasses. If it were practicable to rescue all the adjacent swamps in the same degree, and to place them in a dry condition also, the great advantages that would result can hardly be a matter of doubt.

It could not justly have been expected that a surface, chiefly tilled and carpeted in the vegetable growth of elevated places, occasionally intersected with a canal containing some stagnant water, but generally destitute of moisture as any other rich composition of earth, one hundred and fifty miles in the up-country, should form an apparatus more fruitful in the furnishing of impure gases, than that same surface in its rice field state of bog and ravine. In point of fact, it appears that the negroes inhabiting those grounds have been so far from suffering more from disease than formerly that they have kept better health, and acknowledge that they have enjoyed greater freedom from fever since the cultivation of cotton has been introduced. The overseers employed to superintend them have sustained attacks of the ordinary remittent, which, in some instances, have been slight and short of duration. But there has not been an original case of that destructive grade of fever which prevailed in the city, and which has been attributed to the dry culture. Mr. Howard informs me that there were five white men in his employ on the plantation of Mr. Wm. Mein, not more than a few hundred yards distant across the river during the fall months, who preserved their health, notwithstanding that they constantly breathed this air of the dry culture in all its simplicity and strength. It is singular, likewise, that the sailors along the borders of this plantation, in the occupancy of the ships in the river, have been more exempt from fever this year than usual. Mr. Bolton informs me that it was even a subject of remark at New York, in the exercise of quarantine, in regard to vessels arriving at that place from this port. And Captain Jayne, of the Oglethorpe, who reached Savannah in the month of October, states that the part of his crew which be confined to the ship escaped the epidemic entirely, while all perished that were permitted to come into town. The fact is irresistible and speaks a volume in defense of that system which it has attempted to impugn, and which is not dependent for its soundness on any experiment now to be made. The dry culture is the only great radical mode which can be adopted with any prospect of rendering this city a tolerable residence during the summer and autumn. Under its ancient circumstances, in conjunction with its present accession of population, its calamities will not only continue, but must be augmented.

The mortality of the past season is unexampled indeed ; but when it is considered that much arose from the mere increase of numbers and the foreign materials of which it was composed it does not at last surpass that of former years so much as is imagined. Since the year 1807 there have been nearly four thousand deaths, so that, calculating the average census at that number for fourteen years, to the close of 1820, it appears that the whole population is exterminated at every revolution of fourteen years, and that human life, according to a general computation, is contracted to that term. It is rare, in any part of the State, that *death* draws so tragic a picture of his ravages in such strong colors. I have inquired particularly into the subject of importation, and *there does not appear to be any better reason for ascribing the disease to this source than to the dry culture.* Importation, as it is generally understood, means contagion ; and it would be sufficient to prove that the disease was not contagious to establish the fact of not having been imported. But it is more satisfactory to establish the fact by positive testimony obtained concerning the condition of the vessels to which it has been or might be attributed. *It was said, by some individuals, to have been brought from the coast of Africa,* in a brig called the Raminez, which had on board a cargo of new negroes. Unfortunately, however, for this hypothesis, the Raminez did not only arrive with a healthy crew and an entire freedom from any malignant disease, but she arrived some time after the fever had grown into considerable extent and severity. I have already stated that some rapid and insidious cases occurred in June, and that fourteen deaths took place in that month. I have stated that Mr. Patrick Stanton even died of black vomit on the 16th of July. The Raminez came into port on the 22d. It was not and could not be an African disease. From the 23d of May to the 20th of July there came five vessels from the West Indies and one from New Orleans. I have not been able to learn of any others. On the 23d of May brig Rover, Captain James, from Havana ; on the 2d of June schooner Phantom, Havana ; on the 13th of June schooner Charles, New Orleans ; on the 24th of June sloop Darien, St. Domingo ; on the 27th of June schooner Isabella, Matanzas ; and on July 20th a vessel to Green & Lippit, from St. Domingo.

It appears from inquiry as to the state of these vessels, that the crews were healthy and there was nothing in relation to them which could authorize a belief of their having either severe disease on board, or the power of propagating any disease whatever. Captain Newell, of the navy, who was in the employ of the government during the last winter and spring, on the island of Ossabaw, communicated to me a very singular fact which is worthy of notice. He states that he left the island on the 28th of May, a short time previous to which several of his crew were seized with a violent fever, one of whom died ; another died on the passage to New York, and a third after their arrival at that port ; that the first in the course of his illness exhibited no increase or decrease of fever, and the last was pronounced by Dr. Baylie, the Health Officer, to be affected with as strong appearances of malignancy as any case he had ever seen. These men were cut off from all communication with the main, or with shipping of any kind, until their embarkation, so that the disease was of local origin, and that local origin was a large pond in a stagnant condition. I mention the fact in this place in order to show the contemporaneous commencement of this fever with that of the city ; their proximate characters in point of violence, and their probable alliance through the general morbific constitution of the atmosphere. It tends to prove the locality of the disease. But this is further confirmed by its non-contagiousness. The Board of Health in August, by a communication to the Mayor, unanimously attested to this characteristic of the prevailing fever. I have not heard of one instance of its being communicated from one person to another. Although many have gone into the country and died of black vomit, there has been no further propagation of any similar affection. There have, too, been some very remarkable instances to test the principles which are taught in the school of New York. It is contended there, that although what is commonly denominated yellow fever, may not be readily communicated in a pure atmosphere, it is so, in an impure one, or one

contaminated by marshes. A country like this is supremely calculated to try such a doctrine, because it abounds every year with
an atmosphere contaminated precisely in this way. Accordingly
it has happened, in the late season, that several persons, after
having been attacked with the disease of the city, went into the
neighboring rice plantations and died with the usual symptoms.
Yet there was no evidence of contagion. A negro went from
town to the place of Gen. Rutledge, where rice is cultivated, and
where it is all swamp, and died with black vomit; yet there was
no contagion. Another went to the plantation of Mr. Ebenezer
Jackson and died in the same manner, but no one took the disease. It was not contagious then either on this ground or in
conformity with the common principles.

The only fair way of establishing the New York doctrine is to
prove the importation of the disease, and then to prove its propagation from the vessel in which it may have been imported. To
do this an obstacle at once presents itself, which appears to me
to be almost insuperable. For it is confessed that no propagation takes place without a certain contamination of the atmosphere,
so that it becomes, at least, a matter of doubt whether it be
owing to that contamination or to the matter of contagion. In
order to fix it on the matter of contagion, it then becomes
requisite to prove that such particular contamination is unable
alone to produce the disease, and this can be done only by demon-
strating its positive presence, sometimes without being attended
with that effect. This is impossible in the present state of medicine, because it is not quite ascertained what the circumstances
are precisely which produce it. We say it arises from *miasmata*,
by which we mean a cause of fever consequent on the decomposition of vegetable or animal matter by the influence of heat and
moisture. What the particular nature of the decomposition consists in; what constitutes its whole character; what are the pre-
cise materials of which it is predicated; what are the identical
qualities of the agent which results from it; what quantity or diversity of this agent may be necessary, are not ascertained. And,
until they are ascertained, it is impossible to determine at all
times whether the immediate local cause be certainly present or
not. But further, if it can be shown, in a single instance, that
the disease has been produced without the aid of an imported
virus, it then becomes totally impossible by any mode of reasoning with which I am acquainted to attach it to this source. For

10

if local causes produce it once, why should they not always produce it? The doctrine teaches that they must always be present,
and that the virus is inefficient without them. They are said to
go hand in hand, and step for step. When the local causes are
limited, there also is the boundary of the virus influence; so that
if the effect can be attributed, for once only, to their sole agency,
it becomes no longer expedient to look to contagion for additional
agency. One cause which is equal to an effect, is always sufficient
to account for it; if another be associated with it, which neither
increases nor decreases the effect, I do not know by what rule of
logic it can be supposed to be instrumental in the production of
it. It may have an influence, but I do not know how it is to be
proved to exercise it. Since it is admitted to be impotent in
itself ; since it is said to be more virulent as the local causes are
more abundant, what means are there left to ascertain its coöperation, or to insulate it in such a manner as to consider the part
which it acts? Can it be done by tracing the gradual progress of
the disease from the imported camps? This will not avail because
the local cause may be more dense and active in that situation
also, as appeared in the case of the putrid coffee in Philadelphia
and in the commencement of the violent cases of the epidemic
this year in the eastern wards. Even in our ordinary fall fevers
their violence is not equally developed in all parts of the city at
the same moment. It begins at some point, in subjection to the
course of the winds, and that point has generally been those eastern wards, precisely after the manner of the last season. The
New York contagionist is thus reduced to the shift of demon-
strating that the common impurities of the atmosphere are not
in greater abundance at the commencing point and its nieghbor-
hood than they are elsewhere. If he can do this, it is impossible
for him to show the propagation of the imported virus. This has
never been done in any instance of which I have any knowledge.
The origin of the violent cases of disease has been commonly at
wharves and docks, which are the great repository of all those
local causes which are said to be necessary to the propagation.
To return, then, to our domestic sources, they did undoubtedly
produce the few cases of black vomit of 1817. The epidemic of
that year had been remittent from June till November, with the
exception of a single instance, where it was continued and attended with black ejections from the stomach. About the beginning of November, some of our Northern inhabitants returning

from their summer tour in the expectation that on their arrival the epidemic would have come to its conclusion, unfortunately incurred the disease, which was still prevailing. In these instances, where the system was strong and inflammable, the absence of paroxysms and the symptom of black vomiting made their appearance. I saw five cases of this description. They were unquestionably the common remittent, urged into the continual form by the operation of the usual cause upon a higher state of the excitability. At this period there was little commerce, and few vessels had arrived in port. In one of the cases the patient landed with indisposition from sea-sickness, which gradually, although confined to the house, assumed this formidable shape of fever, and eventuated, after a fortnight's duration, in black vomit and death. There are instances of the local foundation of the disease which I have witnessed personally and am fully satisfied with. *They are sufficient to establish the competency of a domestic cause* without the coöperation of a foreign one, and demonstrated the supererogation of imputing to an imported source any share in a result which the local one is adequate to effect. I have dwelt thus on the hermaphrodite theory of contagion, because it rests on a possibility of truth in consequence of its insuperable alliance with the theory of domestic origin and of the good company which it is constantly made to keep.

To sum up then, all which I have suggested, it appears that the causes of the fever of 1820 have been : First, A general epidemic condition of the atmosphere, of extraordinary virulence, either proved to exist or produced by an uncommon deficiency of the electrical fluid. Second, The early establishment of that condition of the atmosphere by the reduction of the winter of 1819–20 to the temperature of spring, and the reduction of the spring to the heat of summer, thus bringing upon us in the spring the usual evils of summer; in the summer, a combination of those evils with the usual evils of that season, and in the fall an aggregation of the evils which are usually incident to it with this extraordinary combination of those which preceded them. Third, The prevalence of eastern winds, which had been predominant and uncommonly injurious in consequence of the general abundance of moisture and *miasmata.* Fourth, The growth of the city within a few years and the rapid increase of its population, thus producing a source of *putridity* and incorporating it with the soil. Fifth, The unnecessary luxuriance of the trees by the shade and

protection which they afford to dews, and fogs, and moisture of
the atmosphere after rain. Sixth, The great number of small
wooden houses, unpainted, and in a complete state of putrescence.
Seventh, Uncovered vaults and cellars, the consequence of the
fire. Eighth, The remarkable number of foreigners and persons
unaccustomed to the climate, producing not an aggravation of the
cause of the disease, but of its general grade and character. Ninth,
The high position of the city on the borders of extensive marsh
grounds, thus attracting and concentrating upon itself their products of unwholesome vapor and *miasmata*. All these causes
together gives a compound origin to the disease, which is *internal
and external*. The origin is a tangible one, and rests on contin-
gencies which the *strength and ingenuity of man may counteract.
But the task is gigantic* and can only be accomplished by public
wealth, and public spirit, and public firmness. Nothing can be
too expensive—no exertions can be better appropriated than to
give salubrity to a city which it is determined to sustain. Caprice,
however heated and liberal and well disposed, will always lead to
disappointments, if not to disgrace. It is beyond the power of
the corporation to do everything which ought to be done in a
work of such magnitude as the total constitution of a healthy
climate in a place like this which labors under so many disad-
vantages. But what can be done should be done, and done completely, without any tergiversation. Temporary expedients are a
permanent waste, and in public as well as private transactions
lead only to discomfiture and defeat. I have pointed out the
causes of the late epidemic which to me are obvious and plain,
and in which I unqualifiedly believe. It remains for Council to
select among them such as it is practicable to remove, and then
they ought to remove them totally, without being influenced in
their pursuit by individual or popular notions.

Having assigned the probable causes of the epidemic I now
enter upon a history of its character and the modes of treament
which were employed. I have already stated that it was *intermittent, remittent* and *continued.* The intermittent form prevailed
throughout the season, but occurred most frequently in the first
and latter part of it, because the *miasm* which produced the disease was least abundant at those periods, and gave birth to a mild
effect in proportion to its quantity. The remittent form also prevailed throughout the season, but was most rife in the middle of
it, because the *miasm*, at that point, had become too concentrated

for an intermittent effect and not rife enough to produce a higher type of fever. The continued form began early, but was not perfectly established till the last of July. It went on then increasing and extending, and was more and more comprehensive until the commencement of cool weather, because the morific cause was more and more augmented and condensed by the incessant operation of the circumstances in which it was founded, such was the order observed by these forms in their relation to one another.

* * * * * * * * *

[OF STOMACH AND BLACK VOMIT—PAGE 49.]

In one instance only an ulceration took place. There was no instance of gangrene. The inflammation ran highest in the robust and strong, as in healthy foreigners. In these the vessels were so rapidly distended as to burst, and then the stomach was found to be full of blood. * * * * * * *

[OF BLACK VOMIT—PAGE 50.]

* * * Dr. Nicholas Chevin, an ingenious and intelligent French physician, who visited this city during the prevalence of the epidemic for the purpose of adding still more to a long experience in yellow fever, firmly entertained this opinion: "That the black vomit was blood." I confess, however, that his proofs did not appear to me to be perfectly satisfactorily.

* * * In the treatment of the continued form of the epidemic of 1820, specifics as well as principles, were unsuccessful in the majority of cases.

WILLIAM R. WARING.

NOTE.—Sometimes the terms "disease" and "fever," as used in this report, are used to apply, not merely to the whole epidemic, but particularly to the *continued* form of it ; as if such form were considered a distinct disease or fever. This note is inserted, therefore, to leave no room for doubt or misconception.

---

*The remainder of the pamphlet, about thirty-five pages, describes the symptoms and various modes of treatment adopted in that day, with the author's criticisms of each. This is omitted as not pertinent to the purposes contemplated in this publication, which is a contribution to the general knowledge of the causes and prevention of yellow fever epidemics.

Savannah, Ga., January 23, 1821.

Dear Sir : * * * Your views on the subject of fevers, in point of character and origin, correspond with the observations I have made in a *thirty* years' practice in this climate. * * * *

Your report, I am persuaded, will have a salutary influence in correcting many false notions indulged by our people, and much false theory among professional men on the subject of yellow fever.

I am, dear sir, respectfully your obedient servant,

LEMUEL KOLLOCK, M. D.

Dr. Waring.

PUBLISHED BY ORDER OF COUNCIL.

SAVANNAH:

PRINTED BY HENRY T. RUSSELL.

1821.

REPORT OF

JOHN E. WARD,

MAYOR OF THE CITY OF SAVANNAH,

—FOR THE—

YEAR ENDING DECEMBER 30, 1854.

REPORT.

Fellow–Citizens :

*　　*　　*　　*　　*　　*　　*　　*　　*

YELLOW FEVER.

After an exemption from epidemics, unknown to any other city, and the enjoyment of unexampled health for almost half a century, in the month of August last our citizens were startled with the announcement that the yellow fever had made its appearance as an epidemic. The first case of yellow fever occurred on the 5th of August in a house situated at the southwest corner of Lincoln and Broughton streets. Regarded merely as a sporadic case it was not reported as yellow fever. Between that date and the middle of the month a few more cases occurred, but nothing to excite any alarm or create any apprehension of an epidemic among us. About that date it manifested itself in an epidemic form, and swept with a fearful desolation over our city. During that month the total number of deaths was 257, 235 of whom were whites and 22 blacks. Of the whites 156 were foreigners, 42 born in America, 29 in Savannah and 7 unknown—13 under 1 year of age, 12 from 1 to 5 years of age, 9 from 5 to 15 years of age, 120 from 15 to 30 years of age, 6 from 30 to 50 years of age, 12 over 50 years of age and 8 unknown. Of the blacks 1 by yellow fever and 21 by other diseases—7 under 1 year of age, 2 from 1 to 5, 1 from 5 to 15, 2 from 15 to 30, 5 from 30 to 50, and 5 over 50 years of age. In the month of September there died 646, 591 of whom were whites and 55 were blacks. Of the whites 367 were foreigners, 119 were born in America, 94 in Savannah and 11 unknown—39 were under 1 year of age, 45 from 1 to 5 years of age, 39 from 5 to 15 years of age, 287 from 15 to 30 years of age, 135 from 30 to 50 years of age, 43 over 50 and 5 unknown; 381 by yellow fever and 210 by other diseases. Of the blacks 9 died from yellow fever and 46 from other diseases—12 under 1 year of age, 7 from 1 to 5 years of age, 7 from 5 to 15 years of age, 14

ERRATA.—On page 151 add the following after paragraph three:

Various causes have been assigned by different individuals for the existence of the disease during the past season. I have felt it my duty carefully to investigate them. The first cause assigned was the introduction of the fever into our city from the brig Charlotte Hague, which put into Cockspur Roads about the 29th of June. She was a Danish brig, bound from Havana to Copenhagen. She was visited on the 30th by the Port Physician, Dr. Mackall, who reported two slight cases of sickness on board. It having been asserted that some of the men brought from her to the city died of the yellow fever, I have used every effort to obtain evidence to prove the fact, but I have found no proof to satisfy my own mind that there was any case of yellow fever brought up to the city from that vessel, and I herewith submit for your consideration a letter from Dr. Mackall and one from Dr. Wragg, the attending physicians of the Savannah Infirmary, to which all the men were carried. Dr. Chartres being absent, I have been unable to obtain an answer from him.

from 15 to 30 years of age, 9 from 30 to 50 years of age and 7 over 50 years of age. In the month of October there died 137, of whom 108 were whites and 29 blacks. Of the whites 65 were foreigners, 24 were born in America, 17 in Savannah and 2 unknown—10 were under 1 year of age, 8 from 1 to 5 years of age, 4 from 5 to 15 years of age, 49 from 15 to 30 years of age, 29 from 30 to 50 years of age, 7 over 50 years of age and 1 unknown; 67 died of yellow fever and 41 by other diseases. Of blacks 4 died by yellow fever and 25 by other diseases—7 under 1 year of age, 7 from 1 to 5 years of age, 5 from 5 to 15 years of age, 5 from 15 to 30 years of age, 2 from 30 to 50 years of age and 3 over 50.

Total number of deaths for the months of August, September and October, 1,040—934 of whom were whites and 106 blacks.

The disease was exhibited in its greatest violence from the 20th of August to the 20th of September, having commenced as an epidemic in the northeastern part of the city; it advanced directly to the southwest, spreading north and south until its influence was felt in every part of the city.

The next cause assigned was the removal of the mud in the dredging of the Savannah river, and depositing the same on the eastern wharves. I respectfully submit to you two letters, one from Lieut. John Newton, the engineer in charge of the work, and the other from Francis Cercopely, the superintendent of the same, which, clearly establishing the fact that the mud was not placed on the eastern wharves, or in any manner exposed to the atmosphere, destroys the theory of those who had traced the existence of the fever to that cause.

Another cause assigned, has been the condition of the rice lands in the immediate vicinity of our city. These lands at the time of the commencement of the fever, and during its greatest violence, were in good order and never healthier. Vegetation was not decaying, and there was no adequate cause for the disease to be found in them. After the banks had been broken by the storm—with vegetation decaying, the lands overflowed, and everything tending to increase the disease, if it had originated from that source—it commenced to decrease, and before the middle of October, without frost or any other agency to which we had looked for its removal, it ceased to exist among us as an epidemic. I can only regard it as an atmospheric storm passing over the whole Southern country and taking our city in its course. It doubtless followed certain definite laws, but so did the tempest that swept over our city on the eighth day of September. They both expressed the will of the great lawgiver—of Him, at whose command the storm or the pestilence arises and pursues its course, baffling the power or the skill of man, until it has accomplished His wise purposes. It may be that He will again command the pestilence to desolate our city, and to hush the accents of affection in our homes, but there is no more reason to apprehend its return from any local cause existing around us than to dread another hurricane on the eighth of September next. We must still witness, everywhere around us, the memorials of our losses, but with a firm reliance on His mercy, who has so long blessed us with uninterrupted prosperity, and an abiding confidence in His power who has stood between the living and the dead, let us be true to ourselves and the prosperity of our city, and the happiness of her people will soon be restored.

Attacked by the epidemic on the 7th of September, I was for some time unable to discharge the duties of my office. During that period, its arduous labors were cheerfully and zealously performed by Dr. James P. Screven, surrounded by death and despondency, in the midst of dangers which might well have appalled " the bravest of the brave."

Not a candidate for re-election, I avail myself of this opportunity to express my most grateful acknowledgments to the people of Savannah for that confidence which has repeatedly elevated me to offices of honor and trust, for that charity with which my acts have been judged, and for that personal kindness which I have ever received from them.

Very respectfully and truly,
Your obedient servant,
JOHN E. WARD, Mayor.

CORRESPONDENCE.

SAVANNAH, November 15th, 1854.

To Hon. John E. Ward, Mayor:

DEAR SIR: In compliance with your request for a written statement of all the facts coming under my personal knowledge connected with the introduction of certain cases of fever into this city from a foreign vessel in July last, I submit as follows:

On the 30th of June last I was called to visit a vessel at Tybee reported as having sickness on board. I answered the call. Before reaching the vessel (which proved to be the Danish brig Charlotte Hague, Captain Buck), I found the Captain and one seaman requiring medical services. The Captain, however, had no fever, and was evidently recovering from a mild attack of remittent fever, at least such was my opinion. The seaman I found sick with bilious remittent fever. I prescribed for my patients and returned to the city, reporting them to you in accordance with the above facts.

On the 2d of July I was again called on to visit the Charlotte Hague. The Captain met me on the deck—the seaman was also on deck, and much better.

Another seaman was called to me for examination (a similar case). I prescribed for them. Seeing that those patients would probably require more medical attention (which at Tybee was onerously expensive to the owners), I gave the Captain permission to bring his sick to the city; this he did the following day (July 3d), and entered with them the Savannah Infirmary, where I visited them in connection with my partner, Dr. J. A. Wragg, until the fifth, on which day, being compelled to leave for the North on account of my own health, Dr. W. M. Chartres took my place and continued to visit them with Dr. Wragg.

I have only to add that the symptoms these cases exhibited, up to the time I left them, differed in no respect from a number of other cases of remittent fever under treatment in the Infirmary at the same time, and showed no symptoms of yellow fever.

Very respectfully, your obedient servant,

R. A. MACKALL.

SAVANNAH, November 4th, 1854.

To Hon. John E. Ward, Mayor:

DEAR SIR: At your request, I hereby furnish you with the facts in relation to the Danish brig, Charlotte Hague, said to have brought the yellow fever to Savannah. These facts have been taken from the books of the Savannah Infirmary, where the Captain and two of the seamen belonging to the brig were under medical treatment for a few days.

The Danish brig, Charlotte Hague, put into Cockspur Roads about the 29th or 30th of June, 1854, and was visited on the 30th by the Port Physician. On the 3d of July two of the seamen were brought to the Savannah Infirmary, where they remained until the 7th, and were discharged cured. They had not the least symptom of yellow fever. The Captain was also admitted to the Infirmary, and discharged cured. He had not the least symptom of yellow fever. On the 7th they returned to the brig and she went to sea. The brig never came up to the city, and the men brought up nothing but the clothing they had on.

Very respectfully and truly, your obedient servant,

JOHN ASHBY WRAGG.

CHARLESTON, S. C., 9th November, 1854.

Hon. John E. Ward, Mayor:

DEAR SIR: In reply to your letter just received I have to state (without opportunity of looking over returns) that about 90,000 cubic yards have been taken out of the channels over the garden banks and the wrecks.

All the material from the bottom was deposited until July on the South Carolina shore, near Hog Island, distant about four or five miles from Savannah. After that time they were dropped in a pocket channel existing on the wreck bank, and have never, I believe, been exposed for a moment to the air. I regard the assumption of sickness emanating from such cause as the most unwarranted possible. Capt. Cercopely can give you the most minute information on this subject if you require more.

I am, sir, yours, most respectfully,

JOHN NEWTON, First Lieutenant Engineers.

Hon. John E. Ward, Mayor:

DEAR SIR: As you wish information from me in regard to dredging done in Savannah river, I will comply with your request as near as possible. I have been inspector of the dredging under Capt. Gilmer and Lieut. Newton's instruction, and I must, in the first place, say that the material taken from the bottom of the river has never been deposited on any of the wharves. All the material has been deposited at different places, generally in Back river and points near the Carolina shore, as directed by the officers, about four or five miles from the city, and has never for a moment been exposed to the air, excepting at the time the scows were loading, and when loaded they were immediately towed to the places above mentioned, and the mud dropped in six or seven feet water.

You wish to understand how the scows are constructed. They are so constructed that by the means of a trap door the material drops through the bottom. As regards the assumption of sickness originating from such a cause it is, in my opinion, very absurd and inconsistent. Why did we not have yellow fever last year when dredging was in operation from about June to November?

I am, yours, etc.,

FRANCIS J. CERCOPELY.

REPORT

—OF—

EDWARD C. ANDERSON

MAYOR OF THE CITY OF SAVANNAH,

—FOR THE—

YEAR ENDING DECEMBER 31, 1876.

REPORT.

After a period of eighteen years of unexampled health, and an exemption from epidemic of any kind, our community was startled in the month of August last by the announcement that the yellow fever had broken out in the eastern part of the city.

The first recorded death from yellow fever occurred on August the 21st, on Wright street, a short *cul de sac*, about fifty yards long, the culmination of Bryan street, in the northeastern part of the city, viz.: James P. Cleary. The *second* occurred in the same street and same locality, August 22d, viz.: Joseph Lynch. The *third* and *fourth*, August 26th, same locality, viz.: John Lynch and Mrs. John Lynch. The *fifth* occurred August 26th, on East Broad street, two doors north of Broughton, viz.: Michael Delaney. The *sixth* took place August 27th, on Reynolds street, next to Gas House, viz.: Mary Ann Smye. The *seventh*, August 27th, on Broughton street, three doors west of Reynolds, viz.: Mary Kehoe. The *eighth*, August 27th, on East Boundary street, north end, viz.: Catherine Kehoe. The *ninth*, August 27th, on Randolph and President streets, viz: Frederick Lawson.

On the 28th of August there are five deaths recorded, one which took place on Stone street, Mrs. Mary E. Malcomes ; one on State street, between Whitaker and Barnard, Edward L. Drummond, and the remaining three in the northeastern part of the city.

On the 29th of August three deaths occurred: One on Indian lane, W. M. Thompson, the other two not specified.

After this the disease spread rapidly, and was not confined to any locality. The highest number of deaths in the city from yellow fever in any one day was thirty-three, on the 20th of September. The highest number from all causes, forty-two, on the 23d of September. These occurred in the fifth week of the epidemic, embracing the period between the 18th and 24th of September, during which week there are reported 229 deaths from all causes.

From the 21st of August until the 14th of November, inclusive a period of eighty-seven days, the total mortality from all causes, whites and colored, reached 1,351, this number being subdivided as follows, viz.: Whites, yellow fever, 771; colored, yellow fever, 125. Total yellow fever, 896. Whites, other diseases, 160; colored, other diseases, 295; total 455. Of this latter total of 455 deaths from other diseases, there have occurred in this city among the whites thirty-eight deaths, from such diseases as have been reported to the sextons of the three cemeteries, as malarial fever, pernicious fever, fever, congestive fever, bilious fever, convulsions, etc., a large portion of which were probably directly due to the pernicious influence of the epidemic, and many of them, in all probability, were genuine cases of yellow fever.

Among the colored there occurs in the same category 132. If the above inference is correct, the report of the mortality during the epidemic would exhibit the following figures: Deaths from yellow fever—whites, 809; colored, 257; total, 1,066. Other diseases—whites, 122; colored, 163; total, 285. The inference is corroborated by a comparison with the usual death rate of preceding years during the same period when there has not been any epidemic of yellow fever prevailing. In the period embraced between the 21st of August and the 14th of November, the epidemic being declared by the physicians at an end on the latter date, there were forty interments of yellow fever in the several cemeteries of persons who were brought dead to the city from different points, viz.: Isle of Hope, Whitesville, Thunderbolt, etc. After the 14th of November six deaths from yellow fever occurred in the city among the whites and one among the colored, and three white persons were brought dead to the city for interment. The last recorded death from yellow fever in the city occurred December 1st.

The origin of the epidemic is involved in obscurity, and a great difference of opinion exists among the physicians as to whether the disease is indigenous to our climate or exotic. A special committe appointed by Council and the Benevolent Association have this subject under investigation, and will, in due time, report the result of their labors.

Dr. Wm. Duncan has prepared a carefully elaborated history of the epidemic from its commencement to its close, which he has kindly consented to publish as an addendum to this report. I have been permitted to verify the figures given in the brief statement above presented from his data.

The history of the terrible pestilence which devastated our unfortunate city would be incomplete without grateful recognition of the generous efforts made to alleviate our distress. As soon as it became apparent that yellow fever was epidemic at Savannah, almost the entire population, whose circumstances permitted, withdrew from our limits, leaving only those who, from the requirements of official position, or an elevated sense of duty, felt constrained to remain. The small white population possessed of any means or experience were at once burdened with a large mass of their fellow-citizens, both white and colored, entirely dependent upon their daily labor, and who at once lost their only means of support upon the sudden prostration of all business.

*　　*　　*　　*　　*　　*　　*　　*　　*

EDWARD C. ANDERSON, Mayor.

A COMMUNICATION

TO THE CITY COUNCIL ON THE

PRIVY SYSTEM

OF SAVANNAH,

BY JAMES J. WARING, ALDERMAN.

THE PUTREFACTION OF ITS CESS-VAULTS

A DANGER TO THE PUBLIC HEALTH.

THE ONLY REMEDY, THE ROCHDALE PALE SYSTEM — THE ROCHDALE PALE
SYSTEM DESCRIBED — TESTIMONY AS TO THE HEALTH RESULTING
FROM THE PAIL SYSTEM, CONTRASTED WITH THE
SPREAD OF DISEASE FROM THE WATER
CLOSET AND SEWER SYSTEM.

SAVANNAH, NOVEMBER 27, 1877.

SAVANNAH, GA.:
MORNING NEWS STEAM PRINTING HOUSE.
1877.

ROCHDALE CORPORATION.

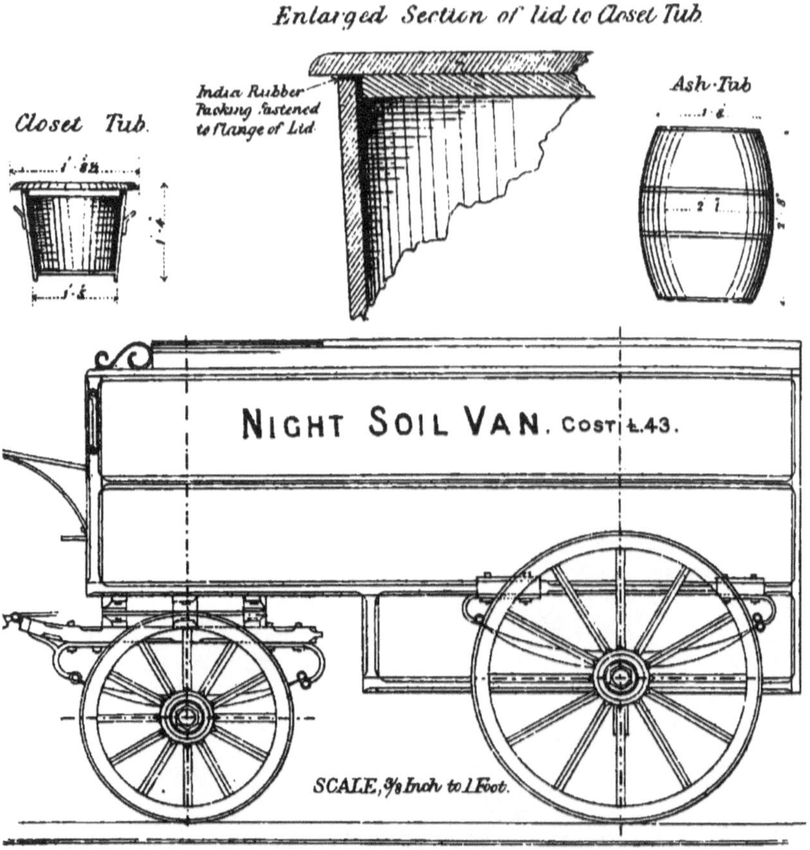
Enlarged Section of lid to Closet Tub
India Rubber Packing fastened to flange of Lid
Closet Tub
Ash-Tub
NIGHT SOIL VAN. COST £.43.
SCALE, 3/8 Inch to 1 Foot.

ROCHDALE
NARROW WOODEN PRIVY

ASH TUB
TUB
TUB
ASH TUB

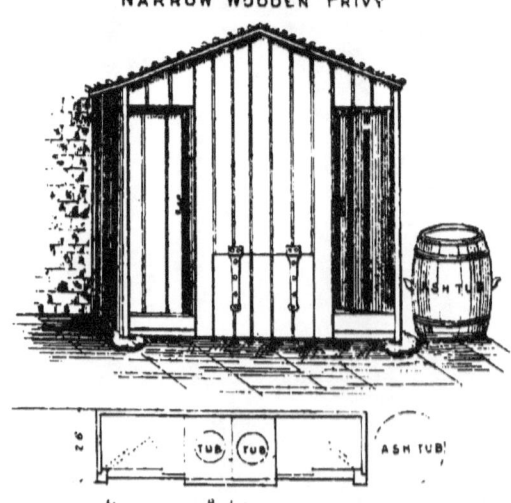

THE EVIL AND REMEDY

—OF—

THE PRIVY SYSTEM OF SAVANNAH.

The population of Savannah by the last census was 28,000. It is probable this number has diminished to 26,000. The plateau upon which Savannah is built is fifty feet above tide water, gently sloping from north to south to an average of forty feet. The water level below the surface of this plateau varies from six feet in the southern wards to twenty feet near the river in the northern wards.

The number of houses in Savannah is near five thousand. The number of water closets is 1,759, (see summary of J. C. Cornell below). And the number of privies or midden vaults is 3,366, (see report of Police Inspectors below).

But the evil of the midden vaults is not to be estimated by this enumeration, for the large majority of the water closets connect with closed or sealed midden vaults, called dry wells, which are (perhaps in lesser degree) nevertheless putrefaction beds, connecting by the waste pipes with the interior of houses.

As the water works of Savannah were established in 1853, and the sewer system not established until 1872, the water closets very generally put into houses after 1853 were forced to connect by waste pipes with such dry wells. I find in the office of the Clerk of Council a record of sewer permits dating only from January 1, 1874, and from that date only 106 permits for water closet connections have been issued. That this record is very erroneous need hardly be asserted. It is safe to say, in the absence of a record, which ought to be taken by Mr. Cornell, that of the 1,759 water closets about 500 only connect with the sewers.

The water supply of Savannah is very abundant. The number of gallons of water thrown upon the plateau for the supply of the inhabitants, averaged in 1876, 47,533,169 gallons per month; and in 1877, for August, September and October, 53,498,939 gallous, (see statement of R. D. Guerard, Superintendent of Savannah Water Works). The refuse water and sewage is conducted by a system of sewers, the main artery of which passes down Broughton and East Broad streets, to its terminus on Bolton street, whose short trunk sewer discharges the whole into the Bilbo canal, now thoroughly flushed and disinfected by the tides which reach up its whole length.

The number of privies in Savannah is 3,366, of which 2,886 are in good condition, 405 need attention and 75 need immediate attention. The privies of Savannah are built with retaining walls of very porous brick and open porous sand bottom, draining laterally and downwards to the water level. A municipal ordinance requires them to be six feet in depth, and requires them to be emptied when they are filled to three feet of the surface. These privies fill slowly with *solid* excremuta, the liquid portion being filtered away laterally through a very porous homogenous sand soil ; hence, the difficulty, if not impossibility, of proper emptying by any process of pneumatic *suction*, such as is sanctioned and encouraged by the present ordinance.

No mild language can fairly describe the nauseating abomination of these middens. Even when clean, the saturated brick sides give off as much odor as the full vault. When it is realized that modern science has proven beyond refutation, that the germs of such diseases as yellow fever, typhus and typhoid fever, diphtheria, etc., are the *pathogenic bacteria* of putrefactive beds and putrefactive fermentations, the grave question of how to deal with this pressing evil comes home to each member of this Board of Aldermen. He cannot thrust it aside.

That the spores, or zoospores, or aurosporen of these bacteria have continued to live through the last winter in lurking or sheltered spots, in spite of the cold, and that they have germinated here and there on some putrefactive bed favorable for such development, we have too sad evidence in the recent death of one of our most valued citizens and the admired associate of this Council. The efficiency of carbolic acid as a destroyer of these bacteria was amply proven at New Orleans in the fatal year of 1876, and I respectfully urge upon Council that large quantities of carbolic acid with no stinting hand be poured into and upon every midden vault and receptacle of putrefaction with an organized force, not only during the winter, but also again upon the opening of April and May.

But such a sanitary measure is temporary, and the following information is submitted, and each alderman is respectfully urged to read carefully every line of these gathered facts.

The Rochdale pail system is practicable and easily carried out. Once it is understood and confidence established in the certainty that the pails will be emptied, it will be gladly adopted by every householder. Such is the universal experience. It is respectfully recommended to incorporate in the tax ordinance an annual tax or license upon the old midden single privies of $15, and upon double midden privies of $30, and upon the Rochdale pail privy of $12. The single pail must be emptied once a week. A van (see plate) with two mules and two men will make three trips per night, carrying away and replacing thirty-six pails. In other words thirty-six pails must pay for a van, and two mules, and two men, fifty-two nights. A liberal allowance will make the following expenses:

Expenses of van . . . . $ 10 00
Two mules for two months at $12 a mule 48 00
Two men for two months of twenty-six workings days, or fifty-
  two days, at $1 00 a day 104 00
Clerks for two months at $50 a month 100 00
                                                        ———
    Total $262 00

Divided by thirty-six, the number of pail privies would make an expense of $7.27 per privy. It is obvious from these figures that a general system would diminish the expense to $4.00. The old privy vaults should be thoroughly cleaned by the town and arched over with brick and cement and a trap communication made for the reception of kitchen slops, thus making of them dry wells. Finally, an ordinance should subject these pail privies to police inspection, and a severe penalty in the police court attached, for emptying into the privies kitchen slops or anything other than the natural accumulation of urine and excrement.

REPORT OF POLICE INSPECTORS OF THE BOARD OF HEALTH.

NUMBER OF PRIVIES.

WARDS.	Good Order.	Need Attention.	Immediate Attention.	Total.
Troup	38	8	. .	46
Lafayette	27	3	. .	30
Derby	12	7	1	20
Reynolds	55	. .	. .	55
Decker	15	6	1	22
Franklin	19	8	. .	27
Jasper and Pulaski	47	14	6	67
Brown	31	3	2	36
Crawford	189	21	8	218
Calhoun	76	6	1	83
Anson	46	5	. .	51
Percival	34	8	. .	42
Forsyth	175	21	11	207
Green and Columbia	60	11	. .	71
Elbert and Jackson	78	11	. .	89
Liberty	40	1	3	44
Heathcote	49	3	1	53
Currytown and Berrien	142	9	5	156
Warren and Washington	68	73	. .	141
Bartow and Davis (Bryan Row)	129	13	3	145
River Front north of Bay street and New Franklin . . .	278	20	31	329
Magazine	247	23	1	271
Choctaw Railroad, O'Neil, Walton and Minis	250	26	. .	276
Outskirts Southwest (Western Division)	175	9	1	185
Outskirts Southwest (Eastern Division	262	24	. .	286
South, North and Middle Oglethorpe	254	55	. .	309
Chatham and Monterey	90	17	. .	107
Total	2,886	405	75	3,366

WATER CLOSET CENSUS.

NUMBER OF WATER CLOSETS.

On River street, from eastern wharf to canal 2
On Bay street from East Broad to West Broad 185
On Bay lane　　"　　"　　"　　"　　" 3
On Bryan street, "　　"　　"　　"　　" 80
On St. Julian street, from East Broad to West Broad 3
On Congress　　"　　"　　"　　"　　" 92
On Broughton　"　　"　　"　　"　　" 154
On State　　　"　　"　　"　　"　　" 41
On President　"　　"　　"　　"　　" 22
On York　　　"　　"　　"　　"　　" 27
On South Broad "　　"　　"　　"　　" 144
On Hull　　　"　　"　　"　　"　　" 16
On McDonough "　　"　　"　　"　　" 8
On Perry　　　"　　"　　"　　"　　" 48
On Liberty　　"　　"　　"　　"　　" 122
On Harris　　"　　"　　"　　"　　" 36
On Macon　　"　　"　　"　　"　　" 16
On Charlton　"　　"　　"　　"　　" 49
On Jones　　　"　　"　　"　　"　　" 104
On Taylor　　"　　"　　"　　"　　" 81
On Gordon　　"　　"　　"　　"　　" 50
On Gaston　　"　　"　　"　　"　　" 65
On Huntington "　　"　　"　　"　　" 21
On Hall　　　"　　"　　"　　"　　" 14
On Gwinnett　"　　"　　"　　"　　" 2
On Bolton　　"　　"　　"　　"　　" 30
On Walburg　　"　　"　　"　　"　　" 8
On Duffy　　　"　　"　　"　　"　　" 9
On New Houston　"　　"　　"　　" 33
On Henry　　　"　　"　　"　　"　　" 5
                                                    ───────
                                                     1,460

On East Broad street from Bay to Liberty street 4
On Houston　　"　　"　　"　　"　　" 3
On Price　　　"　　"　　" " Anderson " 2
On Lincoln　　"　　"　　"　　"　　" 2
On Habersham　"　　"　　"　　"　　" 5
On Abercorn　"　　"　　"　　"　　" 42
On Drayton　　"　　"　　"　　"　　" 30
On Bull　　　"　　"　　"　　"　　" 40
On Whitaker　"　　"　　"　　"　　" 33
On Barnard　　"　　"　　"　　"　　" 35
On Tatnall　　"　　" Liberty to "　　" 20
On Jefferson　"　　" Bay　"　"　　" 16
On Montgomery "　　"　　"　　"　"　" 10
On West Broad　"　　"　　"　　"　　" 37
                                                    ───────
                                                     1,750

On Broughton street from East Broad to Randolph street 1
On Liberty　　　"　　"　　"　　"　　"　　" 2
                                                    ───────
                                                     1,753

On Indian street from West Broad to canal 1
On Harrison "　　"　　"　　"　　" 1
On Margaret "　　"　　"　　"　　" 4
                                                    ───────
    Total in the city 1,759

Alderman J. J Waring :

The accompanying information is the result of the census I have taken of the water closets in the city.   J. C. CORNELL.

STATEMENT BY SUPERINTENDENT OF WATER WORKS.

The average gallons of water supplied to the city of Savannah per month during 1876 was 47,533,169 gallons. The consumption during the months of August, September and October, 1877, was as follows :

August, 1877 . . . . 53,521,904 gallons.
September, 1877 . . . . 52,440,964 gallons.
October, 1877 . . . . 54,533,949 gallons.

Respectfully, your obedient servant,

R. D. GUERARD,
Superintendent Savannah Water Works.

[From the Journal of the Society of Arts, May 11, 1877, p. 569.]

REPORT ON THE PAN, PAIL, AND MIDDEN SYSTEMS OF DISPOSING OF DRY SEWAGE.

GREAT BRITAIN.

BY GILBERT R. REDGRAVE, ASSOC. INST. C. E.

Mainly owing to the exertions of the officers and inspectors of the Board of Health, and the admirable reports of the medical officers to the Privy Council, the abominable midden system, as it formerly existed in all old towns, is fast disappearing, and in its place, we find numerous contrivances for abating the nuisance and evil occasioned by the retention near our dwellings of vast heaps of putrefying refuse. Full descriptions of the improved systems of midden construction, and details of the dry closets, pans, pails and other appliances, for the reception and removal of faecal matters, may be found in the Twelfth Report of the Medical Officer of the Privy Council (1869), and the Second Report (new series, 1874). If we look at the condition of the chief Lancashire and Yorkshire towns some ten years ago we find that the midden or ash-pit arrangement was everywhere in vogue. Into open, reeking middensteads, was thrown the entire refuse of the house, there to undergo slow decomposition along with the excrement and slop water. The Birmingham and Manchester reports of that date give us estimates of the united areas of these masses of putrefaction, and the Public Works Committee of the former town tells us, as late as 1861, that in their town there were thirteen and a half acres of space devoted to such

middens, practically open to the air. The manifest improvements
of the last few years has removed much that was most objectionable in the old midden system ; thus, the Manchester authorities
filled up the midden-pits level with the surface of the ground,
excavating at the same time, and carting away the foul and infected earth which surrounded them. They introduced in their
place the earthenware bevel-midden, which was perfectly impervious, and, from its small capacity, demanded very frequent
emptying. All types of midden construction which limited the
storage area were of necessity improvements, and when the midden took the form of a handy tub, pail, or box, which was entirely
water-tight, and was capable of being constantly emptied and
cleansed, the main objections to the system were removed. We
look upon the pail-system, when properly attended to, and superintended by the local authority, as the most simple and practical
plan of dealing with the excreta of a manufacturing population ;
and it is certainly the only one which holds out hope of the
profitable utilization of fæcal matters in the future. We pro-
pose, in the present report, to examine, first, some of the various
modes of pail-collection, and then to describe briefly the processes
now in actual operation for the conversion of the excreta into
manures. We may consider the pail system under three sub-
divisions :

1. Pails used without absorbents.
2. Pails used in conjunction with absorbents.
3. Pails used for the joint collection of the ashes and the excreta.

Rochdale was the parent of the first of these systems, and,
under the indefatigable care of Alderman Taylor, the process he
introduced some seven years ago seems in a fair way to become
generally adopted in the surrounding towns. The Rochdale plan
has been so often described that it is not now necessary to go
into details. The main features, so far as we need consider them
at present, are the systematic collection of the excreta and the
dry house refuse at short intervals, in tubs of special construction ;
the provision of separate tubs for the excreta and the ashes ; the
careful arrangements for the transport of the excreta to the depot
without smell, by the adoption of an air-tight lid to the pails,
and the use of vans with India-rubber beads round the doors ;
and lastly, the excellent mode of book-keeping, by which the
work of the carters is checked, and records are obtained of the
weight of all materials brought to the yard. In his paper con-

tributed to the conference in May last, Alderman Taylor gave, as the latest result of his work in Rochdale, that there were 5,644 pail closets emptied weekly, used by 52,000 persons, and giving a gross weight of excreta collected during the past twelve-month of 5,398 tons. In an analysis of these results, undertaken by Messrs. Rawlinson & Read in their recent report (p. 60.) it is shown that from this it would seem that 19.1 cwts. were annually collected per tub, and that each tub was used by 9.2 persons, who thus produced only 2.07 cwts. per head. As the weight of the excreta of an average human being, taken at $2\frac{1}{2}$ lbs. per diem, would give an annual total of 1.8 cwts., it is argued that the system fails to account for 6 cwt. per head, or nearly three-fourths of the fæcal matters. The Rochdale pail contents are, however, likely, for several local reasons, to be under the usual average, though by no pail system do we ever obtain more than the solids, together with about three-fifths of the liquid dejections. In Halifax, each tub is used by 10.9 persons living in 2.6 houses (the Rochdale proportion is about 2.2 houses per tub), and the weight collected is 77 lbs. per pail per week, or 1 lb. per head per diem, which is the amount generally assumed as sufficiently correct.

The second sub-division is pails used in conjunction with absorbents. As a type of this system, I must instance the process employed by the Goux Manure Company, and now in operation at Halifax, Aldershot, and in many rural districts. The plan adopted by the company is to surround the bottom and the interior of the pails with a lining of some porous material. In the pails we have seen, the amount of lining is never sufficient wholly to absorb the liquid, and thus, towards the end of the period during which the pail is in use, the contents are found to be in a semi-fluid state. There is certainly some abatement of nuisance arising from the Goux lining, and a partial immunity from the risk of splashing, but the advantages of the lining do not, I believe, counterbalance the expense incurred by the extra weight to be carted backwards and forwards from the depot, and the increased cost of the preparation of the pails. There is, in fact, little sanitary or economic gain in the use of absorbents, and the manure made on this system does not theoretically much exceed in value the simple compost of ashes and excreta.

Under the third head I include those systems where the ashes are introduced into the tubs, either screened, as at Manchester, or unscreened, as at Nottingham and several other large towns. In the latter plan we have simply the substitution of the tub, or box, for the old middenstead. Where Morrell's closet is used, or the Manchester cinder-sifter, the aim is to exclude the larger and heavier matters, and to put the ash only into the tubs. I may at once express my belief that every mechanical contrivance I have yet seen for effecting this is a failure, and I am convinced that the mixture of the ashes with the excreta is unattended with any advantage, either from the sanitary or from the economical point of view. In the summer time, when the pail contents are likely to be most offensive, the volume of ash is small, and the pails arrive at the depot in a very fluid state. Scarcely ever, however, do we find sufficient ash present to absorb the liquids. The ash is said to act as a deodorant ; and it certainly has some small influence in this way, though it merely, I think, retards decomposition, and has no real effect in retaining ammonia and the other valuable components of the fæces. Mr. Leigh says that where an admixture with ashes is made no larvæ are ever found in the pails, but we are inclined to think that with a weekly collection such a state of things can rarely occur, whether with or without ashes. Upon economic grounds, and having in view the preparation of high class manures from excreta, we may repeat that the admixture with ashes, as also with earth, charcoal and other substances used in the receptacles, is undoubtedly a mistake.

Having thus glanced at the chief modes of pail collection, I may lay down the following general rules : That one week is the longest period that should elapse between the times of emptying each receptacle, unless the liquids and solids are kept separate. That the covers used for the removal of the pails from the house to the van should be absolutely air-tight. That the vans for the conveyance of the pails to the depot should have air-tight doors, and be sprinkled at the bottom with some cheap deodorant. That the introduction of deodorants into the pails is of little use, as the quantity that can be applied is almost immediately buried or exhausted. That no system of "filling up" or emptying the pails into liquid manure carts should be permitted, but that each pail, with its contents, should be brought to the depot, and a clean one substituted for it in the privy. That it would be an advantage in the pail system to provide some ready means for the separation, in the receptacle itself, of the solids from the liquids ; and, lastly, that the removal of the pails should be entirely in the hands of the local authority, and should be conducted upon some such careful system as that practiced in Rochdale.

The town of Rochdale, which has thus attracted some attention in the scientific world, is described in the *Journal of the Society of Arts*, May 5th, 1876, page 560 :

ROCHDALE.—Population, 67,590 ; mortality, 24.10. Water carriage sewage contains manufacturing refuse ; is drained direct into the river Roche ; 429 water closets in use.

Pail closets, 5,553 ; middens, 2,276, and ash-pits, 1,590 in use.

Mr. J. Netten Radcliff's report for 1874, states : " The Rochdale system consists in the systematic removal at weekly or shorter intervals of the excrement, and dry house refuse in pails each separate from the other, the manufacture of the excrement with the fine coal ash into manure, and the proper utilization of the dry refuse ;" and mentions that "taking the week ending September 24, 1873, the total net cost to the town for the removal of excreta and house refuse of a population of 36,894 was £10 3s. 3d., being at the rate of £14 6s. 8d. per 1,000 per annum."

A further description of the Rochdale system is found on page 122 of twelfth report of the Medical Officer of the Privy Council of Great Britain for 1869 :

The pails used in Rochdale are made by the committee who have undertaken the system from disused parafine casks, each cask cut traversely in half form two pails. Iron handles are attached to each pail, and the cost of each pail complete for use amounts to 3s. 4d. The pails are changed for other pails belonging to the committee, and this is done weekly, except in the case of lodging houses or closets used by more than one family, when they are changed twice or thrice a week. Before the full pail is moved from the closet it is covered by a lid with India rubber packing attached to the flange. Thus covered it is placed in a closed van for removal to the depot. We are satisfied from the statements made to us by householders, to whose residences pail closets are attached, that the removal of the filled pails gives rise to very little offense, even in those instances where the pails have to be carried through the house. * * * Since last summer, offense from the vans in removal has been obviated by the introduction of the tight-fitting lids to the tubs.

The number of closet tubs in use January 19, 1870, was 580. According to our book, in the week ending January 26, 1870, pails emptied, 582 ; emptied February 2, 481 ; emptied February 9, 581 ; February 16, 410, being an average of 513 per week.

The vans collect three loads per day and one load on Saturday—sixteen loads per week—the average weight of which are believed to be 30 cwt.

	£.	s.	d.
Wages for 6¼	24	19	8
Keep of two horses at £1 each per week	8	0	0
Cost of materials used	5	12	0
	38	12	8

[From the Journal of the Society of Arts, May 26, 1876, p. 656.

ON THE REMOVAL OF THE EXCRETA AND REFUSE OF ROCHDALE BY THE "ROCHDALE SYSTEM."

BY MR. ALDERMAN TAYLOR.

In the year 1864 I wrote to the Night-soil-Committee, detailing to it a method of dealing with night soil and refuse of the town, by which the increasing cost of removal might be lessened, the objectionable privies and middens abolished, and the health of the town improved.

The letter was read, but the plan was not then taken into consideration.

There was also the fellow question of the disposal of the sewage proper raised about the same period, and in 1866 it was distinctly recommended by high engineering authorities to turn the whole of the sewage into the river, so that it might make its way to the sea. The scheme was strenuously resisted by the writer, and, after some lengthy discussion, the Council refused to adopt the wasteful scheme, and decided to further consider the whole question. To the writer it appeared of the first importance that the question of sewage proper, that is, the washing and cooking water of the household, should be kept distinct and treated separately by towns, and I therefore again urged the Council to consider the whole subject. Conjointly with this, the difficulty of disposing of the night soil, the inefficient manner in which the emptying of the cesspools was performed, and the increasing demands of the contractor compelled the Council to give more attention to the ques-

12

tion, and in October, 1868, the recommendation of 1865 was
considered, and in the following December the Council appointed
Alderman Mansell (who was Mayor and Chairman of the Night-
soil Committee), Alderman Taylor, and Councillors Schofield and
Booth, to be a committee to arrange for a trial of several methods
proposed, by which the night soil should be removed. In June,
1869, this committee engaged Mr. J. Havercough, our present
manager, to superintend the removal of the night soil and its
manufacture into a manure. The methods decided to be tried
were the Goux system, the ash system, and the pail system. After
a nine months' full trial, the Council, on the recommendation of
the committee, decided that the pail, now known as the "Rochdale System," was the best.

What then is the Rochdale system?

The answer may be given in a few sentences :

1st. That the excreta and refuse of a household shall be removed within a week.

2d. That the household shall have no care or trouble thrown
upon it.

3d. That the collection be made in pails, not unwieldly, yet of
sufficient size to prevent inconvenience from their being too full,
and so constructed that they may be thoroughly cleansed when
emptied.

4th. That the whole of that which is collected shall be utilized.

These propositions, which seven years ago were looked upon as
chimerical, are now carried out.

The number of closets at this date in Rochdale is 5,644, and
the excreta contained in these, the refuse, including ashes from
the house, are systematically collected weekly, or oftener, without
any notice being required from the householder, and the whole is
utilized by being made into manure, mortar, cement or fuel.

The manner of operation is as follows : The town is divided
into six divisions, named A, B, C, D, E and F. Each division has
its corresponding books, the pages being ruled into thirteen weeks.
In the books every excreta pail and ash tub is entered in progressive number, and the street 'recorded into which it is placed.
Vans and ash carts are appropriated for the collection, and the
guard is furnished every morning with the names of the streets
and the number of closets in that street, written on a ruled blank
list, which he has to collect. When the van or cart returns, it is
weighed, and the list given to the weigh clerk, in the ruled squares

of which the guard has entered the pail or ash-tub number which he has brought in. The van is then emptied, the washer of the pails taking an account of the total number brought in by each van. An inspector daily enters from these lists into the division book, the numbers of the pails brought in, and is thus able to say at the close of the week if every closet has been attended to, and if not, a van is specially sent for the pail omitted. It is found that, with this oversight, the number omitted collecting in regular order has not exceeded thirteen per week.

The pails are thoroughly washed, and into each is put a portion of chloride of alumina and sulphate of lime. The excreta is emptied from the pails into a trench formed of fine ash, which has been sifted from the refuse and cinders collected by the ash cart. A quantity of sulphuric acid, thirty pounds to one ton of excreta, is poured into the trench, and the whole mixed. In three days the trench is turned over with a spade, and again in twenty-one days, by which time the whole will have become in a tolerably dry state, containing about thirty-five per cent. of water. Before the sale of the manure it is again turned over and screened. The quantity of excreta to ash used at present is seven cwt. of ash to one ton of excreta.

The area from which the collection is made is 4,136 acres, and the distance to the manufactory is, in direct line, from the north, one and a half miles ; from the south, one and a half miles ; from the east, one mile, and from the west, one and three-quarter miles. When this site was fixed upon the boundary of the borough was regular, being an exact circle of three-fourth mile radius. The borough was extended in August, 1872. The extension has very considerably disturbed our operations, and increased the costs of the whole work. Three convenient sites would much lessen the cost of carting, and the cost of manufacture would be but minutely increased.

That the inhabitants approve of the system is apparent from the steady increase in the number of pails used. In the first year there were 527 pail closets ; in the second year, 1,070 ; in the third, 1,699 ; in the fourth, 2,509 ; in the fifth, 3,980 ; in the sixth, 4,741, and this year at this date, 5,644, and in no case has legal means been taken to oblige alterations. From the acknowledged advantages the corporation will doubtless compel the whole of the remainder of the old privies—which are now 2,786 in number—to be altered to the pail system, if such compulsion be ever required, but from the present aspect in two or three years the whole will have been altered independently of the corporation.

There is another mode of ascertaining the value of the pail system, if the subject be looked at from the stand-point of seven years ago. At that time the whole of our Lancashire and Yorkshire towns were on what is called the Lancashire privy system, and a terrible nuisance that was found to be. What is the state now? Manchester, Oldham, Warrington, Wakefield, Huddersfield, Halifax and other towns in the country have, more or less, adopted the Rochdale system of collection, that is, by the use of convenient pails. Certainly, some have added what were supposed to be improvements, such as the addition of ashes and lining the pails, but there needs no great foresight to see that they will be obliged to come to the pail, pure and simple. Indeed, there is not a method adopted in any of the towns that was not carefully experimented upon in Rochdale, and abandoned because of its unsuitableness to a town's requirements.

[From the Journal of the Society of Arts, May 26, 1876, p. 662.

THE GOUX ABSORBENT SYSTEM.

BY THOMAS MASON.

A tapering tub or container is provided, say sixteen and a half inches high and twenty inches at its greatest diameter. Upon the bottom of the tub is placed three or four inches of refuse, such as new stable litter, loft sweepings, stack bottoms, ferns, shavings, sawdust, shoddy, flax dressings, speutan or hops, or the various waste materials to be found in town or country; this is mixed with a little soot, charcoal, gypsum or other deodorizer for the purpose of packing or lining the tub. A mould of the same shape as the tubs, but six inches less than the internal diameter, is placed upon the four inches of absorbent material referred to, and the space between the mould and the tub is packed with the same kind of refuse. One boy can pack eighty tubs in an hour, and this is all the manipulation required, except placing and removing the tub at stated times. The absorbent material having been only moderately pressed down, the mould is withdrawn, and there remains a cavity into which the dejections fall, the liquid parts of which are taken up by the absorbents, and retained by them so as to check fermentation.

That the Goux system is generally applicable is proven by its having been five years in use in private houses, unions, hospitals, schools, factories, prisons, camps, villages and large and small towns. It is in use at Aldershot Camp, Sherness, Woolwich and elsewhere for the war office, and the company is in treaty with the government for its introduction at other places. This system of collection is adopted by the sanitary authority of Halstead, in Essex, and worked by their own men under the supervision of Mr. Matthews, the town surveyor, who asserts that it pays for the collection, reduces the cost of the water supply, and generally improves the health of the town.

The villages of Townley, Mickley, Stella, Prudhoe, Walbottle and Seaton Delavel have also the Goux system in use, and the agent to an estate in the latter place, after seeing the good effect it had upon the health of the residents, and the fertilizing properties of the manure, ordered 350 sets, and the same number of new closets or privies. These were placed at only eight feet from the doors of the houses without causing any nuisance.

In the year 1870 the Goux system was first introduced into the town of Halifax, in Yorkshire, and, although no pressure has been put on the property owners, more than 3,000 of these closets are now in use. The health of the town during the period from 1870 to 1875 is shown on the maps before you, which have been prepared by Dr. Haviland, the well-known author of "The Geography of Disease." The deepest red shows the maximum of health, and the deepest blue the greatest intensity of disease, and the various tints show the different gradations.

From the figures on the maps you will notice the remarkable manner in which the extension of the Goux system has coincided with the advancement of the health of the town. I need not weary you by reading the figures. If these do not give proof positive of the value of the system, they at least use strong presumptive evidence that the "Goux" has exercised a beneficial influence on the health of the town of Halifax.

[From the Journal of the Society of Arts, May 26, 1876, p. 664.]

THE PAN AND PAIL SYSTEM IN EDINBURGH.

BY ADAM SCOTT.

THE EFFECT ON THE PUBLIC HEALTH OF THE PAIL SYSTEM AND WATER CLOSET SYSTEM CONTRASTED.

The following interesting statement is made by Dr. Henry Littlejohn, the Medical Officer of Health for Edinburgh. It appears in a report upon the Liernur system made to the corporation of the city of London by their engineer, Lieutenant-Colonel Haywood :

"Edinburgh consists of two distinct towns, and old and a new, but with very different populations. The new town is inhabited by the better classes, and is pre-eminently a water-closet town, whereas the old town consists for the most part of strongly built tenements, which, in the process of years, have undergone repeated sub-divisions, until individual rooms, by means of partitious, are found to contain several families.

"It has been found impracticable to supply these tenants with ordinary water-closet accommodation, and to this day they have to make use of pails for the reception of the excreta of those confined to the house. These pails are brought to the street daily, and emptied into carts provided by the authorities.

"The authorities have also provided numerous public privies, which are daily cleansed by scavengers, and the contents of these pails and pans add largely to the value of the refuse of the city of Edinburgh. From a return made to the corporation in 1874, I find that 41,613 houses were examined. Of these, 27,294 had water-closets, and 14,319 [population about 70,000] none. The latter mainly constitute the worst part of the old town of Edinburgh. Some notion may be formed of the nature of the house accommodation when it is stated that of these 14,319 houses, no less than 13,506 were rented under £12.

"From this state of things—the low morality of the population, the bad ventilation, the crowding together, and the retention of the filth in the living rooms for the greater part of the day, it might naturally have been imagined that typhoid and diptheria were endemic in the old town. This is not the case, however, for, despite the surrounding circumstances, these diseases may practically be said to be unknown.

"In the new and water-closeted town, however, the case is

quite different ; typhoid and diptheria are never entirely absent, are frequently epidemic, and it has been noticed that the ravages of these diseases have been the greatest in the best houses."

I may add to this that the water supply in both towns is the same, that the corporation have, as opportunity offered, introduced water-closets into various houses as improvements upon the old arrangements. Dr. Littlejohn states that whenever this has been done typhoid fever or diptheria has invariably broken out within six or nine months, and Dr. Murchison, in the second edition of his book on "Fever," page 444, states that typhoid fever was unknown in Edinburgh until its sanitary arrangements were altered.

The lesson which this teaches is, that any system of removal cannot be sanitary unless, by it, in the words of Mr. Simon, all the excremental produce of a population is so promptly and so thoroughly removed that the inhabited place, in its air and soil, shall be absolutely without faecal impurities.

[From the Journal of the Society of Arts, May 26, 1876, p. 664.]

EDINBURGH AND GLASGOW WATER-FLUSHING SYSTEMS.

BY ADAM SCOTT.

Dr. Fergus, the President of the Health Section of the Glasgow Philosophical Society, was, I believe, the first to point out the startling fact that, according to the returns of the Registrar-General, the death rate in this country from cholera, diarrhœa, and dysentery, which are recognized as diseases all more or less arising from excremental pollution of air, soil or water, was nearly four times what it was thirty-five years ago. The figures are as follows :

	Deaths per million per annum.
Mean of five years, 1838–42 . .	298
Mean of five years, 1867–71	1,161

During these years there was no epidemic to disturb the normal rate, and typhoid fever, which sickens 150,000 each year, and which is recognized to be solely an excremental disease, is not included in the above figures, as until lately the deaths from this cause were not separated from those arising from other fevers.

Up to the present time neither the government nor any scientific association has ever instituted an inquiry into this subject. Of its importance, no one can have the least doubt, as the question involved is whether the great so-called sanitary movement of the last thirty years, which is every day extending, is really a sanitary movement, or the reverse, and my object in writing this paper is to induce the Society of Arts to undertake an open and comprehensive inquiry into the matter.

The figures obtained from the Registrar-General's return furnish in themselves a *prima facie* case that justifies such an inquiry, but as facts regarding individual towns, which facts are not generally known, can be brought forward in support of the argument founded on such figures, it is important that this should be done.

With regard to Glasgow, I may state the fact that in the period 1838–1842, typhoid fever was simply unknown in that town. My authority for the statement is Dr. A. P. Stewart, the eminent physician of Grosvenor street, who at the time was engaged in the Glasgow Hospital. Dr. Stewart is an authority upon typhoid fever, for it may be remembered that he was one of the first to point out the difference between it and typhus, at the time when these diseases were supposed to be identical. Dr. Stewart, to whom I am permitted to refer, states that typhoid cases did appear in the hospital, but in every case they came in for treatment from Campsie, a place ten miles off. In Glasgow itself the disease was unknown, nor did it appear until the sanitary arrangements of the town began to be altered. Since then that fearful disease has never left the town. The following statements, made by the late medical officer of Glasgow at two different periods, are instructive :

"It was accurately stated that the evils inseparable from the water closet system were likely to be less felt in Glasgow than in many other places, owing to the considerable fall of the greater number of sewers, and the almost unlimited supply of water by which the matter is diluted.

"It has been conclusively shown that houses presumed to be beyond suspicion of any possible danger to health from this cause—houses in which the most skillful engineers and architects had, as they believed, exhausted the resources of modern sanitary sciences—have, nevertheless, been exposed in a high degree to the diseases from air in contact with the products of decomposition in sewers, and this for a very obvious reason. Such houses are usually built on high levels, when the drains have a very rapid fall."

Dr. Stewart also mentions that in Edinburgh typhoid fever was unknown, and this is confirmed by the writings of the late Prof. Reid, of St. Andrew's, who remarks that, like as in Glasgow, the only cases were those not originating in the town, but which were brought in for treatment in the infirmary from the county of Fife. I find this is also confirmed by Dr. Murchison in the second edition of his book upon "Fever," pages 443-4, in which he states that typhoid fever did not exist in Edinburgh until the alteration in its sanitary arrangements took place. As to its prevalence now, the following statement made this year by the Medical Officer of Health, tells its own tale :

" In the new and water-closeted town of Edinburgh, typhoid and diphtheria are never entirely absent, and are frequently epidemic, and it has been noticed that the ravages of these diseases have been the greatest in the best houses."

Can anything be more striking than the fact which he also states (see pan and pail system in Edinburgh on another page) that in certain districts containing 14,319 houses (or, at five persons a house, 70 000 people), where the sanitary arrangements were never changed, typhoid and diphtheria are to this day unknown.

The water supply in Edinburgh for the districts afflicted and not afflicted with the typhoid, is derived from the same sources. The sewage is partly disposed of in irrigation fields, partly carried out to sea and partly discharged into a small burn. The fall of the sewers is great, the whole town being built on high ground. In Glasgow the sewers are of very rapid fall, are nowhere of any great extent, but run direct into the river that passes through the town, and they are flushed by the enormous quantity of fifty-three gallons of water per head per day. The water, which comes from Loch Katrine, is above suspicion.

The sewers in both towns, as in the case of every town in the kingdom, allow precolation of sewage into the subsoil and the formation of sewage gas, and the house drains, like the house drains of all other towns in the kingdom, are frequently imperfect, and also allow free access of the sewage to the soil. It may be that if the sewers were made impervious, and the house drains also made perfect, and of impervious material—it may be that then, but not till then, excremental matter might be safely flushed

into them. This simply means that every sewer in the kingdom
should be rebuilt and every drain examined, and in most cases
relaid. As a system of perfect sewers and drains, however, comes
under the head of "systems not yet tried," I suppose it must not
be discussed. Meanwhile we may well assert that the great principle which the sanitarian should advocate, in regard to water-
flushing towns, is that the filth, which is the cause of disease,
should be utterly excluded from those imperfect sewers and
drains which allow of pollution of air, soil and water, and should
be removed in such a manner that none of these three elements
should be tainted with excremental refuse. In this alone lies the
first great principle of safety.

[From the Journal of the Society of Arts, May 26, 1876, p. 665.]

THE MUNICH SEWERS, AS ILLUSTRATING HOW THE SUBSOIL AND SUBSOIL WATER OF TOWNS ARE POLLUTED BY SEWAGE.

BY CAPTAIN LIERNUR.

The fluid mass in sewers does not flow away without infecting
the soil in which they are built simply because no masonry can contain it. The chemical action of water upon mortar has been repeatedly ignored or denied by eminent sewer builders (they can be no
engineers). They ascribe the percolation of sewage to bad materials, bad sectional profiles, insufficient gradients, or to crevices
caused by subsidence, etc. They say, "build really good sewers
of the best material, keep up a constant flow in them, and there
will be no fear of percolation."

But as it always happens, when scientific truth has been tempo-
rarily silenced through the noisy violence of ignorance or interest
(too often taken as a test of the correctness of judgment of so-
called "practical" men), experience has also corroborated its
dicta. She has shown that the very best kind of sewers, constructed by the very ablest of that class of engineers, with all the
care and skill they could muster, become in a short time as a
leaky basket, and impart to the soil a great deal of the putrid
fluid passing through them.

[From the Journal of the Society of Arts, May 18, 1877, p. 624.]

THE PRACTICAL EXPERIENCE OF THE DRY SYSTEM, SHOWN BY THE USE OF MOSER'S CLOSETS IN A SMALL DISTRICT, FOR TWO AND A QUARTER YEARS.

BY ALFRED CARPENTER, M. D., (LONDON), C. S. S., (CAMBRIDGE).

It may interest the conference to have laid before them the practical facts connected with the application of ash closets in a small district.

It is well known that Croydon is drained in the ordinary way; that is, more or less imperfectly, but there are small areas which are not sewered at all. Among these, is the hamlet of Waddon; it lies between Beddington and the southwestern part of the parish of Croydon. It is a district in which the water line is constantly changing, according to the requirements of the miller who works the water mill, which has existed from time immemorial at the confluence of the several small streams which give rise to the river Wandle. The occupiers of some of the fields close to the hamlet have also the right to dam up the Wandle, and use it as a sheep wash, and also the right to irrigate the pastures themselves. The result of the maintenance of these rights is, that the subsoil is generally water-logged, water existing within a few inches of the surface of the ground. Notwithstanding this state of things, a number of cottages were built on a part of this land close to the left bank of the principal stream of the Wandle. When the plans were first deposited by the speculators who proposed to erect these houses, there was no law by which they could be compelled to provide a dry basement. Application was made by the builders to the local authority to sewer that district at the public expense, but the local board declined to do it except at the expense of the owners. It was contended by the writer that the rate-payers of the parish ought not to be called upon to turn a swamp into building land for the benefit of speculators. Nevertheless, the houses were built, and immediately occupied by a swarm of poor. The result, which was predicted when the plans were deposited with the local board, soon came to pass. The inhabitants suffered continually from the effects of enthetic disease. Scarlatina, diphtheria and fever were constant visitors. The neighbors then began to complain. Many deaths occurred. The stench from the continually overflowing cesspools was plainly perceptible in the public roads, and great pressure was brought to bear upon the local authority to compel them to sewer the district, at an expense almost equal to the value of the cottages themselves. But it appeared to the writer that to put sewers into such a district would be a sanitary mistake. At least one-half of the time they would be waterlogged, and be the means of retaining mischief in close proximity to the houses instead of conveying it away. It appeared that, before sewering the district, the water line should be permanently lowered, that the owners should give up the right to flood the neighborhood, and thus make the land fit for building purposes, before the local authority provided sewers for the sewage. There was also another consideration in the case. The sewage from these cottages would have to be conveyed to Beddington sewage farm. There would then be a twelve-inch sewer, constantly discharging subsoil water instead of sewage upon a farm which already receives more subsoil water than it is entitled to. The owners refused to do this duty, and it was left to the sanitary committee of the Croyden Local Board of Health to devise a remedy for the insanitary state of the hamlet, which state the law had allowed to grow up close to our own noses and in spite of our protests. The year 1874 was a very fatal one to the inhabitants of the cottages. The owners did not—indeed, they could not—empty the cesspools which had been constructed, and it was evident that something must be done. The property had changed hands, and the new owners were willing to do what the sanitary committee recommended. The writer had been much struck with the simplicity and cheapness of Moser's closets, as exhibited at the Social Science Congress at Glasgow in 1874, and ultimately twenty closets were erected by Mr. Moser, at a cost to the owners of something under £3 per closet. They were completed December 24th, 1874. The cottages are in a block close to the road, and about one-third of a mile from the outfall sewer, near to which the town refuse of the Croydon district is conveyed. It was agreed with the owners that they should erect the closets, but that the Croydon Local Board should collect the refuse, and supply the hoppers with dry ashes and the pails with sawdust as often as should be necessary. The whole of the arrangements were carried out, and have since been superintended by Mr. Mitchell, the sanitary inspector of the Croydon Local Board of Health, and I learn from him the following results: He states that, whereas serious illness always prevailed in those houses before the erection of the closets, there has been very little since

and scarcely any of that class of disease which formerly visited
them ; that the houses, instead of being pest houses to the neighborhood, are now perfectly healthy. It is also stated in Dr·
Buchanan's report upon the epidemic of fever which visited Croydon in 1875 that these cottages at Waddon altogether escaped.

[From the Journal of the Society of Arts, June 16, 1876, p. 755.]

FOREIGN SYSTEMS.

FLORENCE.

Mr. C. N. Cresswell said he was in a position to give the conference some interesting information with reference to the city of
Florence. Ten years ago he was engaged in negotiating a con-
cession for improving and enlarging the city of Florence just at
the time it was made the capital of the kingdom of Italy.

The houses were to be drained into cesspools, to be constructed
under the superintendence of the authorities. It was necessary
that he should explain to the meeting the construction of these
cesspools and the mode of emptying them. Every cesspool was
designed and built upon a system approved by the municipal
engineers, and subject to their supervision, the size being fixed in
proportion to the number of inmates resident in each block of
buildings. It was air and water-tight, and provided with a suction pipe inserted at the bottom, and also a tube from the arched
roof of the cistern, carried up to the level of the surface similar
to an ordinary water main. These cesspools were periodically
emptied by the municipal employés by means of an air-tight tumbrel, connected with an exhaust pipe, and drawn upon wheels to
the spot where it was required between the hours of one and four
o'clock in the morning. The process was as follows: The air was
exhausted in the tumbrel sufficiently to produce a partial vacuum;
the hose was then attached by a nozzle screw to the· suction tube
before mentioned, the air pipe was opened to let in the outer air,
and, by atmospheric pressure, the cesspools were emptied in a
minute and a half. The contents are sold for the benefit of the
municipality to the farmers in the vicinity, who compete eagerly
for the privilege, and use this sewage to fertilize the vine, fig and
olive gardens, which abound in the highly cultivated valley of the

Arno. Mr. Cresswell mentioned that the Italians were great con-
sumers of vegetable food, and that the kitchen slop waters were
also carried into cesspools by means of pipes, well trapped to prevent the escape of gases into the sculleries, which, in Italian
houses, were on the same floor as the drawing room. This rendered it the more imperative to take precautions against a nuisance of which Italian noses are peculiarly sensitive. He stated
that the pneumatic scavenging cars were supplied by the municipality, and that, partly from the unpopularity of the Grand Duke
of Tuscany at the time of their introduction, and partly from the
pungent odor which surrounded them, they were styled the Grand
Duke's snuff-boxes. The value of the contents of the Florentine
cesspools was estimated so highly by the neighboring farmers
that they stipulated eagerly for the privilege of emptying them
at an annual rent varying from £3 to £7 per year for each
cesspool. The lessors of the company's offices justified the high
rent demanded for the premises occupied by them in Via del Gig-
lio by the fact that the garden surrounding them possessed the
special advantage of three large cesspools, which would be worth
at least from £15 to £20 per annum to the proprietors. In conclusion, Mr. Cresswell said that he was not prepared to give any
statistical data as to the death rate of Florence, but that during
the last two visitations of cholera, while the neighboring towns
were decimated by that scourge, Florence had altogether escaped
the epidemic.

www.ingramcontent.com/pod-product-compliance
Lightning Source LLC
Chambersburg PA
CBHW020623030726
47497CB00007B/2382